Angels in Arms

MIKE RIPLEY

Angels in Arms

St. Martin's Press
New York

Library of Congress Cataloging-in-Publication Data

Ripley, Mike.
    Angels in arms / Mike Ripley.
       p.   cm.
    ISBN 0-312-07629-0
    I. Title.
  PR6068.I56A84   1992
  823'.914—dc20
                                                     92-2633
                                                      CIP

First published in Great Britain by HarperCollins Publishers.

First U.S. Edition: June 1992
10 9 8 7 6 5 4 3 2 1

AUTHOR'S NOTE

I am indebted to the following for technical help and advice:
Dan Silver and Ritchie Boot;
Fred Dent, JP;
The Rev. I. C. Davies;
M. Lionel Hervé, Château du Val, Plangenoual.
None of them should be held in any way responsible, and
not even taken in for questioning.

M.R.

Respectfully dedicated to the
Lucindas and Werewolves of this world

CHAPTER 1

I was admiring Jasmine's left breast and explaining my latest money volcano idea of having mobile hairdressers on roller-skates serving cocktails while snipping, when Fenella arrived in full Hold-The-Front-Page mode.

'It's dead simple, really,' I was saying, 'because We Have The Technology nowadays.'

'For what?' asked Jasmine, lining up her clippers to the top of my ear.

'To make you mobile. Those clippers are battery powered, right? So you don't have to work near a power point any more. Everything else you use—comb, scissors, clips, so forth—you carry on you. There must be the technology now to have a battery hair-drier and you could wear it in a gunbelt. Then you'd be completely mobile. The clients wouldn't have to sit in a row at a central console, you could move them around. Redesign the salon every day. Get all the cutters on roller-skates and you could zip from customer to customer. Pump up the volume on the old sound system and maybe stick a few more monitors around the place so everybody can actually see the music videos, and you'll have the wickedest hairdresser in town.'

'Where do the cocktails come in?' she asked. That's why I always ask for Jasmine; she's done basic level Conversation. Most of them have only two things to say: Did you have a good holiday/Where are you going on holiday? depending on the time of year.

'Now that,' I said, proudly, 'is the clincher. The juniors don't have much to do—'

'They wash the client's hair.'

'Yeah, but apart from that, they just hang around and occasionally get the brush and pan out to clean up.'

'They're observing,' she said primly. 'And learning all the time. I was a junior once.'

'If that's what they do, then I still am one,' I said, thinking it odd that I should get some of my most profound thoughts while sitting back with a breast in my face. 'But the plan is that they double as cocktail waitresses—on roller-skates, of course—which would add at least another fiver per punter—sorry, client—to the old cash flow. We could call it *Snipadrome* or *Curl Up And Boogie*. They'd be beating the door down to be seen in here.'

'You'd never get a licence,' said Jasmine gloomily. She stood behind me and took a strand of hair from above each ear and sized them up in the mirror. 'Now look what you've made me do.'

'It's not my fault one's longer than the other. You're the one with the scissors.'

'You talk too much.' She trimmed one side carefully, concentrating hard and not realizing her tongue was sticking out.

I must have giggled.

'Sit still! You're more trouble than any three of my other regulars put together. Most of them just go red and all coy when I stick my bazookas in their face.'

'I bet it helps with the tips.'

'You ain't kidding. And, boy, am I glad designer stubble's out of fashion. That was painful, man.'

'Yes, I suppose—'

That was as far as I got down that particular conversational cul-de-sac because suddenly there were two women in the mirror.

'Angel! I knew this is where you'd be!' she said, flapping her arms as if her Paddington Bear brown duffel coat was fighting back.

'Hello, Fenella, why aren't you at work?'

'Because I'm here looking for you because—'

'Lisabeth told you I'd booked in for a trim because she was listening in when I phoned to make the appointment yesterday. I must have told you about Lisabeth,' I said pointedly to Jasmine, 'my downstairs neighbour. Not that you'll ever meet her. She objects to hairdressers on principle and the idea of a unisex salon would—'

'And you didn't put the phone call in the log book, you know,' Fenella blustered. 'She's keeping a record for when the bill comes in. And anyway,' she sniffed, '*I* cut Lisabeth's hair when she requires a tidy.'

'Have you thought of a new style yourself?' Jasmine asked her.

In the mirror I could see Fenella sizing her up.

'Why do you say that?' she asked, bobbing her fringe with an imperious twinge of her head.

'Well, that page-boy look just doesn't do justice to your cheekbones, my dear.' Jasmine reached out a finger and flicked expertly at the hair covering Fenella's left ear. 'I'd suggest a top box cut, quite short, with a high shave up the neck, but leaving enough at the front so that it could fall over one eye. Have you thought about streaks? A couple of blonde streaks could really highlight your natural colouring.'

I couldn't tell if it was a wind-up or not, so Fenella certainly couldn't.

'Was there a reason you came looking for me, Fenella?' I said into the mirror. The two women looked at me as if they'd just realized I was there.

'Oh yes, you had a phone call, just after you went out, about half past eight. Lisabeth answered it and said you'd better come home quick.'

She relaxed having delivered her message and smiled at Jasmine as if to say that the rest of the day was her own now.

'Do you really think a blonde streak would—' she began.

'Straight up,' said Jasmine, giving her the professional once-over. 'Not too loud and maybe just in a couple of—'

'Excuse me,' I said loudly. 'But why do I have to go back to the house?' Then to Jasmine's reflection: 'You can't get the staff these days, can you?'

She smiled at that. Fenella didn't.

'Because he's ringing back at ten-thirty,' she said primly into the mirror with an if-you-really-have-to-know sneer.

'Who is?'

'Maybe a streak of red, too,' Jasmine said almost to herself, still checking out Fenella's scalp. 'Blue, even.'

'Blue? Oh, I don't think so . . .' Fenella began to blush.

'Seriously. Just a highlight. It makes all the—'

'Excuse me,' I said, louder this time. 'Who?'

'Who what?'

'Who's ringing back?'

'Oh. A Mister Gurney.' I could see Fenella was pleased she'd remembered that.

'I don't know anybody called Gurney.' I settled down deeper into the chair. 'Must've been a wrong number.'

'But he asked for you, Angel, by name. Well, so Lisabeth said.'

That was odd. No one I knew would recommend me to anyone. Well, not to the extent that they'd give out my number without checking first. That's standard. And getting the wrong Angel was unlikely too. There are eighty-three Angels in the London (Residential) phone book. I'm not one of them.

'No chance. Snip on, Jasmine.'

'But Wilf said it was a matter of life and death. Or maybe life or death. But it was important.'

'Wilf?'

'Wilf Gurney. That was the name. I'm sure of it.'

'Fenella, do I look the sort of person who knows Wilfs?'

'Well, don't shoot the messenger, I'm only doing you a favour. Some people!'

This last was to Jasmine, clearly looking for sympathy. Jasmine, scenting new business, took her side.

'Right on, sister. You tell him!' Fenella looked over her shoulder to see who Jasmine was talking to. 'You're welcome to him, 'cos I've just about finished here.'

She held up a hand mirror so I could see the back trim. I nodded an OK.

'And now for the bit I like most,' said Jasmine, reaching over me and dipping a hand into a jar of hair gel. She scooped out a gobbet and smacked her hands together in a sucking, squelching clap.

'I love it when you talk dirty,' I smiled into the big mirror.

Fenella went a pinker shade of blush and averted her eyes.

I strolled back to Stuart Street with that extra spring in the Reeboks which you always get after a haircut. This is partly due to the new zappy image you think you've just acquired and mostly due to the tiny bits of hair which always go down the back of your T-shirt.

I've lived at No. 9 longer than I'd lived anywhere at one go, in London at least, and Lisabeth and Fenella had shared the flat below mine from the off. The other two flat-lets, one on the ground floor and one above mine taking in the old attic space, had been occupied by, respectively, the mysterious Mr Goodson and the Celtic Twilight. Mr Goodson kept himself so much to himself that we often forgot he was there. You couldn't say the same about the Celtic Twilight, the name I'd given to Inverness Doogie and his girlfriend Miranda in case they ever formed a folk group.

Doogie was a chef at a posh West End hotel and loved talking about pastry cases, delicate sauces made from kiwi fruit, street fighting and the chances of Dundee United winning the Scottish football league. Miranda was a straight-faced, dark-eyed Welsh lady whose sense of humour had fled screaming some time before puberty, due to too many Sunday School sessions in chapel back home in the Valleys. They were an unlikely couple, but then this was Hackney and despite the irresistible yuppification, there was still room for people like that.

I had walked round to the *Cut and Thrust* salon (not bad, not bad) because parking in the little shopping precinct is a bitch even with a delicensed black London cab. And there was always the hazard that my Austin FX4S—the classic design diesel cab, accept no substitutes—would be mistaken for a real cab by the women waiting at the back door of the supermarket for the 'shop and ride' car they'd phoned for.

Sometimes, I'd met some interesting people that way. I mean, if you don't actually notice that the light on top of Armstrong saying TAXI is permanently off, or that the fare meter has been replaced by a cassette tape-deck, then he doesn't look any different from a few thousand other black London cabs. Now if someone weighed down with the weekly shopping needs a lift somewhere, and then insists on pressing money on me, who am I to refuse?

Actually, unless times are really hard, I do refuse these days ever since picking up, and yes, I do mean in the biblical sense, a young lady who eventually grassed me to her mini-cab-company-owning husband.

Armstrong was parked neatly outside No. 9. As the only motorist in the house I had my pick of parking space, so he always got poll position. All seemed right with the world until I noticed the flysheet stuck under his windscreen wiper.

One side was printed: SAY NO TO THE POLL TAX, and was designed to go in a window facing out. I preferred to say nothing to the new poll tax on the basis that if you say no, somebody might hear you—and find out you haven't paid.

On the back was felt-tipped a Lisabethogram in her usual cryptic style.

'*Phone for you at 10.30, then every hour on the ½-hour. L,*' it said. Then: '*PS: Some of us have jobs to go to.*'

My, but Mr Wilf Gurney, whoever he was, seemed keen. Maybe it was a job offer. If that meant an unofficial taxi service or playing trumpet for a few nights in a seedy club, then I could handle that. After all, that's what normally kept the rentlady at bay. But if it was an insurance salesman or a double-glazing salesman, or the tax man, or a poll tax inspector, or the father of—

Stop it, I told myself. All this paranoia over a phone call you haven't had yet. Why worry?

As I put the key in the lock of the front door, the phone started to ring.

Our communal house phone is nailed to the wall in the hallway, just inside the front door. I lifted the receiver in one fluid movement and only disguising my voice slightly (just in case), I said:

'Hello dere! Dublin Pizza Express. Can I help?'

The Irish accent had been a shot in the dark. Honest.

'Angel?' came the voice down the line. 'Stop fucking about. It's Werewolf. I'm in Guernsey and I'm in deep shit.'

Time to press the Worry Button.

Warp Factor Five.

My Rule of Life No. 6, although highly adaptable, goes something like: Never refuse to help a genuine old and distinguished friend. The trick, of course, is not to have too many of them.

Werewolf and I went back quite a way. If he'd never left the one-pig town he'd been born in, the Irish would have written folk songs about him by now. Or given him a job in the government; if there is a Ministry of Loud Music over there, that is.

He is an above average musician and could have made it in the rock music scene were it not for the booze and drugs and fast women. He liked them so much he never had time to play anything. So he did the next best thing and became a roadie, which gave him the sort of hours he liked to work, cash in hand and a chance to travel all over Europe. Since the cracks started appearing in the Iron Curtain, Albania is about the only gig he hasn't done. (And let's face it, that would be a one-night stand.)

He's the sort of Irishman who's always thirsty and when he says he's popping out to buy cigarettes, could be gone for up to three months. Which doesn't really narrow it down.

He's taller and leaner and meaner than me and dresses down in none-too-fashionable scruffy chic. He has a beard which could double as a duvet for a dachshund and for some reason appears wildly attractive to women.

He'd also saved my life once, more or less, and wasn't the type to have forgotten either.

The last time he'd been in London, he'd renewed his friendship with Sorrel, a fine, iron-willed blonde lady whose antiques business probably didn't even need subsidising by her incredibly rich daddy these days. Mind you, her ski-ing holidays probably did.

I'd had a card back in January from her complaining about how little snow there was on her particular piste that year. It had been a bad year for second-holiday skiers snow-wise and some of them had even had to go as far afield as Austria to show off this season's day-glo gear. They didn't usually mention places like Austria. After all, it's so cheap compared to Switzerland and what's the point of having it if you can't flaunt it?

I decided to look up Sorrel, partly to see if she knew anything and partly because Werewolf's phone call had worried me. And where he's concerned, you can only talk it through with someone who knows him. It would be no good ringing the Samaritans. They'd be slashing their wrists by the time you'd told them about his first traumatic experiences with women and drugs and booze. And after puberty, things got worse.

I nosed Armstrong through the late-morning traffic and ended up parking him on a taxi rank near the Aldwych. It meant I had to hoof it into Covent Garden but it wasn't far and no one would turn a hair at a black cab unattended on a rank. They'd just assume, as they usually did, that the driver was making a pit stop, or had nipped off for lunch or was just being bloody-minded.

On Bow Street I ran into Touting Terry, a permanently resting actor who had found touting tickets paid better than spear-carrying, and we blagged for a few minutes on what was the hottest seat in town at the moment. Andrew Lloyd Webber show tickets still proved more valuable than coin of the realm, so nothing new there, and Terry had caught a cold on a block of seats at the Hammersmith Odeon for the Bob Dylan tour. That didn't surprise me much either.

In the rear end of the Garden I scouted the flea-market stalls until I spotted Sorrel's pitch. In the main piazza, the fire-eaters, white-faced clowns and jazz 'cellist with a synchrobeat synthesizer were warming up the noonday crowds. It's a good place to work, if you can pass the audition.

My first thought was that Sorrel had sold her pitch to the anorexic Hippy Romantic who was sorting the china goods, the old patent medicine bottles people turn up in their gardens and the motly collection of horse brasses. Then I saw the back of Sorrel's blonde hair down behind the trestle table. She was sitting on a folding camp stool (which had a price tag tied to one leg) and she had a portable computer on her knee, screen up, green digits flashing.

The Hippy Romantic smiled at me from beneath his headband. He was wearing a sleeveless Afghan over a flowery shirt and the headband matched the shirt. It looked suspiciously like Laura Ashley material. He wore jeans with flares so wide they went out of fashion with sailing ships, let alone the real hippies. God, I hate revivals.

'Excuse me,' I said to the HR, 'but I'm trying to get a valuation on my grandmother's collection of porcelain dildoes. She's used them as jelly moulds, would you believe it?'

Sorrel answered without turning round and before the hippy's jaw had dropped.

'Hello, Angel. Nice haircut.'

It took me a second to twig that she could see me reflected in the computer screen.

'Thanks. The antiques business gone hi-tech now?'

'You bet. Come see.'

I strolled around the back of the stall and bent over to kiss the cheek she tilted towards me. She looked as good and smelled better than I remembered. She jabbed a column of green figures on the screen with a manicured finger.

'There's my latest acquisition—Hales Limpton.'

'What's a Hales Limpton?' As far as I could see, the screen was giving out a list of things, some of which I could recognize. Flintlock fowling pieces (8), Q. Anne tables (2), escritoires (4), late Vic. toy theatres (6)—and so on.

'It's a place,' said Sorrel, 'in Norfolk. A village, with three antique shops. Everyone has a personal computer nowadays—'

'I don't.'

'—so I borrow their stock list disc and do an evaluation.'

'So it's like mail order antiques? You buy what takes your fancy?'

She gave me the sort of look I reserve for people who buy Richard Clayderman tapes.

'I buy the lot.'

'Pardon me? You'll have to go slower. I'm computer-hostile, remember. The thought of using all that green Tippex to correct your mistakes—'

'Idiot. I value the stock of all three shops and then at the optimum point, put in a bid for the entire stock. Having the stock list helps identify the odd item which might be really valuable. The rest go job-lot when we send in the truck.'

'Truck?'

'The container lorry that comes across from Denmark. I've worked out that three shops just about fills an empty container on the return journey. I sell to a consortium of Danish dealers on a one-trip, bulk purchase basis and they split the goods how they want. The Danes are into antiques at the moment and this way they don't have the hassle of coming over here to sort out what's real and what's fake.'

'And you get a good discount for clearing the shop, of course.'

'Absolutely. The shops will cut their margins to the bone thinking that if the worst came to the worst they can buy stock from the other ones in the village, especially now they're cash rich.'

I must have grinned because she stopped.

'Sorry,' I said. 'It's just that the words "cash rich" always excite me. Doesn't Shop A get a bit pissed off when they find Shop B has done the same deal?'

'Probably. That's their problem.'

'Doesn't anyone object that you're selling an entire village to the Danes?'

'Maybe. Maybe the place is a dump. I don't know, I've never been there. It's all done in here.'

She patted the computer screen and flicked the off switch.

'Well, that's all right, then,' I said, keeping the sarcasm toned down. Hales Limpton, wherever you were, that was your life. 'Got a minute to talk?'

'Sure. Let's walk. Redvers will mind the shop.'

Redvers? No wonder he needed to be a Hippy Romantic. Anything but a Redvers.

We strolled around Covent Garden and I bought us both ice-creams from a bicycle-powered vendor brought out earlier than usual due to the mild winter. Sorrel's mini skirt and long expanse of legs in black woollen tights ending in spiky-heeled Edwardian lace-up ankle boots brought admiring glances from every male in the area. The way she flicked her tongue at the maple and pecan cone just brought sharp intakes of breath. Mostly from me.

'It's about Werewolf,' I said, glancing around for a litter-bin to dump my ice-cream in. (Why does pistachio always taste of diesel in this country?)

'I thought it might be,' Sorrel slurped.

'Know where he is?'

'Europe?'

'There's no need to be so specific. You'll be giving me grid references next.'

'Oooh, sharp! You'll cut yourself one of these days. What's up, is he overdue on his rabies booster?'

I flashed my most disarming smile. I've got good teeth; so flash them is what I say.

'Now, now. Do I detect a certain coolness in your once white-hot relationship?'

'Not at all. Werewolf just decided he didn't fit into my lifestyle on a regular basis.'

'He didn't like some of your friends?'

'Got it in one.'

'Did he get physical?'

'That was the one thing he had going for him . . . Oh, I see what you mean. Yes, there were a couple of unpleasant incidents. Do you know how much it costs to respray a Porsche?'

'I can guess. So when did you last hear from him?'

' 'Bout a month ago. Got a letter from Germany. He was on tour with a band. No, not a band as such, a new singer, does Revival Soul—Belinda O'Blake, that's it.'

'She's good,' I said.

'So Werewolf thought.'

Oh dear.

'And you've heard nothing since?'

Sorrel shook her long blonde hair. 'Nope. He should be back by now. If he rings, he rings.' She reached out and grabbed my wrist. 'You worried about him?'

'Sort of.'

'Is he in trouble?'

'Could be.'

'Nothing trivial, I hope.'

'Really, Sorrel.'

'OK, OK.' She smiled. She had good teeth too. 'Only winding you up. I know you two go back a long way. Code of the Old and Distinguished Friends. Isn't that what you called it?'

'Something like that. Listen, you're sure you haven't heard from him?'

'Positive. Hey, if he's really in schtuck I'll help if I can.'

'And your relationship is lukewarm, shall we say?'

'We are not—' she paused for effect—'an "item" as the Americans would say.'

'And you're pretty sure he's not back in the country?'

'Not as far as I know.' She screwed up her eyes. 'Why the twenty questions?'

'Oh, nothing, nothing.' I exercised the teeth again. 'Doing anything tonight?'

CHAPTER 2

I surprised myself by making it out to Heathrow the next morning in time for the 8.20 a.m. flight to Guernsey. I surprised the girl selling tickets by presenting an American Express card for the £158 she stung me for the round trip. For that sort of money you could cross three states in the US—big ones at that. For less than double that you could actually get to the US itself.

The girl at the desk had heard it all before. And she double-checked the signature I gave her, though goodness knows why. After all, 'Roylance Maclean' was what it said on the card. Some people are naturally suspicious.

I had time for a styrofoam cup of coffee and a Danish pastry from the hospitality trolley before we were ushered along a corridor to the plane. The stewardesses were well practised at it; we didn't get anywhere near a Duty Free shop, not of course that we had any right to, it's just nice to live in hope.

The plane was a turbo-prop German affair, Guernsey not being too keen on jet propulsion. I was the only passenger not wearing a suit and not carrying a combination lock BMB (Busy Man Bag). As we settled down, and I grabbed a double seat near the rear of the cabin, the two suits sitting across the aisle from me went into a 'Chocks away/Squadron scramble!' double act. Then one told the other, in a very loud voice, the old gag about the retired Wing Commander giving the end of term speech at a posh girls' school and reminiscing about the time 'six Fokkers came out of the sun' at him. The headmistress, natch, has to interrupt and explain that Fokkers were a type of German fighter plane. 'Yes, ma'am, but these Fokkers were flying Messerschmitts!' I mouthed to the stewardess checking our seatbelts, getting to the punchline before Biggles did. She joined in as well, having heard it more times than I had, and by the time we were over the Channel she was sitting in the spare seat next to me with her shoes off, telling me how much she hated getting drawn for these 'island-hopping' shifts.

She asked me if I was hiring a car while I was on the island, as she could have got me a good deal as long as I didn't mind driving a Metro. I told her that as long as nobody I knew saw me, I didn't mind, but I was out of there later today. I asked her if she knew St Peter Port, the island's capital.

'Oh sure. You'll need a taxi from the airport but if you're looking for a fun time, keep the engine running,' she said like she'd said it to her friends on long-haul routes who boasted about stop-overs in Honolulu or San Fran.

'How about a bar called the Pony and Trap?' I tried.

'It'll be down near the harbour in St Peter Port, no doubt. Ask the guy driving the cab. They know most things.'

I hoped she was right. This one at least knew her London phone number before the pilot applied the brakes.

'You're not one of those real ale nutters are you?' asked my cab-driver.

'No. Why?'

'Well, asking for the pub like you did. We get the real alers coming over here from Jersey all the time. Bit of a pain they are, too. They say there's no real ale brewed on Jersey, so they have to come and sample the Guernsey Brewery. Bunch of wallies if you ask me. I mean, what's the opposite of real? Unreal?'

'I know,' I sympathized, cabbies-in-arms and all that. 'It won't cut much ice when the cops pull you and you've had a skinful and you try saying "But it's all right, Officer, it wasn't *real* ale."'

'Too bloody right, mate.'

I don't know what it is about cab-drivers. Maybe it's sitting looking at somebody's rear licence plate all day brings out the natural philosopher in them.

The driver actually pointed out the Guernsey Brewery as we turned on to the sea front in St Peter Port. There was a dray lorry outside, being loaded up, with 'Pony Ales' written down its side. I asked my driver why Pony?

'Buggered if I know,' he said. Obviously an island guide.

He dropped me a hundred yards beyond the Pony and Trap after identifying it for me. As I fumbled for some money to pay him, he pointed out the tourist sights like the fort out in the harbour and the fact that the island policemen were just like our own boys in blue on the mainland. He'd be telling me they didn't carry guns next.

Werewolf had said to meet him at the pub at noon, which gave me over an hour to kill. The cab-driver told me where I could get a cup of coffee and where there was a cab rank for the trip back to the airport. He clearly thought I was two bricks short of a wall, having asked for a particular pub which I then seemed to be ignoring, but he took his fare and, as is the way with cabbies, as soon as the door clicked shut I was history.

I spun out a cup of coffee and a cheese roll much longer than was either natural or economically viable for the café the cabbie had recommended. It offered me a window seat where I could watch the front of the Pony and Trap pretending I was a private eye or similar, and nobody complained as it was still out-of-tourist-season and they were probably grateful for the sale of the cheese roll.

I rewound what Werewolf had actually said over the phone and did a mental remix.

He'd said he was 'on' Guernsey, so he was here already. No why or how or even 'having a marvellous time wish you were here'. He'd said he was in big trouble, which on most days was like saying that come nightfall it'll get dark. He'd said he needed me here pronto. No pleading or sugaring the pill. No 'come on down there's a gig/party/sure-fire-way-of-making-money on'.

He had said he was in trouble and he needed to see me, and he'd said it about four different ways. He'd also said it would be OK and 'no sweat' to try and reassure me, leaving me feeling as secure as a battery-farmed turkey at the end of November.

He'd also slipped in the peculiar phrase: 'Do this thing for me, Roy, and I'll rule out the seventy-four favours you owe me.'

Now I hadn't actually asked him if he could talk freely or if someone was listening in. With old friends, you don't have to do that, though Werewolf took no chances and got in the word 'rules' and seventy-four before I could blow it.

My Rule of Life No. 74 is that you can work your way out of most situations if you give yourself enough thinking time.

If I were Werewolf's 'thinking time', then I was right to start feeling like a turkey.

And somewhere across the farmyard I could hear the sound of an axe being sharpened.

They came at about quarter to twelve and even I couldn't miss them. If they'd had a marching jazz band going before them with a troupe of baton-twirlers, then maybe, just maybe, they would have been less obvious.

The leader, or at least the one walking out in front, got christened Belmondo straight away. Two-tone brown and white brogues, trousers with flares and turn-ups (and, I bet myself, Paisley braces), a grubby off-white trenchcoat and

tweedy flat cap. His sunglasses were the thing that stuck out
a mile, though, apart from him being the only person in
Guernsey wearing them that day. They were dark brown pol-
arized Highway Patrolman shades. Right period, wrong
style. Clash, clash, clash.

The two bringing up the rear were hardly less conspicuous
in their own way. There was a thin one with skin-tight black
jeans, a fur-lined leather bomber jacket and cowboy boots,
for goodness sake. And there was a fat one, and I mean fat.
We were talking Sumo here. He wore a striped Breton
fisherman's pullover stretched so tight it looked like the hori-
zontal hold had gone on a black and white TV.

They came up from the harbour and made to cross the
road to the Pony and Trap, like all innocent pedestrians
should, at the zebra crossing. As they trooped over it, I
wished I had a camera because it looked for all the world like
a surreal version of the Beatles' Abbey Road LP cover.

Belmondo, hands in pockets, swaggered out front. Then, in
a line, came Sumo and the thin cowboy. Oh yes, and Werewolf
was there too, being pushed in a wheelchair by Sumo, his leg
encased in plaster sticking out in front of him like a bowsprit.

I thought for a minute that they would have to take the
door off the Pony and Trap in order to get the wheelchair
inside, but they managed it with only slightly less disturb-
ance than the Keystone Cops changing a light-bulb.

I let them get inside and then I left the café and strolled
across to the harbour wall. There was a positive forest of
masts from yachts large and small, mostly with covers on
having overwintered there, but little activity. The only
sounds were the usual harbourside backing track; the
chink-chink of loose bits of equipment, the slap of water
between boat and harbour wall and the occasional com-
plaint from a seagull. Way down the harbour, a diesel engine phut-phutted into life.

I kept walking round the wall until the boats to my left stopped being the rich people's yachts and got scruffier and older until they turned into working boats.

The fifth one tied to the harbour wall was the one I put money on. Just to be sure, I walked straight by it; then, after another fifty yards, casually turned and sauntered back. I had my hands stuffed into the pockets of my blouson, reaching for the cigarettes I'd given up using the month before. Again.

Yes, that one would do me.

When it comes to anything you eat or drink, the French get quite specific. In a country where you can buy a shot of brandy as a suppository, this is not surprising. Though the brandy might be. I knew they had different names for fishing-boats depending on what the boat was designed to catch. The nearest equivalent to a small British trawler would be a *thonier*, ostensibly a boat that caught tuna fish. A larger, ocean-going trawler would be a *chalutier*, and a shrimp or oyster specialist would be a low-decked, front-cabin *langoustier*, or shrimper.

The *Cendrillon* out of Roscoff on the Brittany coast was a shrimper if ever I saw one. This took no great feat of detection as the crew had conventionally left plastic crates on deck, each one stencilled with the name '*Cadic*' and the legend '*Langoustiers de Roscoff*'.

The boat's crew were on board, a father and two teenage sons so alike they could have been twins. They were involved in a heated argument in thick Breton dialect, about one word in six of which I could understand. They didn't spare me a glance as I walked past them heading back to the main street and I managed to catch just enough of the Breton verbals to decipher that they were debating what to have for lunch.

By the time I got back to the main street, I had convinced myself that the *Cendrillon* was the only boat with any

sign of life on it and so that must have been where Werewolf, Belmondo and his two goons had come from.

So I knew how he'd got to Guernsey. Did it help? Did I
feel any better for having found out?

I looked across the road at the Pony and Trap and
thought the best thing to do was go in and ask the son-of-a-
bitch what was going on.

It was nine minutes past High Noon.

'Well there, you old bastards! Whose round is it anyway?' I
breezed in moving straight to the table where they'd settled
themselves, the cowboy and Sumo on either side of Werewolf's wheelchair.

'Another Guinness, Francis?' I smiled sweetly and took
the empty glass from in front of Werewolf. 'My, but you
look rough, old son.' He did too. 'What about the rest of
you smegheads? Absinthe and blackcurrant, isn't it? Do
they serve that here?'

The Cowboy started to stand but then thought the better
of it. Sumo watched me open-mouthed as I collected
glasses. Belmondo shifted on his seat so I could see inside
his trenchcoat.

I dropped any idea of putting a glass in his face and starting a knock-down-and-drag-out. Best plan was to keep the
blag going. The only plan.

'OK then, three small beers it is. I think I'll have a pint
of the local brew. When in Rome, as they say. My, but you
look like you've been in the wars, Francis. And tell me, is
your friend that pleased to see me?'

'No,' said Werewolf through a fake smile, 'it really is a
gun in his pocket.'

'I'll just get the beers in then, shall I?'

Cowboy and Sumo looked at each other mystified.
Belmondo moved his hand inside his coat and said: 'Please
stay within full view at all times.'

'But of course,' I said equally politely. But I decided not to tell him about the sunglasses.

I made it to the bar without my legs giving way. Guns do that to me, even when they're not pointed directly at me. The one Belmondo had under his coat, pointing at Werewolf's kidney, was a big black ugly thing—they always are when you're not holding them. The most frightening thing about it was that it looked perfectly at home in Belmondo's hand.

I ordered a load of beers from a barman who came out of the pub's kitchen to serve me. He didn't notice my hands shaking and totally ignored my telepathic messages for him to phone the cops. Typical. I knew pubs where they called in the Riot Squad if two people laughed at the same time. All this guy wanted to do was get back to making sandwiches, though God knows who for. Me, Werewolf and the Hole-in-the-Wall Gang were the only customers.

I kept talking as he pulled beer. Mostly it was nerves.

'Bet you didn't think I'd turn up,' I said too loudly, over my shoulder.

'Nah, I had faith,' said Werewolf.

'Come off it.' I grinned inanely, carrying three glasses of lager to the table and amazing myself by not spilling much. 'What odds were you giving on me showing? Six-to-two against?'

Werewolf sucked air in through his beard.

'After what's happened to me lately, I wouldn't give six-to-one,' he said, making eye contact so I was sure he'd caught on.

So I could be right about the three on the boat backing up these three musketeers. Too many, especially without transport. For a moment I remembered what my air hostess had said and cursed myself for not hiring a car. Then I thought about getting Werewolf and a wheelchair into a Metro and didn't feel so bad. (Rule of Life No. 47: When there's really nothing you can do about a situation, it's time to have another drink.)

I returned to the bar for my pint of bitter and Werewolf's pint of Guinness. I put money down in London prices, without thinking, and got change in Guernsey prices which meant I had a lot of loose coins but a warm feeling.

'Dontcha just love these prices? Must be a nice place to retire to and run a pub,' I babbled as I picked up the drinks.

'Sure, you get a lot of trouble from customers,' said Werewolf putting on the Irish.

'Who said anything about customers?' I asked dead straight. It was a routine we'd rehearsed. It didn't get a laugh there either. 'No go, though. You have to have been born on the island to qualify for a licence.' Where did I remember such stuff from? A previous life?

'I don't suppose any of you gentlemen qualify?' I risked, smiling at Sumo. The three beers I'd brought them remained in the centre of the table.

Sumo looked blankly at me, then at the Cowboy.

'Sit down,' said Belmondo as he shuffled inside his trenchcoat.

I sat, my knees up against Werewolf's plaster-encased foot.

'My name is Yannick Guennoc,' said Belmondo.

'I knew someone else called Yannick once,' I said stupidly. 'Well, I suppose he still is called that. He—'

Belmondo-Guennoc stared me down, which is not easy when you're wearing sunglasses.

'—was a Breton too,' I finished quietly.

Guennoc said something to Sumo and Cowboy and they shrugged in stereo. Maybe it was to test me.

'Who said we were Bretons?' he snapped.

'That wasn't any French I understood,' I said truthfully, 'but Yannick's a dead give-away as a name. My friend

Yannick had a Welsh wife and when they had a row he'd swear in Breton and she'd curse him in Welsh and they understood each other. It added a lot to their marriage.'

Guennoc sunglassed me some more, then shifted position so that the nasty round O of the barrel and the shark's fin front sight of the gun were visible through the material of his coat.

'True story,' I said, to break the ice. I felt Werewolf wince.

'Cool it with the crap, eh?' Werewolf grimaced.

I held up two fingers in the Scouts' Honour pledge.

'Crap cooled. You got it.'

I sipped some beer, then put the glass down before they saw my hand shaking.

'So. Here we are then,' I tried. 'You been dancing the Lambada again? I told you, at your age—'

Guennoc leaned forward as if to reach for his drink but in doing so, he pressed the gun through his coat into Werewolf's thigh. Werewolf sucked in breath quickly.

'Explain to the fool and tell him what he has to do, then we go.'

The Cowboy said something to him in an accent it would take me days to get tuned in to and he answered him curtly. Cowboy and then Sumo sat back with their beers and gradually Guennoc eased back too, releasing the pressure on Werewolf's leg.

Werewolf massaged his thigh and began to speak quickly. I was pretty sure that Cowboy and Sumo hadn't a clue between them as to what was being said. Guennoc was another matter, though. And I was wondering just how much Werewolf understood of what they'd said—and how much he'd let on.

'I was on the Belinda O'Blake tour,' he started.

'I heard,' I said, but thought it best not to mention where from.

'Small stuff, mostly university gigs. Fourteen of 'em in nineteen days. Germany, then Amsterdam, Rotterdam, Leuven in Belgium and then two in France. The first was Rouen, and that went OK, then the last was going to be Rennes. After that it was up the coast to Roscoff and the ferry back to Plymouth.'

'The cauliflower run.'

'Yeah, that's right.'

At this time of year the Roscoff–Plymouth ferries carried a few tourists, mostly French truckies loaded with vegetables. It was also one of the least monitored Channel runs if you were thinking of any other sort of cargo.

'Like I said, the Rouen gig went off without a hitch and I gets an early start the next morning heading west on the old autoroute, just trucking along minding my own business. Suddenly, somewhere out in the fucking sticks, I hit a patch of oil and now I'm going sideways instead of west. I try to correct the steering but the back axle clouts something, God knows what, and must've ripped the hydraulics. The rig starts to jackknife on me and I've seen that happen before now so I does what any sane person would do, I show the truck a large proportion of leg and jump for it.'

'Sad choice of words there,' I observed helpfully.

'As it turned out, yes. Me leg goes snap under me as I hits the tarmac. Worst of all, the fucking truck waltzes full circle and comes to a gentle halt up a grass embankment.'

'So the truck's OK?'

'Yeah, thanks a bunch. That's what Belinda's bloody management said. Bugger the driver, is the gear in one piece?'

'Trucks are insured.' Freelance roadies like Werewolf usually aren't unless they've taken out cover themselves and they rarely do.

'You're telling me. The insurance assessors were flown over the next morning. This was after a couple of nuns in a 2CV had stopped—the only spot of Christian charity in Normandy that day, I can tell you—and taken me to the hospital back in Rouen.'

'Nuns?'

'Don't knock it. I was well pleased to see them. So there I am, just time to phone the management back in London when they jab the hypo up me backside and I come to the next day with this thing in plaster up to the goolies.'

He paused to finish nearly all of a pint of Guinness in one go.

'That's it? You were just tooling down the autoroute minding your own business when you—you?—lost control?'

'That's about the height of it,' said Werewolf philosophically, wiping stout cream from his beard. 'Difficult to believe, isn't it?'

'Imfuckingprobable, to say the least.'

I sneaked a glance at Guennoc. He looked puzzled. Good. Maybe his English wasn't all that hot.

'What were you on?'

Werewolf attempted to look surprised and hurt. I suppose it could have fooled lesser mortals.

'Nothing, man, honest. Not a whiff, not a trace element of any noxious substance, sullied my system. The traffic *flics* never even bothered to test me.'

'Speed?'

'I just said—'

'How fast were you going?'

'Ah, well, there was that. About a hundred and ten.'

'Kilometres?'

'Sadly, no. It was miles per hour.' He showed me the palms of his hands. 'It was one of the new Volvo rigs and up till then I'd never had a chance to put it through its paces. This was the first bit of straight road I'd hit this side of the Rhine.'

'And the road hit back, so to speak.'

'You could say that.'

'I just did.'

'You would.'

'So then what?'

'So I'm in hospital, dying of thirst—' he rolled his empty glass—'and Belinda turns up to see if I'm in one piece and to offer to pay any bills.'

'That was nice of her,' I offered.

'Oh sure. Superstar Belinda O'Blake turns up with her agent, with her publicity agent and with a sodding photographer. Caring popstar pictured looking after her injured staff, I don't think. Half a dozen carefully posed shots round the hospital bed and she pisses off. They wanted one for *New Musical Express* that week. Did you see it?'

'You know my views on that: reading the *NME* gives you cancer.'

'Well, she's out of it and on with the tour. Then the management turns up with a French lawyer to see about the truck.'

'Which management?'

'Box Pop.'

I knew them; a smallish outfit, pretty second division, working out of a warehouse near Heathrow, leasing equipment rather than owning it. Their drivers and roadies were officially 'self-employed', which meant no tax, no paperwork, no pension plan, no comeback.

'And?'

'And they decide I haven't damaged it enough to stop my wages but obviously I can't drive it back, so they hire some gink to get it back home.'

'For the concert in Rennes?' I asked.

'Nah, too late for that. The Volvo goes back via Cherbourg on the first available ferry. Yours truly left well in it trying to reverse-charge the phone calls to Box Pop to wire me some dosh.'

Werewolf leaned forward and relieved me of my half-drunk pint.

'After three days or so one of the nurses tells me that someone is coming to spring me and like a right airhead I go along with it.' He slid his eyes towards Guennoc.

'And where have you been since?' It was worth a shot.

Guennoc shifted his chair around and let his coat fall open again. I got a really good view of the gun that way. I could even read the letters 'P.38' on the shiny black metal breech.

'Your friend stays with us,' said Guennoc quietly. 'It does not matter where.'

Sumo and Cowboy relaxed and Sumo even wrapped a hand around his beer, then supped it in one go. The plan had been to let Werewolf talk and Guennoc coming in like that had been a signal that things were going to plan.

Plan? What plan?

'And you are?' I turned the smile on Guennoc and wondered if it would help if I told him he looked like Belmondo. I decided against it, even if I'd stressed the 'younger version'.

'We represent the FPB,' he said proudly, pronouncing the letters the French way: eff-pay-bay.

'And that is?' Still smiling, but getting a bad feeling about it all.

'The *Front Populaire Breton*.'

Silly question. The FPB was so bleeding *populaire* I'd forgotten about it. No, be honest: I'd never heard of it.

I waved a hand limply, which in other circumstances could have been taken for the offer of getting another round in.

'And your interest in my friend here . . . ?'

Guennoc took his left hand out from under his coat, laced his fingers and cracked his knuckles. A nasty habit, but effective.

'M'sieur Dromey here—' I did my ritual double-take

when someone used Werewolf's real name, but it didn't throw Guennoc—'was carrying something for us. Property of the FPB. We want it back.'

'Drugs,' I said fatalistically.

Cowboy sat up with a start and tried to look mean. That was at least one familiar word of English for him. Probably picked it up from the Eurovision Song Contest. Sumo also sat to attention and because of his size, he didn't need a refresher in menace.

'I said nothing about drugs,' Guennoc hissed.

'OK, so the truck had come from Belgium via Amsterdam and Rotterdam. The Belgians don't export anything more lethal than cherry-flavoured beer, so that leaves the Dutch. Don't tell me, you've cornered the market in Edam cheese, is that it?'

'I didn't know, Roy, honest,' said Werewolf. Knowing him, he only had to say it once and he knew I'd believe him. That's what friends are for, but it doesn't mean you should let them off the hook.

'And you told these Provos—' I hoped they hadn't heard that one on the news lately—'that I was just the man to help get them back, eh?'

'Something like that,' he said grinning.

'Thanks. Thank you, Monsieur Francis X. Dromey.'

'What's the "X" for?'

'I'll think of something. I ought to slug you.'

'You'd hit a cripple, wouldn't you?'

I never knew just how much Guennoc understood of all that, but I got the feeling that he was sure he had another recruit to the *Front Populaire*. He hadn't touched his gun for nearly a minute, he was so confident.

'It was in the truck?' I asked him.

'Yes, though we were not told exactly where.'

Great help.

'What were you carrying?' This is Werewolf.

'Back-up light show stuff, a spare generator and a bank
of speakers. Nearly all doubled-up with the other two
trucks.'

'No essential gear for the gig? Costumes, instruments?'

'Nah, nothing they'd really miss. The stuff would probably have gone back into store once it got to England, back
at Box Pop.'

'You haven't asked anyone there to check it out?' I asked
half-heartedly. Last-ditch attempt to stay uninvolved. Fat
chance.

'You kidding? That mob? They'd be retailing at fifteen
quid a tab in Milton Keynes before Saturday night.'

So it was Ecstasy tablets was it? Great.

'I needed someone I could trust,' said Werewolf lamely.

'Someone who can move freely in England,' said
Guennoc, going quiet again. 'Someone who can find our
property within five days.'

'Why five days?' I asked, knowing I wouldn't like the
answer.

Guennoc smiled.

'Because in five days we kill him.' He jerked a thumb at
Werewolf.

Werewolf shrugged his shoulders. 'It's a bummer, isn't
it?'

CHAPTER 3

I had no choice in the matter, had I? I mean, what are
friends for? If you can't respect that, then you're no better
than an animal, are you?

Animals. More hassle, but that could be sorted. First
item on the agenda. Second item, contact Box Pop and find
out what happened to Werewolf's truck, or rather its con-

tents. Third item, locate aforementioned naughty substances, secure them and then wait for Guennoc's phone call in five days' time. No sweat.

Not too much to do for an old and distinguished friend, was it?

After all, when you've lost your wheels, broken your leg, been kidnapped in a foreign country, are held to ransom for a consignment of drugs you didn't even know you were carrying, and have five days before you're executed by a bunch of urban terrorists you've never heard of, who else you gonna call?

I was back in London by 4.30 that afternoon.

Guennoc had instructed me to remain in the Pony and Trap for thirty minutes after the travelling circus had left. I gave it twenty and that allowed me a sight of a fishing-boat heading for the harbour entrance. No prizes for guessing it had *Cendrillon* on the stern. There was no sign of Werewolf but in his condition, he'd hardly be shinning up the mast spotting whales. I could make out Sumo, though, arguing with one of the crew; probably about lunch.

I cabbed it back to the airport and blagged my way on to one of the early afternoon flights. I rescued Armstrong from one of the car parks (actually the yellow-lined area near the terminal entrance which says TAXIS ONLY) and ignored half-a-dozen suitcase-laden tourists who tried to flag me down. At any other time, I could have shown them the scenic route into West London—the one that takes in Eastbourne—but I had things to do.

By the time I reached the West End, the traffic had glued up, though most of it was running against me, trying to get out of town. There was still time to pull a Middleditch and sort the first of my problems.

I picked a big oil company office just off Oxford Street (and driving down there is another perk of being thought of as a taxi) and pulled up right outside the front glass doors.

In the glove compartment I keep a small package with the words 'Mr Morton Middleditch—By Hand' typed on an address label. Actually, it's an envelope containing a copy of *The Story of O* in a well-thumbed paperback edition, and while I know of no such person as Middleditch, one day I'll meet one and probably be very embarrassed.

I smiled my best flossed smile at the receptionist who was actually more interested in the clock above her desk creeping round to five-thirty than she was in me.

'Package for Mr Middleditch,' I said sweetly.

She wrinkled her eyebrows, then looked over my shoulder at Armstrong parked outside, then at her mini-switchboard.

'No one here of that name. Are you sure?'

'Sure I'm sure. Well, I'm sure that's what I was told.' I gave her the full but-you-know-what-people-are look.

'Definitely—' she ran a red fingernail down a type-written list—'no Middleton here.'

'Middleditch,' I said.

'Him neither.' Then she turned her head to a middle-aged doorman wearing a security man's uniform, who had emerged from a glass cubicle by the door. 'You ever heard of a Mr Middleditch, Frank?'

Frank shook his head and massaged his Adam's apple.

'No such person,' he said with the confidence that a uniform and a peaked hat always imparts to the wearer.

I looked at the envelope and then scratched my head.

'Bloody dispatchers,' I said to Frank the Uniform and he nodded wisely. 'Could I use your phone, mate? Find out what's going on?'

''Course you can, squire. In there. Dial 9 for an outside line.'

'Cheers.' It never fails.

*

'Lloyd Allen, please.'

'Lloyd's not here, man.'

'Any idea where I can get him?'

'Lloyd's not here, man.'

Why couldn't he have an answerphone?

'Tell Mr Allen that Mr Angel wants a word in his shell-like, bloody quick, OK?'

'Hold that thought, man.' There was a thirty-second silence. Well, that's not strictly true. Nobody spoke but I could hear a Gypsy Kings record playing loudly in the background.

'Chill out, man, you're on the list,' the voice came back. 'You can get Lloyd the Droid on his car phone.'

'Hang on.' I pinched a pencil from the security man's desk and scribbled a Vodaphone number on the back of my Middleditch package. 'Got it. Thanks.'

So much for Brixton Directory Inquiries.

I don't know what they do to the calls, but ringing into a car phone seems almost as expensive as ringing from one. Those things eat money, so I was glad it wasn't mine.

'Lloyd?' I squeaked, amazed at getting through first time.

'Maybe.' It was Lloyd.

'Angel here, in need of advice.'

'Angel, my main man! What sort of advice? Financial, sexual, social or you just out to improve your street cred?'

'What do you know about Box Pop?'

'The tour managers? Bit of a cowboy outfit. You playing for them?'

'They got any jobs going?'

'Not for you. Not your scene at all, Angel.'

'Hey, man, jazz is back, you know.'

'*I* know that, baby, but did *you*? Your sort of jazz never went away, just stayed where it was . . .'

'You're getting very faint, Lloyd,' I lied. 'I said, do you know anyone in Box Pop?'

'Is the Pope free on Easter Sunday? Of course I do. Ritchie Fortune's the man to see. Do you want a number for him?'

'I'm impressed, Lloyd; having it at your fingertips right now.'

'Hey, man, that's not all I have at my fingertips right now.'

Then I heard: 'Pass my Filofax, honey . . . No . . . no . . . ooh . . . No, the other pocket . . .'

'You're fading on me Lloyd.'

He came back with a 486 London number, which meant inner city. I scribbled it on my envelope.

'You sure, Lloyd? That's a West End number. I thought Box Pop was based out near the airport.'

'Ritchie's a Turk and lives above the family restaurant. There's nothing at Box Pop 'cept a warehouse, man, and that's mostly empty these days. Ow! Cut those nails, babe . . .'

'Lloyd, you're not driving, are you?'

Lloyd had a customized old Ford Zephyr complete with multi-choice furry dice in different colours depending on his mood. It had most of the luxury accessories you'd get on a standard Porsche these days, but automatic pilot wasn't one of them.

'Hell no, I've got one of the Dennison boys driving. I'm in conference with my new personal assistant—and, trust me, she is into assisting.'

'Have fun. Can I mention your name to Ritchie?'

'Yeah. My credit's even good at his restaurant but take a tip, don't have the liver.'

'Thanks, Lloyd. Listen, I'm in in your debt.'

'As usual, Mr Angel, as usual.'

'Well, you take care. Oh, Lloyd?'

'Yeah?'

'Why do they call you Lloyd the Droid?'

'Who does? Who laid that on? Which—'

'Sorry, Lloyd, you're fading out. See yer.'

'Excuse me, but do you guys have an office on Duke Street?'

'No chance,' said Frank the Security Man; with authority.'

'No way,' chimed in the receptionist, looking round for her coat. It was on the back of her chair, but I thought I'd let her find it herself.

'Then they've screwed it again, the bastards.' Then I made a big open-pupil stare at the receptionist. 'I'm sorry, pardon my French.'

'That's all right,' she said, ignoring me and reaching for her handbag. But Frank the Security Man looked impressed.

'Would you excuse me—again?' I asked, jerking my thumb at his office, and the phone.

'Sure, son, you help yourself.'

It's a shame to take the money sometimes.

'Hello, Aunt Dorothea?'

'I don't want any.'

'Aunty, it's me, Roy.'

'Double-glazing salesmen will be shot on sight as soon as they enter my property. How many times—?'

'Aunty! Pay attention. It's Roy.'

'Are you selling double-glazing?'

'Of course not . . .'

'Conservatories?'

'No.'

'Roof insulation?'

'No! Will you put a fucking sock in it, Aunty?'

'Oh, hello, Fitzroy, I didn't recognize the voice.'

'That's—'

'It's been so long, after all—'

'Aunty—'

'Not that there actually is any money left from the Will, but—'

'Social call, Dorothea.'

'Then why didn't you say so, dickhead? What's cooking?' I felt one of my headaches coming on again.

'I want you to look after Springsteen for a few days, that's all.'

I was beginning to regret this already.

'That black moggie? You mean you haven't got that stuffed and nodding in the back of your car yet?'

'Not yet, Aunty.' Was the woman mad? 'He isn't actually . . . Oh, skip it. Look, will you take care of him for me? Just for a few days.'

'Usual charge, board and lodging?'

'Whatever you say, Aunty.'

'Cash?'

'Of course.'

'In advance?'

'Naturally.' It's good to have family.

'Very well then, just this once.'

'Thanks, Aunty. I'll bring him on the train.'

'Give me a bell and I'll meet you at the station.'

'You got it.'

'Fitzroy?'

'Yes, Aunty?'

'Why aren't you my favourite nephew?'

'Can't think, Aunty.'

'Neither can I. Byeee.'

I came out of Frank's cubicle and I was already saying:

'Typical! They change shifts and now nobody knows . . .'

Then I realized I had the foyer to myself.

I made one more call, booking a table for later that night at the Fortuna restaurant on the number Lloyd had given me. Then I walked out to Armstrong.

'Don't worry,' I said aloud to no one in particular, 'I'll lock up.'

I'd better explain.

Lloyd Allen, the ace Brixton entrepreneur, is The Man when it comes to deals, wheels and wheels-within-wheels, especially in the music business. What he doesn't know wasn't worth forgetting. He's a very dangerous friend to have, and also a very reliable enemy. But if he said Ritchie Fortune was the one to hit, that's who was going to get hit.

Oh yeah. Springsteen.

He's a cat and we sort of share the same living accommodation.

It's a fair divide. I buy the food and pay the rent.

Fenella was horrified at first, then she saw the sense of it.

It was not so much Springsteen himself, more the six half-Springsteen, half-Siamese kittens we still had which were the problem. They had been a belated Christmas present from Springsteen himself—and that nice Mr Tomlin down the street who had tried to breed pedigree Siamese. Well, if he can't control the women in his household, what did he expect? What I hadn't expected was to be lumbered with a boxful of Springsteen's offspring on New Year's Eve.

They had now got to the stage where they should be able to stand on their own four feet. Typically, this was the only time Springsteen showed any interest in them and every time someone came round to suss one out as a prospective parent, he would either attack them or do something unspeakable on the hall carpet right in front of them. It was like people going to an adoption agency with the best will

in the world and being met by a ground-level attack from
F-111s.

'A few days in the country will do him the world of good,'
I said to Fenella, making sure HE was out of earshot, 'and
it'll give you a chance to get rid of the kittens.'

'But they're so sweet,' she whined. 'And you make it
sound like you want me to put them in a sack and throw
them in the river.'

I whipped a hand across her mouth and said loudly:
'That's the last thing I said, Fenella. And I don't know how
you could even think such a thing.'

I scanned the landing but there was no sign of Springsteen.

'Have you no sense, woman?' I hissed under my breath.
'Don't you know that cat can pick up satellite TV?'

'Sorry,' said Fenella quietly. 'I'm sure it's for the best.'

'It's your responsibility to find them good homes while
he's away,' I said reasonably.

'Yes, I accept that,' she said seriously.

There's one born every minute, isn't there? And I don't
mean just Springsteen's.

'I'll do my best,' she promised. I could have kissed her.

'I know you will Fenella, thank you.'

'But—this sort of responsibility—'

'Yes? Tell uncle.'

'You won't let on to Lisabeth that I've taken this on, will
you?'

'Won't say a word, kid. Promise.'

The Fortune family restaurant—Fortuna—did a good job
at hiding itself in an alley off Great Titchfield Street over
towards the BBC. The entrance lobby had a counter for
take-away kebabs, although not in business during the evening, and a couple of hatstands groaning with coats. Once
in the restaurant proper I could see where the coats had

come from. There were tables for maybe two hundred diners disappearing in a dog-leg to the left to the back of the building. Like Dr Who's time machine, it was much bigger from the inside. And doing good business, making the Fortunes' fortune.

A white-shirted waiter with a blue cummerbund showed me to a wall-table for two half way down the dining-room and left me with a menu and a wine list. I didn't recognize any of the wines except Keo, which comes from Cyprus, and in other circumstances I would have had great fun experimenting. I'd discovered some great Lebanese reds that way in the cluster of Lebanese restaurants in 'Little Beirut' down the south end of the Edgware Road. Of course you can make mistakes and pick the ones that come with a HAZ CHEM. warning on the label. I settled for an Efes Pils beer, and, remembering Lloyd's advice about avoiding the liver, ordered humous and the spiced lamb patties.

When my beer arrived I asked the waiter if Mr Ritchie was in tonight and he jerked a thumb at a reserved table in the corner and said 'Nine o'clocks', giving that it was no big deal to get to see the man himself.

I was into my main course, the plate stacked with food as I should have expected, when he arrived. He just appeared from out of the back, or the kitchens, or somewhere. Suddenly he was there at the table and two waiters were fighting to be the first to pull out a chair for him.

He looked around mid-twenties, with unfashionably long hair and small circular steel-rimmed glasses with tinted lenses. He was dressed in regulation cool: jeans, leather jacket and a Friends of the Earth sweatshirt. He laid out a mobile phone and a bulging Filofax, which just went to prove that even though no one is seen in public with one any more, addiction can be a terrible thing.

Once settled, a waiter brought him a bottle of red wine and a bottle of Badoit mineral water (the one that has a higher sulphur content than hell) and one big glass. He mixed himself a half-and-half and sipped. Then a second waiter appeared with two filing trays, one empty and the other stuffed to overflow with papers, including a wedge of computer printout and an inch-thick pile of flimsy fax messages. He settled down to work as more waiters dropped off dishes of crudités and dips.

I gave him ten minutes or so, then sauntered across.

'Mr Fortune?'

'One of them,' he said without looking up.

'Can I bother you for a minute?' I put my hands on the back of the chair opposite him.

'It won't be a bother, will it?' he asked, unfolding a computer printout.

I realized I had two of the waiters on either side of me. Both were a foot shorter than me, both at least twenty years older, both tough as old boots.

'Lloyd Allen told me I could find you here.'

'And that's a recommendation?' He refolded the printout and slipped it into the empty tray. Still no eye contact.

'Best I've got.'

He looked up at me. Then frowned.

'Seen you around. Don't tell me.' He pointed a finger. 'Horn player. Did you do some session work on a demo cut down at Boot-In for a spade chick called Beeby Bee?'

'Yeah, last year.'

'Flugelhorn, wasn't it?'

'No, bass trumpet.' My lip had taken a week to recover.

'What happened to the chick?'

'Disappeared almost as fast as the demo tape did.'

'Mmm. Figured. Sit down.'

The waiters had gone. Maybe they'd never been there.

'You tried the liver here?' Ritchie asked, moving one of his trays so I could rest my forearms on the tablecloth.

'I've eaten, thanks. Excellent.'

'Yes, but did you catch the liver?'

'No . . .' No point in blagging, he could check.

'I'll get you a plate. It's our speciality starter. Drink?'

'Beer. Efes.'

'Good choice.' He waved a hand and beer, cutlery and then a plate of liver cut into triangles and deep fried appeared almost instantly.

'Talk while you eat,' he said, leafing through a four-page fax message.

'Box Pop put together the Belinda O'Blake tour of Europe, right?'

'Yep, just finished. Good gigs. Hardly stadia rock but not small change either. What's it to you?'

'I'm a friend of the driver of the truck you lost.'

'The Irishman? Sheeiit! I've told them never to hire Irish or Greek. It's always trouble. If it isn't booze, it's women. Still, the truck was OK, there was that. But so what?'

I forked another piece of liver and chewed slowly. The soft fried onions with it had been marinated in something I couldn't quite identify. Gasoline; that was it.

'Well, Mr Fortune, I just thought you'd be needing another driver. I've got a clean HGV and now Francis is laid up . . .'

'You're talking to the wrong dude. I put the tours together, that's all. I don't run trucks, don't own gear. It's all hired in. You'll do better talking to Candlepower.'

'Candlepower?' I choked down another piece of liver and smiled. Not easy.

'The lighting company I used for the O'Blake gigs. I'll take a PA set-up from one company but the light show and staging comes from another. Usually, the trucks come from a third source but it just so happens Candlepower own a couple, so the truck came with the deal.'

'Why doesn't someone offer the whole lot in one go?' I

asked, sidetracked but interested, for a second. 'Trucks, sound system and lighting all in one package.'

Ritchie Fortune looked at me with genuine pity.

'Then nobody would need me to put the deal together, would they?'

'Oh, of course not. Sorry. So you reckon this Candle-power may have a job going?'

'Maybe.'

He looked at my plate of liver. There were two pieces to go. I forked them into my mouth quickly and washed them down with the last of the beer.

'Know where I can find them?'

'Yeah, sure. They have the next unit on the industrial estate out at Heston.'

I was beginning to see the light. The trucks and light shows were nothing to do with Box Pop Ltd; they just happened to come from their next-door neighbour.

'Ask for Jev Jevons,' he said, putting me out of my misery. 'He's the head honcho out there.'

'Thanks,' I said, swallowing hard. 'Can I get you another drink?'

'No way, I've got work to do.' He reached for his In-tray again. 'You pay on your way out.'

I stood up and saw that my table had been cleared and a young yuppie couple were being seated. There was a waiter at my elbow with a bill on a plate.

'Thanks again,' I said. 'And thanks for recommending the liver. I'll remember that.'

'Tastes like shit, doesn't it?' he said quietly, without looking up again.

'Yeah, but organic shit. No preservatives or anything.'

He snorted a half-chuckle and reached for his mobile phone.

At the desk on the way out I found that my bill had had the liver and the extra beer added to it. I didn't complain.

Too many complaints in a place like that and you could
end up starring on the menu.

Back at Stuart Street I started to put myself on a war foot-
ing.

The first thing to do was to round up Springsteen's six
Siamese clones. I don't know what they'd inherited from
their mother, probably their ability to shout instead of
miaow, but Springsteen had given them speed, that was for
sure.

Eventually, I had Ella, Billy, Sarah, Louis and Dizzy
locked in the downstairs back kitchen, which nobody used
these days, but I couldn't find Miles. And Springsteen had
disappeared, so he was being no help at all; although staying out of the way probably was helpful in his case.

A muffled scream from the flat below helped me narrow
my search area. I was half way down the stairs when Fenella emerged holding Miles.

'He was in Lisabeth's bed,' she said, mock sternly. Then
she raised her voice: 'And it had better not happen
again!'

'I'm sorry. It won't. Come here, you little hooligan.'
Then, quietly: 'And I'll give you a medal.'

Fenella giggled.

'Poor Ella,' she whispered, stroking the kitten's head.

'This is Miles,' I said.

'Are you sure?'

'Yes.'

But I wasn't. I'd just named half of them female and half
male. I had no intention of looking to see how accurate I'd
been.

As I locked Miles in with the rest, I told Fenella: 'Now
remember, do not open this door until I'm well clear of
the house tomorrow morning. I'll be leaving early, so it
shouldn't be a problem.'

'You were up and out early this morning,' she said suspiciously.

'Yeah, I had to fly over to the Channel Islands for a drink with some old mates.'

'Not that I'm the slightest bit interested in where you really were, but you must think I'm stupid to believe that one,' she snapped and flounced back upstairs.

Sometimes you just can't win. I really should know that by now.

Back in my flat I cleaned up the kitchen so that I wouldn't come back to a fresh crop of penicillin when I returned. There was half a bottle of Chardonnay left in the fridge and I decided that wouldn't keep either. Anyway, I still needed to chase the taste of liver away.

I drank from the bottle to save on the washing-up and put Hugh Masekela's version of *No Woman No Cry* on the CD. It lacked the religiosity of the Bob Marley original, but it had a trumpet solo I could mime along to.

I took out a copy of Hugh Brogan's *History of the United States* and opened it up. This was not an academic exercise. My copy had been converted by a miscreant called Lenny the Lathe into a fireproof combination-lock safe. Ideal unless you get turned over by intellectual burglars.

This was my war chest, such as it was, containing a couple of building society books, spare cash and credit cards, some of which were in my name, or most of it. I mean, I can't help it if people get my name wrong, can I? So sometimes I'm Roy Maclean, sometimes Fitzroy Angel, sometimes F. M. Angel. Nobody really believes Fitzroy Maclean Angel.

My literary safe also contained a broken-spined address book and under 'W' for Werewolf there were at least eight numbers. One of them wasn't a Werewolf number at all, it was Werewolf's brother, and Werewolf had given it to me

once—when drunk and getting emotional—in case anything serious ever happened to him.

I'd remembered saying at the time that the address had
seemed familiar. Not surprisingly perhaps, it was a pub;
but a pub—the Sundial—in a place called Donhead St
Agnes in north Dorset. Now the reason I knew such a way
out place was that Aunt Dorothea, the recently appointed
custodian of Springsteen, lived not a million miles away
near Salisbury.

I carried the wine bottle with me to the phone by the
front door. As I dialled I checked my Seastar. It was 10.45
p.m. Surely even in Dorset the pubs would still be going.

'Sundial Inn,' came a female voice, 'how can we help?'

If I'd expected 'Oo-Arr, pass the cyder jug, m'dear' then
I'd got the wrong pub.

'I'm trying to get hold of a Mr Gearoid Dromey,' I said,
trying to remember how Werewolf had told me to pro-
nounce the Irish version of Gary.

'Oh, you mean Werewolf's brother?' she said.

I might have known.

CHAPTER 4

The war of nerves with Springsteen went on most of the
night. He long ago mastered the techniques of sleep depri-
vation and when he wasn't employing them against me, he
was prowling noisily around the flat checking and recheck-
ing that the cat flap was locked and the kitchen windows
shut. Then he would come into the bedroom and just eyeball me, as if he couldn't believe I'd dared do this to him.

First thing next morning I grabbed a shower and a cup
of coffee, then dressed in jeans, sweatshirt, trainers, leather
jacket and black leather gloves. Just to be on the safe side,

I wrapped a black wool scarf around my neck and mouth. Then I tuned the radio into Jazz FM and turned the volume up to drown the howls of protest as I stuffed Springsteen into his carrying basket.

I had allowed myself plenty of time to find a parking space for Armstrong near Waterloo Station, but even so, I only just made the Salisbury train. I had bought a cheap day return ticket on the first train to run outside the Crush Hour, but once I had left Springsteen's basket in the guard's van—and advised him to lock the door—I made my way to the First Class dining-car, picking up a copy of the *Financial Times* which someone had left to guard their seat, en route. Even with the continental breakfast, it's cheaper than paying for a First Class seat and it put the entire length of the train between me and Springsteen.

Round about my second croissant and honey, I picked my target.

There were three mobile phones on show in the dining-car, all carefully displayed by their suit-wearing executive owners. I picked a guy two tables away who was chatting up a middle-aged power-dressed woman with plucked eyebrows and a ski-slope suntan. She looked bored and nowhere near as interested as he did. He wouldn't want to be shown up as a tightwad in front of her.

Making like I'd just seen something dramatic in the *FT*, I sat bolt upright, mugged a double-take, then, folding the newspaper over to quarter its size, I looked around anxiously. I made eye contact with the guy and sprang out of my seat. Clutching the paper, I made my way over and leaned against his table to counter the sway of the train.

'Do excuse me, but could I possibly borrow your telephone. It's something of an emergency.'

'Well . . . yes, of course,' he said, handing it over.

I stepped through the automatic door into the corridor, switched the phone on and dialled.

'Hello, Aunty.'

'Who is this?'

'It's Fitzroy, your nephew.'

'Just checking.'

'I'll be arriving at Salisbury station in about half an hour. You haven't forgotten you're picking me up, have you?'

'Of course not. What size helmet are you?'

'Pardon? What was that?'

'Never mind. See you soon.'

She hung up, leaving me more than a little puzzled.

Through the glass of the sliding door I could see the guy I'd borrowed the phone from flicking through his copy of the *Financial Times* to try and spot what I'd seen.

He had the good grace to blush with embarrassment when I handed back the mobile, catching him at it. He didn't even complain that I'd smeared honey over the push buttons.

I've never asked, but Aunt Dorothea must be pushing sixty-five. I had once seen a photograph of her from around 1950, which could have been captioned Shortest Debutante of the Season. In her strapless posh party frock flared out by enough petticoats to support the Parachute Regiment, she needed four-inch heels to bring the top of her head anywhere near the shoulder of the shortest of her contemporaries. She looked even shorter in the saddle of the 750 cc BMW motorbike when she met me outside Salisbury station.

'Hop on, Fitzroy, and hang on to the moggie. There's a helmet in that basket thing on the back,' she said cheerfully, sliding up the visor of one of those crash lids which look like a stormtrooper's helmet from *Star Wars*.

I must have just stared. Even Springsteen stopped howling. I was dead now. He'd never forgive me for this.

'Hello, Aunty. I was sort of expecting a car,' I said stupidly. A Morris Minor perhaps, or a Renault 4.

'Oh, I sold the Jag,' she said casually, tweaking the throttle. 'Too expensive to run. Mind you, the insurance on this is an absolute bugger.'

'I bet it is. Are you sure . . . ?'

'Oh, come on. Where's your spirit of adventure? Big city got your balls, has it? I had the local vicar on the back last week.'

There was a white shopping pannier on the back which had a circular sticker saying 'Pensioner Power' on the lid. Inside was a regular black crash helmet. I pulled it on, grateful now that I'd brought gloves and scarf. Springsteen yowled once, as if asking where his was.

Aunt Dorothea revved up again as I straddled the bike behind her, clutching Springsteen's basket to my chest. That left me without hands to hang on with, so I tensed my knees so tight I knew I would have the cramps before we got out of the station car park.

Not that that took long. Nor did the rest of the ride to Dorothea's village down a hair-raising spiral of country lanes out beyond the racecourse. I missed the views, the pastoral scenes, the hill figures carved by primitive man. I had my eyes shut. So did Springsteen.

To be fair, Dorothea did slow down to a blur as we went through her village of Chalkeford and then she had to change down to turn into her cottage through a set of oversized (but no doubt at some point in the past, cheap) wrought-iron gates. Hence, she had called the place Heaven's Gate—and where else would an Angel live?

I peeled myself off the bike with the distinct feeling that my legs might never meet again at the knees. I put Springsteen's basket down and tried to massage some feeling back into my thighs. Aunt Dorothea laughed as she took off her helmet.

'It's all right for you,' I said petulantly. 'You're wearing leathers.'

She put the BMW up on its rest and took off her gauntlets.

'You'll have to help me get the boots off,' she said, giving me a peck on the cheek but not taking her eyes off the handle-bar mirror in which she was tweaking her hair back into shape.

'Anything you command, Aunty. I'm not going to cross a Hell's Angel.'

'Gosh,' she said sarcastically, 'that's an original. No one's *ever* said that before.'

'Where's Bishop?' I asked as she took my arm and led me round the side of the cottage.

Bishop was Dorothea's twelve-year-old black Labrador. I knew from her last letter that she had spent a fortune on him and a hip replacement operation, necessary due to some unspeakable doggy disease.

'He'll be in the kitchen, toasting himself near the Aga. He can't get out much nowadays.'

As we turned the corner round the back of the cottage, I could see why. One of the outbuildings near the kitchen door had had a fencing extension built on to the front. Heavy-guage chicken wire went up to about twelve feet in height and then formed a flat roof back to the old wood store, or whatever it had been. It looked like the lion house at a third-rate zoo, but somehow a polar bear had got in there.

'Jesus!' I yelled, jumping back a good two feet.

Springsteen hissed viciously, but he was probably spoiling for a fight.

'That's a fucking bear, Aunty!'

The thing was huge, standing on its hind legs, paws up against the wire at my head height, bending it outwards. I had to look up to see its head, and jaws, and teeth.

'Actually, Fitzroy, its an Akita. Down, Cherry!'

The huge white beast took no notice, just showed more teeth. It hadn't barked, though, but I didn't know if that was a good sign. I was more interested in checking the stables which kept the wire in place.

'Cherry?'

'That's right. And that's Blossom,' said Dorothea as a second white wolf emerged to press a head no bigger than a bison's up against the wire. 'They're from Japan. Cherry blossom—geddit?'

'Mutant Ninja Rottweilers, more like it. Dotty, they're fucking monsters.' I found myself backed up against the wall of her cottage.

'I certainly hope so,' said Dorothea with a big grin.

It dawned on me.

'Aunty, you're not breeding them, are you?'

'No, I'm teaching them to play cribbage!' She shrieked with laughter. Then she nudged me in the ribs with an elbow. 'What's got four legs *and* an arm?'

'A Rottweiler.'

'You've heard it.' She sounded genuinely peeved. 'Well anyway, Akitas eat Rottweilers for breakfast. Did you know that a Rottweiler's bite strength is fifty per cent more than an Alsatian's? Well, an Akita's is thirty per cent bigger than that.'

'Who on earth wants one? Who can afford to feed one?'

'You'd be surprised. No, maybe you wouldn't. I've got three on the waiting list for puppies already.'

I checked the cat basket. Springsteen's tail had fluffed up to the size of a fox's brush.

'I think we'd better go inside,' I said, keeping my back to the wall and edging towards the kitchen door.

Dorothea banged the flat of her hand on the Akitas' cage wire. Cherry fell back on to all fours with a nasty gleam in his eye.

'Don't just stand there, fool around!' she hissed at him, but he showed no sign of doing that. He just lumbered off to the end of the cage as far away from Blossom as possible.

Bishop the labrador gave a half-hearted bark as I entered the kitchen. He was cowering round the corner of the Aga range and didn't offer to come and greet me. I put Springsteen's basket down on a chair and went over to scratch his ears. The old hound dog looked really sorry for himself. Even without his replacement hip joints, he was no match for King and Queen Kong outside. The poor old sod must have developed a bad case of the inferiorities. I patted him some more and realized that he now had Springsteen as a house guest.

'Sorry, Bishop,' I whispered. 'This just isn't your day, is it?'

'Coffee's on,' said Dorothea, rattling a kettle under the tap. 'Are you staying for lunch?'

'Actually, I was hoping to pop over to Donhead St Agnes for lunch.'

'Good. I didn't think to get any food in. I've got work to do and I'll just munch a ship's biscuit or something.'

Dorothea was an artist, and a good one. In recent years she'd made a good living painting plants and flowers for gardening books, Sunday newspaper supplements and seed catalogues. She used to do illustrations for children's books but blew it with a much too close to the bone version of Goldilocks and the Three Bears for a very straight publisher. (Family rumour had it that she later sold the illustrations to *Playboy*, but she'd never confirmed that. Never denied it either.)

'I was hoping I could borrow some wheels . . .' I said lamely.

'Well, you've seen 'em. Take 'em if you think you can handle them.' She tossed me the keys to the BMW. 'What's in Donhead St Agnes to interest you?'

'Brother of a friend of mine lives there. Couldn't pass up the chance to say hello as I was this close.'

'Must lead a quiet life if he lives in St Agnes,' she said, fitting a filter paper into a filter which she balanced over a jug bearing the legend 'Gordon's Gin'. 'People from Donhead regard Chalkeford as the big bad city. There's a good pub there, though.'

'The Sundial?'

'That's right. Good ale and decent food, too.'

'Care to join us?'

'No way,' she said, pouring hot water on to coffee. 'I can't. The landlord banned me. He put a sign up saying "No Bikers". Pompous sod.'

Aunt Dorothea didn't appear to own a map but she gave me explicit directions on how to find the Sundial. The instructions were of the 'Go through Ebbesborne Wake, then turn right just after the stile and then you cross the A30 and turn right at the telephone-box' sort. They included the priceless piece of information that if I found myself in Sixpenny Handley, I'd gone entirely the wrong way.

Mindful of Dotty's warning about the pub's landlord, I drove by the Sundial before parking and locking the crash helmet away in the pannier. From the look of Donhead St Agnes, cattle-rustling was more likely than anybody joyriding the bike. But then, you never know. If Dorothea had local customers for her Akitas, it probably meant they had some sort of kamikaze Neigbbourhood Watch running; the sort that bit first and asked questions later.

I couldn't see any notice about bikers in the Sundial itself. Aunt Dorothea had probably been at the paintbrush cleaner again. I could quite accept that the landlord had banned *her*. She would give his normal Hell's Angels customers a bad name.

The pub was filling up for lunch-time, with about half

the scrubbed wooden tables set out for meals. I ordered a pint of the local Gibbs Mew bitter from Salisbury, having checked that at least one other customer was drinking it. (A useful tip for pubs, especially out in the sticks, where there are slack periods.)

The beer was delicious and the landlady smiled at me when I asked if Gearoid Dromey was in.

'Sure he is,' she said in a sing-song voice. 'And it's good to hear the Irish spoken properly. Gearoid—' she pronounced it 'Garrodth' as I had—'is over there by the fire. You're not from the old country yerself?'

''Fraid not,' I said, though sometimes I think I'm the only one who isn't, or at least claims to be.

'Pity. There's them in Dublin can't say the West of Ireland names properly to save their souls.'

I buried my face in my beer and over the rim of the glass checked out the horse-brass-covered fireplace at the far end of the pub.

There was a red-haired guy, about mid-thirties, with a moustache and chin beard but no sideburns. He had his elbows on the table and his hands clenched as fists, knuckles to knuckles. As I got closer I could see he was concentrating on a travelling chess set on the table. He wore a khaki duffel coat with floppy hood and wooden toggles. It had seen better days. So had the empty glass next to the chess set.

He looked up as I approached and his eyes flashed clear blue. I could see the family resemblance.

He spoke before I could.

'Good morning. Do you play chess?'

I looked down at the board and shook my head.

'No,' I said. 'You can't deal at chess.'

Gearoid roared with laughter and held out a hand as he stood. 'You must be Angel.'

As we shook hands, his duffel coat fell open to reveal a

six-inch-long thick wooden cross hung from his neck by a leather thong, and under that, a light brown monk's habit.

'Jesus Christ!' I breathed, unable to stop myself.

'No, no,' said Gearoid with a smile, 'just one of his soldiers.'

'When Werewolf—sorry, Francis—told me he had a brother, I didn't realize he meant a *Brother*, if you see what I mean,' I said sheepishly after I'd refilled Gearoid's glass with stout.

'To be honest, we're not really proper monks, but it helps the image.'

'Er . . . image?'

'For the business.' He saw my expression. 'I'll show you.'

He went over to the bar and chatted up the darlin' Irish landlady. I could definitely see the family resemblance. He returned carrying a bottle in one hand and a plastic bag of mushrooms in the other.

'See?' He held out both for me to see.

The bag of mushrooms had a preprinted label with a picture of a monk's cowl and the description: MONK'S HOOD ORGANIC MUSHROOMS. The bottle, a deep golden liquid, had the same design on its label with the words: MONK'S HOOD MEAD—*Alc. 27% by vol.* Under each was the legend: *Produce of the Community of St Fulgentius, Donhead St Agnes, Dorset.*

I pointed to the bag of mushrooms.

'Isn't monk's hood a . . . ?'

'I know, I know. It's called marketing.'

He returned the bottle and bag to the bar and rejoined me.

'St Fulgentius?' I tried.

'I spent three months trying to find a monastery named after St Sexburga. Don't laugh, there really was one. A Saint, that is.'

'And there was a St Fulgentius?'

'Absolutely. One of the best-known sixth-century theologians ever to emerge from Tunisia.'

'Tunisia,' I said in the sort of voice which hinted that maybe something stronger than beer was called for.

'It's a cracker, isn't it?' Gearoid grinned. 'Real conversation-stopper. OK, what the official guidebook—yours for only 50p—says is this:

'In the second half of the nineteenth century a loony, but rich, Yorkshire mill-owner called Webster decided to recycle his ill-gotten fortune and looked around for a suitable cause. The one thing that got him hot under the wing collar was the growing rate of illegitimate children being born to the women who worked in his own factories. Now the trendy thing at the time was to go Catholic, but Webster couldn't quite stomach that, so he did the next best thing. He found himself a Saint and set up a religious retreat in perpetuity—God and the poll tax allowing—to perpetuate his beliefs. Of course, I've paraphrased a bit.'

'And St Fulgentius got picked?'

'Yup. Good old Fulgentius. St Fulgentius of Ruspe, actually, which really is—or perhaps was—in Tunisia. He had, shall we say, rather forthright views on unbaptized babies. So forthright he ended up being banished to Sardinia.'

'I can think of worse fates,' I said.

'Well, Corfu was probably *passé* even then. Anyway, old Webster, and here I quote, "shocked by the laxity of prevailing Anglican baptismal policy"—' I like that bit—set up the community of St Fulgentius to dedicate itself to promoting the teachings of the need for baptism of all God's children. And there was enough cash in the bank to see us through to today, although of course we now have to sell mead and honey and organic goat's cheese and so on.'

'Here in Dorset?'

'Yeah. The big house down the road, you probably passed it on your way in.'

'No, I mean, why Dorset? I thought you said Webster was a Yorkshire mill-owner.'

'He was. Would you want to invite your friends to weekends in Bradford?'

'I see your point. Can I ask why you?'

He pursed his lips. His glass was empty. Genetics again.

'It's not something I think of more than twenty times a day.' He looked down at the chess set and moved a rook, which seemed to me to put himself in checkmate.

'I was looking for somewhere to hide, I suppose,' he said softly. 'And they needed someone to look after the bees, and I'd always been fascinated by them. And it's not too rigorous, no auditions or credit-rating before they let you in. Did you know that the Benedictines used to leave prospective monks knocking at the front door for seven days just to teach them patience?'

'I do the same with Mormons,' I said, and he laughed.

'The community is also much freer and easier than the real monks. The Benedictines—well, they're probably Egon Ronay listed these days. And the Jesuits have gone from slightly to the right of Attila the Hun to Militant Tendency and are well into revolution. The Anglican orders tend to take life as it comes, even if they are trying to get as close to Rome as they can get away with.'

'So it's an Anglican order? Like Church of England?' I asked.

'Of course it is.' Gearoid rapped his empty glass on the table, and his face lit up. 'Who'd think of looking for a good Irish Catholic boy among heathens like that?'

The Dromey family continued to run up my bar bill.

I ordered the pub's special Ploughman's Lunches for us, mainly because they featured Monk's Hood organic cheddar, organic lettuce and organic tomatoes. Fortunately the pickle was stuffed with additives and so tasted of something.

'So what's my darlin' younger brother been up to?' Brother Gearoid asked between mouthfuls. Then he moved on to his fourth pint of Guinness.

'The Community doesn't worry about the drink, then?' I said, putting on the Irish.

'Nope. I checked the small print before I joined. Now, come on, tell me what's wrong.'

I took a deep breath in through the nose, held it and let it out slowly through the mouth. Like the shrinks tell you to.

'Were—Francis—has been in an accident.' I held up a hand to dispel panic. None showed. 'A road accident, in France. He's OK apart from a broken leg.'

'So it's hospital bills, is it? No medical insurance, something like that?'

'Not quite,' I said, picking my words. 'Some stuff has gone missing and Francis is sort of being held responsible for its recovery.'

Gearoid stroked his beard twice.

'Would I be right in thinking that what was missing I'd better not know about?'

'No. I mean yes. Point is, I think I can get it back. It's just that I thought someone ought to know what the situation was.'

He shook his head. 'I'm not much wiser, Mr Angel. It's Fitzroy, isn't it? No matter. Perhaps it's better I don't know any more. Unless there was something you would have told Francis's brother if you hadn't found out he was a *Brother*?'

I felt myself blushing and I shrugged a 'No, it's not that . . .'

Gearoid reached inside his cassock.

''Scuse me while I whip this out!' he said loudly.

'*Blazing Saddles*,' I came back.

'A great movie,' he said making a big show of plonking a thick A5-sized brown envelope on the table. 'That's what Francis called his emergency fund. Three thousand pounds English, not Punts Irish. To be truthful, three thousand seven hundred and sixty-two as a result of a slight indulgence on my part on last year's Irish National. Don't worry, the rest of the winnings went to a good cause.'

I must have reached out for the envelope, because the next thing I knew my wrist was in Gearoid's left hand and the grip was not to be argued with.

'To be used in an emergency. That's what Francis said.' He said it in a voice which made me wonder how I'd ever queried he might be Werewolf's brother.

'It is an emergency,' I said, staring him out.

'Will money help?' Still the eyeball.

'Can't hurt. If it's not needed, you'll get it back.'

'Now that,' he said with a smile, 'was never in doubt.'

He released my hand.

'Drink up. It's my round.' He stood up and collected our glasses. 'And try not to worry so much, Angel. If you get into trouble, give us a call.'

'At the Community?'

He raised his eyes upwards and tapped the wooden crucifix round his neck with an empty glass.

'Why not? We have branches everywhere.'

I saw two neolithic hill carvings on the way back to Aunt Dorothea's. Fortunately, I realized I was riding round in circles before anyone called the cops and I got back on the side roads as soon as I could. I could see it all—up in court for drunk-driving a stolen motorbike after an afternoon's boozing with a monk from a religious retreat started by a nineteenth-century nutter and named after a Tunisian saint. Thank you very much, Mr Angel. Take him down, Officer. Yes, the padded cell.'

Dorothea was in her studio at the front of the cottage when I got back.

'Brought you a prezzie, Aunty,' I said, relieved to have made it in one piece.

She looked up from her easel, a paintbrush between her teeth.

'What is it?' she said indistinctly.

'Mead. The beverage of our forefathers. The natural elixir distilled from the purest Dorset honey.'

'You're pissed,' she said, turning back to her canvas. It looked like a sunflower but I couldn't be sure. 'And I suppose you want me to take you to the station?'

'Yes, please, dearest Aunty. Where's Springsteen?'

'Upstairs somewhere. I let him out of his cage and he shot up there. Probably frightened of Cherry and Blossom,' she snorted.

I knew better.

Springsteen was just gaining height so he could come at them out of the sun.

Dorothea put down her brush and palette of oils. With one fluid movement and a ripping of Velcro, she removed her ankle-length artist's smock. Underneath she still wore her leather riding gear.

'You'd better hang on to your girdle, young Fitzroy. I always like a burn-up on the highway this time of day.'

I was glad I wasn't staying the night. I couldn't stand the pace.

CHAPTER 5

On the journey back to town I sobered up on British Rail coffee, chocolate biscuits and sleep. The sleep did the most good, and didn't leave an aftertaste.

Armstrong was where I'd left him, unmolested and unclamped. Who'd have a Porsche?

I took Southwark Bridge to get back across the river and into the City. At Christmas, the crane operators working for the developer there on both sides of the Thames had vied with each other to decorate the arms of their giant War-of-the-Worlds machines. This had involved hundreds of coloured lights and in one case—the one which got my prize—a six-foot Christmas tree, fully decorated, right at the end of the gantry a couple of hundred feet up. You can keep your Regent Street illuminations; it's the little things like that which make living in London worthwhile.

Once in the City, I headed due east, avoiding several potential fares as drunken city slickers got thrown out of the wine bars which insisted on closing by nine. I didn't even bother to stop. None of them would be going to Barking.

Duncan the Drunken, probably the best car mechanic in the world, lived in Barking, though his neighbours would say that he'd taken it over rather than moved in. If I was lucky, tonight would be his night for sitting in and watching the TV. If I wasn't, then I'd have to scour six or seven local boozers to find him, always assuming I could escape the clutches of his wife Doreen. Not that there's anything going on there. Duncan and Doreen's marriage had been forged in Yorkshire and whether it was an act or not, Doreen played the dutiful, obedient Northern wife to perfection.

Any day now Duncan would tell her she had the vote.

'Angel! Long time no see, my lad. Eee, but you're thin. You haven't been eating proper, have you?'

Doreen; the last of a breed of women who distrusted any man less than thirty pounds overweight.

'Hello, snakehips.' I put an arm half round her for a quick cuddle. 'Is that boring old fart you call a husband in or have we got the place to ourselves?'

'He's in,' she said, raising her eyebrows. 'Sheffield Wednesday are playing in the Cup. It's on telly—the Big Match Live, they call it.'

I didn't like to say that 'live' was probably pushing it in the case of Sheffield Wednesday. Soccer fans, especially Northern ones, take things very seriously.

'Go through,' said Doreen, holding the door for me. 'Can I get you a drop of his home brew?'

'No! Er, no, thanks. I'm driving.'

'Oh, it's non-alcoholic.'

'Really?'

'Oh yes. He only made it yesterday. There can't be any alcohol in it yet. It's in a dustbin in the airing cupboard. I'll get you a glass.' She strode off to the back of the house, then yelled over her shoulder: 'A clean dustbin, mind you.'

Duncan was sitting in the living-room (the 'front' room) with his feet up on a glass coffee table. A giant television dominated a quarter of the room even though the sound was turned down.

'Wotcher, Dunc.'

'Aye-up, young Angel. Doreen getting you a beer?'

'So she says. What's with the alcohol-free home brew, then?'

I perched myself on the arm of a chair and pretended to be interested in the soccer match. I'm not that good an actor.

'Couldn't wait,' said Duncan simply. Then, to the screen: 'Pass it, you daft bugger!'

Doreen returned with a pint glass of dark brown soup; from the number of solids in suspension, probably vegetable.

'Get that down you, Fitzroy,' she beamed. I managed a sip and a non-committal smile. 'And alcohol-free as well,' said Doreen proudly, disappearing kitchenwards again.

Duncan stuffed a hand down the back of the seat he was in and produced a half-bottle of vodka. Without taking his eyes off the television, he handed it to me.

'It tastes much better cut with this,' he said.

'It would, but no, thanks. It's already been one of those days.'

'Suit yerself.' He took the glass from me and put it down on the coffee table. Then he put his feet back next to it. 'So what you after?'

'A motor, for tomorrow and maybe a few days.'

'What sort?'

'Nothing that draws attention to itself. Something a low-grade insurance salesman might drive, say.'

'Got an old Cortina Estate. There's a fair few miles on the clock but it's almost two litres and it's clean.'

'Sounds good.' Apart from the 'almost' 2.0 litres. But Fords are one of the easiest engines to get at if anything went wrong, and in an emergency you can always kip down in an estate car. 'As long as you put in a full tool kit.'

'Fair enough.' Duncan's car deals may be suspect but his tool kits are legendary.

'And you'll look after Armstrong for me?'

'Sure. Can I have him for Saturday?'

'Have you got a wedding booked?' I asked suspiciously. It was one of Duncan's sidelines.

'Might have.'

'Well, clean the sodding confetti out of the back this time.
And no more second-hand condoms, either.'

'Ah yes, sorry about that. I'm not doing any more Greek
weddings, I can tell you. Do you want me to drop the Cortina round to your place?'

'First thing?' He nodded. 'OK, then I can give you the
spare keys.'

'Got some,' he said into his glass.

'What?'

'When you asked me to cut some spares after Christmas,
I must've done one too many.'

'I see,' I said, knowing when I was beaten.

'Do you still keep that one on the magnetic pad near the
exhaust pipe?' Duncan asked conversationally.

Was nothing sacred?

The train journey had provided me with thinking time, as
well as taking care of two practical problems—Springsteen
and touching base with Werewolf's brother. That had been
important just to make sure that a third party knew roughly
that something was going down, even if they didn't know
exactly what. Gearoid's contribution to operational funds
had come as a bonus.

I had reasoned from the start that I would have to be
prepared to stay loose. Werewolf had been pretty vague
about what his truck had been carrying when he parted
company with it. Perhaps he was being clever because
Guennoc had admitted he didn't know exactly where the
stuff was stashed.

He knew I would know what sort of thing was in a back-
up truck. He and I had done the road in the past, before the
business changed so that for most bands now you needed a
degree in electronics, or, for the big acts, a diploma in
crowd control for the stadium concerts.

My best guess was that he would have been carrying

mostly lighting gear—lamps, spots, beacon towers, gantry poles, dimmer boards and so on. There would have been back-up amps and spare bulbs and such. But the key thing was that any electronic equipment, especially amps, speakers and dimmer boards and the computers which controlled them, would have been automatically stripped down and checked as soon as they got back to England.

The lighting gear itself, the spotlights, the lighting trusses and the floor spots and strobes, they would have been tested, sure, but only to the extent that they would be turned on. If they worked, fine. If they didn't, replace a bulb. And then sign them out for another gig a.s.a.p. Equipment costs if it isn't working.

Ritchie Fortune hadn't raised an eyebrow when I'd inquired after Werewolf's truck and the Belinda O'Blake tour. He wasn't that good an actor and he'd been happy to pass me on to this guy Jev Jevons at Candlepower to get rid of me. As he would have had to check the returning contents of the truck against his manifest (if only for the Customs clearance), surely he would have twigged if there was a consignment of naughties in there too.

So it had to be in the lights. Next problem: getting Jev Jevons to tell me where the lights were.

Maybe Ritchie Fortune was so relaxed because he knew, as I did and Jevons would, that it was virtually impossible to get a driving job on a tour once a tour has started. Even if you claim to be a friend of the management. Sometimes, especially if you claim to be a friend of the management.

With a bit of luck, he wouldn't have bothered even to mention me to Jevons. With Werewolf's current luck he certainly would have, and anyway, the lights would be en route to a charity concert in Namibia or somewhere by now. Still, if Jevons was expecting a taxi-driving unemployed trumpet-player, I'd better give him someone else.

Back at Stuart Street, I crept upstairs to avoid having to

meet any of the other inmates. I had assumed that Fenella would have locked the kittens away in the downstairs kitchen by then but I still found Miles asleep on my bed despite the locked door and the locked (from the inside) cat flap. The boy showed promise. I prodded him playfully in the stomach and he yawned at me, showing his fangs as if saying wait-till-my-daddy-gets-home. I decided to leave him where he was.

While it's not exactly a Rule of Life, I find it good working practice never to throw away a visiting card. Not that I'm in the lifestyle where it is common to exchange cards and what on earth would I put on mine if I had one? But over the past few years the wine bars and some of the flashier pubs in the City and the West End have had pinboards up where the punters stick their calling cards and once a week there is a draw out of a hat and the winner gets a bottle of champagne or similar. Occasionally, there are some interesting ones worth lifting. Bankers and stockbrokers are always good value; brewery sales representatives are definitely prized. But insurance salesmen are useful too.

I rummaged through my collection, which I keep in a video cassette box, though God knows what had happened to the tape of *Rio Grande* which was supposed to be in there.

Vic Hewitt, Insurance Broker, said the one I chose, and there was an address in Milton Keynes and a phone number. That would do, even though there was a hole in the middle where it had been drawing-pinned to the side of a bar.

I laid out my one suit and my one tie. The suit was perhaps a bit flashier than a real Vic Hewitt would wear and the tie was past its smart-by date, though that would be in character. I had possessed another tie, a black felt one for funerals, but it had never recovered from being used to clean records at a rather taxing party in Brixton. (It had given up on Day Two; so should I.)

Then I dug out a holdall which gave Marlboro cigarettes a blatant free advert, though I never smoked them, and began to pack. Just the essentials: spare socks, knickers, jeans, T-shirts, and a small pack of washing powder, working on the assumption that I'd never be too far from a launderette. I added a new toothbrush from my stock (I always keep a few on hand; they're fairly impressive first thing in the morning), a towel and a battery razor which had an extra cutting edge for trimming your designer stubble according to settings Day 1, Day 2 or Day 3. Presumably Day 4 was 'beard'.

From my combination safe/*History of the USA* I took cash and credit cards and then I rooted up a courtesy sewing kit which I'd lifted from a Holiday Inn ages ago and settled down to one last bit of packing.

Baseball hats were all the rage at the time, though I'd been wearing them for years off and on. If they stayed fashionable, I'd have to get something else.

I got to work on it. It was dark blue with a red peak and inside the rim it said it was official Major League Baseball merchandise, made in Korea. On the front it had just a single capital A surrounded by a halo; the logo of the Californian Angels.

What else?

The next morning I waited until everyone had gone to work, then I locked Miles in with the other hell kittens and checked outside the front door. Duncan had been as good as his word. Where Armstrong had stood the night before, there was a dark blue Cortina estate with no obvious signs of rust and a tax disc good for another three months.

Propped up behind the wall phone was an envelope with

'Angel' scrawled on it. The keys, which Fenella or Mr Goodson or some kind soul had picked up off the doormat for me.

I used the phone while I was there to try Vic Hewitt's number in Milton Keynes. An answerphone said that 'Vic Hewitt, Insurance Broker and Mortgage Consultant' wasn't available but I had to leave a number.

As long as he stayed unavailable for the next two hours, I'd call that good insurance.

I put my holdall in the back of the Cortina next to the tool kit Duncan had thrown in with the deal and headed across town, feeling my way into the moods and nuances of the Cortina. I had to get used to wearing a seat-belt again. Taxi-drivers can get away with things respectable, suit-wearing insurance brokers can't.

Just after the Fuller's brewery at Chiswick, I picked up the A4, the old Great West Road, until it was time to turn north and head for Heston and the new industrial parks sandwiched between the M4 motorway and Heathrow airport about four miles away. The jets came in and went above me and for a moment I was tempted to keep going, check in and fly out. But only for a moment.

I knew the general location of Box Pop and Ritchie Fortune had said that Candlepower shared the same section of the industrial park. I stopped at a newsagent's near a school and checked my directions with a surly pensioner who looked as if he prayed for the school holidays. I bought a red-cover notebook and a couple of ballpoint pens from him and, back in the Cortina, I scribbled a few notes and some fake addresses in the first three or four pages, to make it look used.

On the Industrial Estate—or Industrial Mall as they tend to call them now—I checked with one of the big road-side boards which gave the layout of the place. Candlepower were down for Unit 234B, a small office unit fronting

a roll-door garage. They must keep their trucks somewhere
else because that sure wasn't big enough.

There was a discreet notice on the door to the office saying CANDLEPOWER in a computer-style script and above the
roll doors were twin security lights, the sort operated by
infra-red which came on if anyone moved into a 70 degree
arc. They looked to be the latest generation, the ones which
set off an audio alarm signal as well. Through the office
window, I could see one guy working at a VDU and an
internal door open into the warehouse.

As I locked the Cortina I checked the road both ways.
There was no sign of Ritchie Fortune, or anyone else for
that matter. There were a couple of anonymous white box
vans zipping around the park, which was par for the course,
and a white Mercedes sports car parked about twenty yards
away. The driver was reading a newspaper and rocking
gently to himself in time to something coming down the
personal stereo headphones he was wearing. Above me,
another jumbo headed somewhere nice.

The Candlepower guy working the VDU had a pencil
between his teeth and didn't seem too keen to remove it.
His long black hair was tied back in a pony tail with an
elastic band and he wore a Stones' Urban Jungle tour
T-shirt which I knew was fake, and a Rolex Oyster which
I knew wasn't.

'Can I help you?' he asked, politely enough, though it
came out as 'Kag I gelt u?' because of the pencil.

I took the notebook from my pocket and flipped it open.

'I'm looking for a Mr Jevons. I was in the area and
thought I'd chance it. You know, drop in on spec sort of
thing. He's not expecting me.'

'You're right there, I wasn't,' he said. 'So?'

I took the visiting card out of my suit's breast pocket and
handed it over, then offered my hand.

'Vic Hewitt, Mr Jevons. I'm following up a claim we're

brokering involving a Francis Dromey, one of your drivers.'

He took the pencil from his teeth, but stayed seated at the console, tapping at the keyboard.

'Correction. One of our part-time, self-employed relief drivers. Certainly not one of our employees and, in truth, I know not where he is, nor do I care.'

'Don't worry, Mr Jevons, it's not a claim involving your company, or at least not from our end, that is.'

He looked up at me then and picked up the card from the desk.

'I don't follow, Mr—Hewitt.'

'Vic, please,' I smarmed. 'Mr Dromey is claiming medical expenses from one of our policies after an accident abroad.'

'Oh yeah, I know about that,' said Jevons, his eyes drifting back to the VDU screen. 'So what? You suggesting liability on our side?'

'Not at all, Mr Jevons. All I have to do is check that there will be no additional claims against Mr Dromey before we settle. It enables the policy issuers to spread the risk burden, so to speak.'

'Oh, I see,' he said. Thank heavens one of us knew what we were talking about. 'You want to know if we're going to stuff him for totalling our truck?'

'It was hardly a serious accident, from what I hear,' I said with a smile. 'And I don't believe a claim has been filed . . .'

That was a guess but a good one.

'Nah. The truck's OK and everything else was covered.'

Of course it would be and Jevons wouldn't want to have to explain how the gear was well-insured but the driver didn't even have a regular address in England.

'It's the "everything else" I was worried about,' I pressed. 'I understood the truck was carrying valuable light and sound equipment.'

'It was, but that's all accounted for.' He played with his computer some more.

'No damage?'

'Some lamps bust, but the amps and dimmer boards are all flight-cased these days, you know, like photographers with expensive gear, it's all cushioned.'

And I bet he had got his insurance company to cough already.

'So, no damage to equipment,' I said, writing in the note-book. 'So no extraneous liability there.'

'Guess not,' he said, bored with me by now.

'Would it be possible to see the equipment which Mr Dromey was carrying?'

That brought a suspicious stare.

'Not for me myself,' I went on. 'But if it could be located, one of our assessors might want to check it out. Some-one who knows what they're looking at.' I beamed foolishly.

Jevons sighed. 'No need.'

He reached into a box of computer discs and slotted a new one into his machine. He tapped in a codeword and then a search instruction.

'Inventory of that particular truck,' he explained over his shoulder. 'We have to do this for customs clearance.'

A list of numbers and shorthand descriptions came up on the screen. He pressed another key and a laser printer on the other side of the office hissed into life.

I ended up with about nine feet of printout. The contents of Werewolf's truck had included sixty-three numbered items including twenty-two lighting trusses.

They were the only items, along with one 'Dmmbd'— which I assumed was a dimmer board—which shared the same code in the last column of the printout. That column was headed 'Status' and next to each truss and the dimmer board was printed OUT—LLL. Every other item had a different status code ranging from FOR SERVICE, TO REPAIR or IN STOCK to RIGHT OFF or just SLIGHT DAMAGE. Most of the entries for lamps and bulbs had RIGHT OFF next to them, as opposed to 'RIGHT ON', I presumed.

I asked Jevons what OUT—LLL meant.

'That stuff's already back out on the road. It must've been OK so it's been hired out.'

'To LLL?'

'Yeah, that'll be the name of the management.'

'Can you trace it on your computer?' I asked innocently.

''Course I can. This baby can tell you where each piece is on any given day,' he said proudly.

'Really?'

'Sure. I'll show you. What's the code number for any of those pieces?'

My Rule of Life No. 83 is that, approached in the right way, anyone will tell you anything. Computer freaks are easy.

'There you go.' He flashed fingers across the keyboard. 'Dimmer board DB8893 is currently appearing on tour with a band called Astral Reich and tonight it will be being plugged into a no doubt faulty electric socket in some crummy hall smelling of beer, at—' he paused for effect— 'Leicester Polytechnic.'

'Amazing,' I said, then to show him I was all business: 'So that all seems to be working. I mean, no damage there for a claim.'

'No,' he said slowly. 'I told you, we won't be claiming against the driver.'

'Fine. Thank you, Mr Jevons. Would you mind signing a waiver to that effect, if necessary. Not now, of course, but my secretary could send one on, if it was necessary.'

'I'd have to take advice about that,' he said, palming the Vic Hewitt card from the desk top and slipping it into the pocket of his jeans.

'Naturally, naturally.' I closed my notebook. 'Thank you for your time.'

'You're welcome,' he said but not like he meant it.

I bet myself he would try Vic Hewitt's number as soon as I'd got out of sight and if he got the answerphone he might even leave a message.

If Vic was a good insurance broker, he'd get back to him and probably end up selling him something. I hoped he would. It would make me feel better about borrowing his name and it would serve Jevons right for being such a computer bore.

Leicester is only about a hundred miles from London, but it took me the best part of an hour to get round the orbital M25 to the M1 and point the Cortina north.

At the first big service station I pulled in, though not for petrol. All Duncan's cars come with a full tank.

I took my holdall from the back of the car and left my suit jacket and tie across the back seat. I emerged from the station toilets ten minutes later wearing trainers, jeans, a Jive Afrika! T-shirt and bomber jacket.

I decided to eat in the plastic restaurant, if only to get me psyched up to being on the road again. But before that I stopped at the bank of pay-phones and called Lloyd Allen in Brixton.

My luck held. He was in. Well, he was in the house, said the voice answering the phone. He'd get him.

I swore to myself and dropped the holdall to the floor. Keeping the phone locked into my neck, I searched my pockets for extra change to keep feeding the phone. Come on, Lloyd, this thing was eating coins.

Out of the corner of my eye I spotted a car waiting at one of the petrol pumps across the car park. A white Mercedes sports just like the one I'd seen parked outside Candlepower earlier.

Couldn't be the same. Why should it? What if it was?

I tried to remember the driver, but he'd been hidden behind a newspaper and had been plugged into his Walkman, so I'd never seen his face.

I glanced over to where I'd parked the Cortina. It was in full view of the Mercedes—if that's what he was looking for. If he was looking for Vic Hewitt, insurance salesman, I just hoped my appearance had changed enough to throw him.

I found myself crouching down at the pay-phone. This was crazy. There wasn't even anybody in the Mercedes. Come on, Lloyd. Down the phone came the sound of a saxophone—probably Tommy Smith—belting out of one of Lloyd's CDs.

Then a young guy came out of the shop where you pay for petrol and walked across the forecourt.

He was in his early twenties, but dressed like a thirty-something; Lacoste shirt and slacks and a light blue sweater tied round his neck by the arms so it hung down his back. I didn't like him already.

He carried two cans of Diet Coke, a bag of popcorn and a large format AA road map of Great Britain, all of which he put on the empty passenger side before climbing into the Mercedes and driving off, heading north.

Not once did he look in my direction or at the Cortina.

I sighed loudly.

'Hey, I've got an obscene phone call!' yelled a voice in my ear.

'Lloyd, it's Angel. Sorry about that, man. I thought I might have been in trouble for a minute.'

'Only for a minute? Mr Angel, quit putting yourself down. What can I do for you this fine day?'

He was in a good mood, so cash in on it.

'A band called Astral Reich. Ever heard of them?'

'Yup. Second division heavy metal. Cut one LP 'bout a

year ago but it did squat. It was called *A Eunuch in the Devil's Harem* or similar. They got some hype recently since the Bishop of New York said that Metal was music of the devil. Now there's a guy who's seen too many slasher movies.'

'Are they on the road?'

'I'd guess so. That's what they're good at. Their studio sessions are crap, but they're a good live act. They're into Lemming Metal.'

'What?'

'Lemming Metal. It's like slam dancing, man, where've you been? The fans queue up at gigs and go up on stage with the band, then dive off into the first three rows of punters. And they pay for this, would you believe?' Lloyd chuckled.

'Pay?'

'Sure. The security men sell tickets with numbers on. Like in a supermarket at the meat counter. When they pick your number it's your turn. Some say they make more dosh that way than actually playing. I've heard their album, man, and I'd pay to be a lemming and get thrown out of there.'

'Any idea where they are at the moment?'

'I could find out if you wanted me to. Is this on the house or are you hiring my services?'

'As what?'

'As a consultant. Everyone has consultants these days.'

'I'll stick to freebie favours, Lloyd.'

'Suit yourself. Anything else while I'm still giving charity time?'

'One thing. A management outfit, tour organizers or something, called LLL—ever clocked them?'

'So she's back, hey?'

'She who?'

Lloyd laughed. It was a sound I didn't like.

'What's happening to your brain cells, Angel? Don't you remember anything these days?'

'Of course I do,' I snapped. 'Who is this, please?'

'This is Lloyd to Planet Angel, come in to the Twilight Zone, will yer? Jesus, man, you introduced me to her, coupla years back.'

'Not . . . ?'

'Yeah, man. LLL is Lucinda L. Luger, your old partner, Lewd Lu-Lu. The Bitch Queen of Schlock and Roll herself.'

Now I was in trouble.

CHAPTER 6

For the drive up the motorway I unpacked the four cassettes I'd stuffed into the side pockets of my holdall. The tape-deck in the Cortina was well shot, one previous travelling salesman owner having rung up a hundred thousand miles of Barry Manilow on it, no doubt, and it only had the two speakers. The trouble was that my Bonnie Raitt tape reminded me of Lucinda. So did the Notting Hill Billies, even the latest Frank Zappa. I think anything short of the San Francisco Gay Male Voice singing *The Man I Love* would have made me think of Lu-Lu.

Werewolf and I had first met her on the road, three or four years back. She was singing then, fronting a designer band put together to promote something called Country/Funk fusion, which basically stole bits and pieces from other bands and styles, including the Gypsy Kings who were virtually unknown outside of France then. The 'funk fusion' part of the act was basically me with trumpet, a soprano sax player who didn't speak English (and I never found out what it was he did speak), and a pair of twins from Jamaica who did the vocals on the choruses. The

Country half of the band was so bad they'd had to get Werewolf in to dub the lead guitar on the live performances while a Boston-born Ivy League student with more money than sense, a crush on Lu-Lu and a passion for bad dope freaked out on stage with his guitar unplugged.

The band didn't last long and even I can't remember its name now. We did a few gigs in pubs and clubs in London and an ill-fated appearance at the Cambridge Folk Festival where we went on as the warm-up act for the warm-up bands. Then the Ivy League kid's money ran out and he went back to college and the rest of us split to the four winds. That last night, in a motel in Cambridge, Lu-Lu had burst into my room around midnight to find me in a compromising, and upright, position with one of the Jamaican twins (now one third of a successful rap band). We'd left the lights on, so all I could do was smile my best smile at her and say: 'I suppose this is what's called being caught with a smoking gun,' which I didn't think was bad under pressure. She'd looked me up and down and then said, 'You may call it a pistol, honey, but I don't see any smoke,' then she'd slammed the door behind her.

In the morning, she'd gone and I hadn't seen her since. I hadn't lost much sleep over it. I mean, we'd quickly es-tablished a relationship as good drinking buddies, but nothing more than that. Lu-Lu had decided to have a good time 'in Europe' and try and make it in the music business, and in her book that meant staying clear of drugs and messy emotional relationships. That was cool, I could ap-preciate that. But the Cambridge disaster had convinced her that most of the band couldn't play even when not spaced out, she couldn't actually sing all that well, and the whole Country/Funk idea was a toilet concept any-way.

Maybe that night she was just looking for comfort and instead found the backing group bonking away, having much more fun than she was. I had assumed she'd gone back to Georgia and gone through a real Georgia Peach wedding to a Coca-Cola vice-president or suchlike. She should have been lunching other Georgia Peaches by now, in aid of Distressed Antebellum Mansions of the South. Instead she was back, managing a shady Heavy Metal band on tour. Perhaps life was too quiet in Georgia. Didn't they do alligator-wrestling any more?

I came off the motorway at Junction 21 and threaded my way through Leicester's quaint traffic flow system into the city centre. I knew I must be getting close to the Polytechnic when the fly-posters started appearing on bus shelters and lamp posts.

They were amateurish but effective, the main design being a searchlight in the shape of a pentangle beaming heavenwards to illuminate the words *Astral Reich* in runic script. The word 'Tonite' had been handwritten in blood red across a bottom corner, followed by a rubber stamp which said 'Doors: 8.30.'

I found the entrance to the Poly and left the Cortina round the block in a space saying Staff Only. It was just after 4.0 p.m., so the band should be well into setting up, or rather the roadies would be. The band would be either still sleeping off last night's gig or preparing for tonight with a case of Carlsberg Special Brew each.

I pulled my baseball cap down over my eyes and followed the signs saying Students Union down a labyrinth of corridors littered with styrofoam cups and upturned tinfoil ashtrays. Posters on the wall told me to save the whale, be green, say no to student loans and free Lithuania. Appropriately enough for Leicester, there was one which just said: 'Bosworth was a stitch-up: Richard III is Innocent.' I'd go along with that one too.

The third student I asked knew where the Social Sec-

retary's office was, though there they referred to it as the
Ents. Office. The open door at the bottom of a stairwell
next to a fire exit had a handwritten sign saying 'Box
Office' Sellotaped to it. The Ents. Office was a matchstick
girl in baggy black sweatshirt and black ski pants which
disappeared in Doc Marten kickers. Her hair was so closely
cropped she could pass as bald in neon light. She was smoking a black roll-up cigarette made with liquorice paper and
dropping ash on to a solar-powered calculator.

'Astral Reich?' I said tentatively.

'Uni, non-Uni or unwaged?' she asked, reaching for a
stack of tickets.

'What's the difference?'

'Three pounds unwaged, four for Students Union members, six for—Hey, you don't get a fuckin' choice, man.
Show me a union card or a UB 40 form, then we'll decide
the price.'

'Relax, just winding you up. I don't want a ticket,
just the band. I've got some gear for them out in the
van.'

I thought it a safe bet that she wouldn't come and inves-
tigate. She didn't look the outdoor type.

'What sort of gear?' she asked, suspicious but not hostile.

I showed her the palms of my hands. Body language:
open, non-threatening.

'Not that sort. A spare dimmer board from Candlepower.
Know where they're setting up?'

'Main hall, one floor down, turn right after the Games
Room.'

'Thanks. Who's the boss roadie?'

'Ask for Mitch.'

She turned to the telephone on her desk and picked up
the receiver with one hand, flicking through a rotadex with
the other, screwing up her eyes from the smoke from her
cigarette.

Body language message: Piss off, you're of no interest any more.

I went.

I found the first two roadies in the Games Room playing pool on a pub-sized table in a windowless room which stank of stale beer and crisps. Only one was playing, and not really that—just hitting balls aimlessly. The other was sitting in a low-slung foam chair which was pitted with cigarette burn marks. He was just about flying and had got careless. His razor blade was still on the wooden edge of the pool table and I'd bet anything he had a cut-down drinking straw about three inches long in his jacket pocket.

I never did understand it, but show a roadie a flat surface two inches wide and four feet long and he has to snort a line off it.

'Mitch around?' I asked like I couldn't care less.

It was the right sort of attitude to have.

'Sound check. Turn left and just follow your ears, man,' said the one sitting down, which impressed me. I wouldn't have thought he was in a fit state to handle long words like 'follow'.

I flicked him a one-finger salute off the brim of my hat and let my ears do the guiding.

Not that they found any music to follow, just shouts of 'Over here, goddammit' and various crashing noises.

The Main Hall, as it was called, had double doors with FIRE EXIT KEEP CLOSED stamped all over them. Naturally, they were propped open with a pair of fire-extinguishers. There were no seats in the hall, except for the few low-slung foam chairs which had been dragged in there by students trying to find a place to work, or sleep or something, from elsewhere. The centre of the hall was a sunken dance floor, two steps down. The far side had been adapted for the stage, with boxwood staging units laid out into the dance floor. I estimated that with a band on, the hall could take maybe two hundred and fifty audience—legally. If you stacked them right, maybe six hundred.

I did some maths in my head. Say four hundred audience at five pounds a go (averaging out the discount for the un-employed and the premium paid by non-students); that was two grand. Take off the Students' Union cut to cover ticket-printing, posters, hire of hall and free tickets for the Ents. Officer's friends (and she must have at least two), and their profit, and the band would be lucky to get £1,200.

There was no way this could be profitable unless the band were on zero wages or being subsidized by a record company. Christ, Lucinda could run up a car bill of more than that in one night at a Holiday Inn.

Which reminded me.

Relax. All clear. Of the dozen or so characters roving the stage area, all were male and all under six-foot four.

One in particular stood out front, directing operations. He wore a long, sleeveless leather coat with big baggy pockets, the sort tank commanders wore in black-and-white war films. He had a clipboard in one hand and a long thin cigarette in the other.

'More blocking stage left!' he yelled, though no one took much notice. 'I want that area sealed off or the punters'll be up there with the fuckin' band. And don't leave the smoke bombs there, for Christ's sake. You'll gas the first three rows. Where's Elvis? I want those fliers up by six o'clock tops.'

'He's gone to the local Tandoori for a take-away,' some-one yelled from behind the assembled pile of equipment on stage.

'Shit! He'll have more than a bad case of munchies if he's not back in fifteen minutes. Who's gopher today?'

A fresh-faced youth, probably one of the local students, piped up.

'I am.' The unpaid help. Go for this, go for that.

'Fuck off and find Elvis. If you can't, don't come back.'

'You got it,' said the lad, and belted off stage.

There were in fact about a dozen students scattered around the hall, just watching, maybe hoping to pick up the odd job, or more likely thinking they'd get invited to some orgiastic thrash by the road crew after the show. They had more chance of that than of picking up a free ticket for the concert, that was for sure.

The stage crew worked mostly in silence and at incredible speed, the equipment stacks growing visibly and the stage itself disappearing under a clutter of guitars, floor pedals, a massive two-bass drum kit and a snake's nest of wiring. Most of them wore T-shirts advertising every Heavy Metal band except Astral Reich, including a Russian one, proving that Metal got to Moscow before McDonald's did. (Rule of Life No. 65: Never wear the T-shirt of the gig you're working on.)

'Don't come too far forward,' shouted the tank commander, 'we've got the ground supports to go in yet.'

'The light truck's outside,' someone yelled from the back of the stage near the double doors which opened on to a loading bay.

'So is Elvis—somewhere. That's the fucking problem!' the tank commander yelled back.

I moved alongside him. There was never a good time to interrupt a boss roadie when he was working, so why wait?

'Mitch?'

'Yeah. So what?' He looked at me for maybe a second, then he went back to scanning the stage.

'Is Lucinda around?' I tried.

'No chance. When the going gets tough—'

'—the tough go shopping,' I completed. It had always been one of her favourite bumper stickers.

'So you know Lucinda. I'm impressed. I'm busy, I have

morons to work with, we're forty-five minutes behind
schedule, I'm being hassled by the local Fire Prevention
Officer and there's no sign of the band yet, but I'm impressed. So what?'

'So could you use a hand flying those lighting trusses
while I'm waiting?' I nodded towards the loading bay
where a roadie was pulling a thirty-foot triangular aluminium truss from the back of a truck.

'Do you know what you're doing?' asked Mitch suspiciously. 'I mean, are you likely to go round a brewery and
come out sober like most of the wankers we've met here so
far?'

'I ain't a student,' I said, 'I'm on your side.'

'What've you done?'

'I've worked Wembley,' I lied.

'Stadium or Arena?'

'Both. The Stones, Springsteen, Genesis,' I lied.

'Yeah, well somebody had to, I suppose,' he conceded.
'OK, look: I can't put you on the cash roll without an
approval from Lu-Lu. You say she knows your work?'

'You could say that,' I said, biting my tongue.

'She should be back in an hour. You help get those
trusses up for no pay and no insurance cover, remember,
and I'll put a word in for you. Fair?'

'Seems reasonable,' I said like Richard Widmark used to
say it. 'What's the lay-out?'

He flipped over a page on his clipboard and showed me
a sketched-out plan of the stage.

'Ground supports for up lights run here and here at
forty-five degrees from these amps, right? Don't worry
about the electrics—that's Elvis's job if he bothers to come
back. Just make sure they're clamped down, 'cos it gets
rough up there when the show's on. We'll bring in another
stage block here, just off centre. That's where the lemmings
queue up to slam.'

'I hear you sell tickets,' I said innocently.

'You don't. I don't. The Reich has a couple of minders who do it. They're mean sods, so don't try and get in on that act, OK?'

'Gotcha.'

'Now, the ground supports have numbers marked along them and so do the lights. It shouldn't be too difficult to get the right light to the right place, but for Christ's sake make sure they're facing the band, right?'

'I think I can grasp the concept. What about the flying trusses?'

Mitch dropped his cigarette to the floor and ground it into the carpet.

'We're working with a low ceiling here, so Elvis will have to re-align them. But you can see the stanchions built into the roof.' I followed his pointing finger and nodded. 'You'll have to use those for the pulleys but don't haul 'em up until the motors have been fixed and Elvis checks out the angles.'

'No follow spots?'

'Yeah, usually, but not here. No clearance. You won't need to attach the rope ladders tonight. Willy usually does that.' Then he yelled at the stage: 'Where's Willy?'

'Pigging out with Elvis,' someone shouted back.

'Shit. OK, let's go for a sound check first, then.'

He looked back at me.

'Still here?'

'Long gone, boss, long gone.'

I walked across the well of the dance floor, peeling off my jacket as I went, though not before transferring my wallet to the back pocket of my jeans. I bench-pressed myself up on to the stage and threaded myself between the speakers and over cables until I got to the doors leading to the loading bay.

The open rear doors of the truck blocked out most of the daylight but the interior of the truck had its own lighting system. With that and the fold-down bed and fridge in the cab, it was probably better equipped than most people's homes.

The driver had almost finished unloading. Jev Jevons had been right, most of the lights were flight-cased in shiny stainless steel boxes which could be secured by straps to the sides of the truck. Just about the only things unboxed were an extendable aluminium ladder and the lighting trusses themselves.

It was the trusses which interested me most. Thirty feet long, but light enough to carry, they were constructed of three hollow aluminium poles set out as a triangle, with zigzag supports. They could be clamped to the stage and individual lights clipped to the top edge of the triangle, or hoisted and rotated on motors with lamps hanging from them when 'flown' from above. It was the job of the missing Elvis to make sure that the lamps came on, went off and dimmed on cue, probably using a computerized master board.

'Mitch's told me to give you a hand,' I told the driver as I put my jacket in the back of the truck.

'Nearly done,' he said, 'but you can cop that ladder. You'll need it in there.'

I climbed into the truck and began to unfasten the ladder from its restraining straps. As I did so, I counted the lighting trusses stacked against the right side of the truck. There were twelve of them.

'Hey!'

I spun round to face the driver, instant guilt all over my face. Or so it felt.

'You'll need these,' he said, offering me a pair of reinforced cotton gloves.

'Thanks, mate,' I said as I took them. 'Thanks a lot.'

I meant it. It hadn't occurred to me until then that it might not be clever to leave fingerprints about.

I pushed the ladder over the edge of the truck and jumped down to carry it into the hall. Inside, Mitch was shouting orders again, demanding a sound check. I dumped the ladder near the two trusses already laid out on the stage and went back outside to help the driver lower two flight boxes of lamps. We laid them just inside the hall and then he moved to close the truck doors.

'What about the other trusses?' I offered.

'Elvis said just the four for tonight, and I've put them out.'

He bolted half the doors closed. One had CANDLE stencilled on it, the other, POWER.

'You brought enough, didn't you?'

'Sixteen thirty-footers. Bloody daft if you ask me, but you know the motto when it comes to metal bands.'

'The more trucks the merrier?'

'You got it. And Jerry's got half-a-dozen thirty-six-footers in his rig for tomorrow night. It's a bigger hall, they say. We're only carrying this amount because of Saturday's gig at the football ground.'

'Which one?'

'St James's Park, Newcastle.'

That began to make sense. No band would need twenty-two trusses—that's what Jevons's print-out had said had been in Werewolf's truck—to do Student Union gigs like this one.

'So Jerry's got the rest in Newcastle?'

'Uh-uh.' He shook his head as he locked the doors. 'Huddersfield.'

'Oh, the gig tomorrow night,' I said knowledgeably. 'It's at the Polytechnic there, isn't it?'

'Yeah. Jerry leap-frogged me with all the extra lighting gear so he could get a head start setting up.' He winked at me. 'Well, that's what we've told Mitch. Jerry's got a bit of stuff lives in Sheffield and this way he gets two nights with her instead of one.'

'Nice work if you can get it,' I said.

He opened the passenger side door of the truck's cab and reached in for a light blue satin-finish blouson. He pulled it on and it said 'Stevie' across the back in gold lettering.

'Tell Mitch I'm going to park the rig, then I'll be back to help Elvis.'

'Elvis is missing, or he was. Gone hunting for a curry.'

'Typical. The man has a permanent case of the munchies,' said Stevie. 'Won't be long.'

'They got you somewhere to park?'

'Yeah, about two blocks away. They've done a deal with the local council for some corporation space overnight. About the one thing that's gone right. See yer.'

I flicked him a wave and stepped back into the hall as he gunned the big truck into life.

Mitch was still directing the chaos.

'Can we at least do a mike test on the PA? Or is that too much to frigging ask for?'

'Testing—testing—one, two, one two . . .' boomed a voice.

I stopped one of the roadies who was prowling backstage and asked if there was a tool kit around. He pointed to a metal suitcase laid open behind one of the speaker towers and I helped myself to a half-inch spanner.

Then I began to drag the trusses to be used on the ground into position, clipping the anchoring suction cups over the bottom tubes and then working my way down their length on my knees levering the cups into place. It wasn't difficult. The cups had locking levers and could be clicked into place with one hand. Once done, I tested them with my foot and they seemed solid enough. I reckoned I had more chance of picking up the staging block than pulling the clamps free.

The spanner? I needed that to tap along the length of the three aluminium tubes which formed the frame of the truss.

I did it quietly and discreetly as I crawled along on my knees. And every time I got a distinct ringing metallic note. The tubes on both trusses were as hollow as a policeman's promise.

It was the same story on the two other trusses to be flown from the ceiling, and I had plenty of time to check as I clipped on the pulley chains.

By then, another roadie—probably Willy—was following me around fastening coloured spotlights to the trusses and a heavy long-haired guy in biker leathers was following him connecting up wires. I was up the ladder fastening the second of the pulleys to a stanchion when they started the sound check proper.

One of the crew had produced a battered red guitar and plugged it in. He hit a chord—at random, I suspect,—which bombed out so loud I felt the ladder shake. The roadies just kept working but there were howls of protest, if not downright pain, from the few students squatting about the hall watching the proceedings.

From my vantage-point I saw Stevie the truck-driver enter the hall and bend his head into Mitch's ear to say something. Mitch pointed at the stage where Elvis was working and Stevie jumped up to join him, feeding back cables to a dimmer board off stage left.

I slid down the ladder like roadies are supposed to, grateful for Stevie's gloves but feeling the friction heat on the insides of my trainers. Two of the crew helped steady the ladder as I dropped the extension part of it and then laid the whole thing down at the back of the stage. Neither of them spoke. Roadies don't much; or at least not before they hit their hotel bar in the wee hours.

The crewman who fancied himself as Clapton had moved on to working the foot pedals though he still wasn't playing anything recognizable. I stepped over his guitar lead and tapped Stevie on the shoulder.

'I left my jacket in the truck,' I shouted into his face. 'Got my dosh and keys in it.'

I spread my hands in stupid supplication.

He reached into his own jacket pocket and produced a bunch of keys, holding one out of the bunch for me. The key ring they were on was the radiator emblem from a VW Golf. Another yuppie had bit the dust.

'Out the main door, first left, first right and across the road. She's parked in an old Freightliner depot. Can't miss it.'

'Thanks,' I said, thinking what a great, trusting camaraderie there was between the real workers in the music business.

'Don't try the cab,' Stevie added, 'I've set the alarms.'

Once I'd found Stevie's truck it took me less than ten minutes to spanner my way along the lighting trusses stacked in the back. Apart from a ringing in my ears, it got me nowhere except half an idea for an alternative comedy routine as a mad percussionist.

I pulled my jacket out from under the bottom stack of trusses, where I'd pushed it so that Stevie wouldn't see it as he closed the doors. Out of spite, I kicked the stack but it got me nothing except a bruised toe.

If the stuff was inside one of the triangular trusses, then it had to be one of the 36-footers that had gone on ahead to the Huddersfield gig. That meant it was probably sitting in a lorry park in Sheffield while the other driver—Jerry?— had the night off. Or on, if he was lucky.

If it wasn't in the lighting trusses, I didn't have a clue where it was and I couldn't see any way round wasting another day trying to find out. Trouble was, I didn't have that many days to spare.

It *had* to be in the trusses. Sure it did. That's the way I'd have done it.

*

I jumped down from the back of the truck and shut the doors so they read CANDLEPOWER again. Walking back across the dirt car park trying to figure my next move, I almost missed the white Mercedes parked behind a corporation rubbish collector (or 'TT'— trash trasher—as the kids call them in Brixton).

It was locked, so I had to resort to peering in through the windows. If anyone saw me, all I was doing was admiring a class set of wheels, so I kept nodding to myself and made approving low whistle noises.

There was nothing in the car except an empty Coke can and an open road map on the passenger seat, but that was enough for me. I made a mental note of its number and then, walking round the back, I noticed that it had a car hire firm sticker in the rear window. There was a phone number and a phone code prefix I didn't recognize. Scrabbling for a piece of paper from my wallet, which turned out to be the bill from Ritchie Fortune's restaurant, I made a note of it and just in case I forgot, I wrote the number down too.

There was no sign of the driver in the car park, nor in any shop doorways or round any corner as I walked back. I checked.

The noise level had risen considerably in the hall, with one of the roadies laying down a neat eight-bar bass line at max volume. I hope the foundations could take it.

Stevie was near the entrance, talking to Mitch and laughing. I strolled up, making a thing of pulling my jacket on, and handed his keys back. He put his hands to his ears, then ripped them away suddenly and laughed some more. Mitch allowed himself a smirk.

'What's funny?' I asked.

'Just set a new record,' Stevie grinned, leaning in towards me so I could hear. 'There was this student, right? Comes in to rubber-neck like they do and he sits down and puts on his Walkman.' He gestured someone putting on headphones. 'Then Julian gets up on stage and plugs in the bass. Christ knows how, but this kid's Walkman must have picked up on the main amp and he gets a zillion watts per channel in both ears. The kid freaks, right? Rips off the 'phones and does a runner out the Fire Exit.'

He laughed again.

'First time we've busted eardrums during the sound check!' He slapped a fist into the palm of a hand.

'Nice one,' I agreed, wondering why I felt worried. But I didn't get time to dwell on it.

On stage, the floor lights came on, flashing in time to the bass player. Then the PA system whined and a voice boomed out, 'Is this show going to happen tonight or what? That's right, it's ass-kicking time, so let's hustle!'

I slid away from Mitch and Stevie and climbed up on to the left-hand block of the stage.

'Get some lights on me, Elvis. You know I love it!' screamed the PA.

I made my way centre stage, cutting behind the bass player, until I was behind the tall figure clutching the central microphone with both hands and threatening to decapitate anyone within range with the mike stand.

'Come on, team, let's get sweaty here! Work, work, work!'

She was six-foot four, that I knew, but the red stetson she was wearing gave her another foot. As more lights came on I could see that she was dressed in black shirt with a fringe across the shoulders, a pair of Harris Tweed hot pants and brown and gold cowboy boots with rattlesnake motifs.

I came up behind her and made the first two fingers of my right hand into a gun. I stuck them in the small of her back.

'This is the Fashion Police,' I said in her ear. 'You're under arrest.'

CHAPTER 7

'It's Angel! The ultimate party animal!'

Lucinda screamed into the microphone and her voice boomed out over the PA system. Even a couple of the roadies stopped to look. Then she swung round and I got a face full of shirt and fringe and some of her softer bits.

'Hello, Lu-Lu,' I said, but it was well muffled.

'Oh, Angel, am I glad to see you!' She closed her grip and lifted me an inch off the stage. 'Are these guys brain dead, or what? We gotta show 'em how to party!'

I felt my face flush red but I wasn't sure whether it was a blush or just that she'd cut off a couple of vital arteries.

'So where've you been, Angel-man? What yer doin' here?'

I struggled free from her grip, then slipped an arm round her waist.

'Calm down, Big Lady. You know I'm yours if you want me.'

She pushed her stetson back with a red-painted fingernail and bent over to kiss me. Then she drew back and showed me her dental work.

'You sho' know how to sweet-talk an innocent young Southern girl, Angel-man. You always did.'

'Especially the ones I know I can't beat at arm-wrestling. Can we go somewhere and talk?'

'With two hours to go before show time and these zombies screwing up on me? Sure, why not?'

She turned back and grabbed the mike.

'Mitch!' she boomed, 'your ass is on the line. I'm going to be in conference in the nearest bar.'

'Now that's what I call delegation,' I said.

Lucinda linked arms and we headed for the rear exit where I'd helped unload Stevie's truck. Before we got to the edge of the stage she stopped and tapped the bass guitarist on the shoulder.

'Hey, Julian.' The guy stopped playing. 'This is Angel, he's with me.'

Julian looked at me, shrugged, and went back to work.

'Is he your security man?' I asked as she linked arms again.

'No way. He's a faggot.' She smiled sweetly. 'And I just can't handle competition these days.'

The rumour that the pubs could stay open all day hadn't reached that part of Leicester yet, so Lu-Lu frogmarched me over to the Holiday Inn and we hit one of the residents' bars.

The barman was hiding behind a copy of the *Leicester Mercury* and not just because he'd seen Lucinda coming. In one corner of the lounge two guys with the longest hair I'd seen this decade had settled themselves down with their feet up on a table-top covered in peanuts and empty bottles of lager which they were drinking by the neck. One was reading a pasteboard edition of *Thomas the Tank Engine*, the other was doing *The Times* crossword. Judging from the empty bottles, they were set in for the day, like rain.

'Barkeep!' yelled Lucinda across the room. 'Build us a coupla cold beers! Big ones. And lay some down for my friends here.'

The barman took up a stance behind the lager pump and tried to make himself a smaller target.

'This is Rory,' said Lu-Lu, pointing to the one reading about the days when railway engines ran on coal and had smiling faces.

'Delighted, old boy,' said Rory in a public school accent and he offered a hand without getting up.

'And this is Neep.'

Neep scowled at me and went back to 14 Down.

'They're writing,' said Lu-Lu.

'Dare I ask what?'

'Songs,' she said dismissively. 'For the Festival of Metal in Newcastle.' She pronounced it Noocassle. So did people who lived there.

I suppose I could see the logic. Steam engines were sort of heavy metal and most Metal songs I'd heard did sound like the answers to a crossword. No clues; just the answers.

'So you're not trying to fill the stadium just with Astral Reich?' I asked.

'Fat fucking chance, old stick,' drawled Rory. 'Lulubelle here has us booked on second, would you believe? For heaven's sake, half our fans will still be buying solvents late-night-shopping at Sainsbury's when we finish our set. They do have Sainsbury's this far north, don't they?'

'They're getting here,' I reassured him.

The barman arrived with two open bottles of lager and two pints of draught on a tray. Lu-Lu took the bottles and dumped them on the table, crushing the peanut debris to fine powder.

'Put 'em on the bill, my man,' she said.

'Room 216, miss?' asked the barman cautiously.

'You got it,' beamed Lu-Lu, slapping him on the shoulder.

'You been here long?' I asked.

'Checked in 'bout an hour ago,' she said. I was impressed. 'Let's sit over here. Leave the guys to it.'

I nodded to Rory and followed her across the bar until she sat down at a table from which, I noticed, the bowl of peanuts had been removed.

Lucinda downed half her beer before she sat, then she swung her chair to face mine and leaned forward and put her hands on my thighs.

'OK, Animal, talk dirty to me and tell me where you've been all this time. You still living in that pit in Southwark?'

'Oh no, I've gone upmarket since then.' I'd had to. That house had sort of blown up. 'Found a nice place in Hackney. Good neighbourhood, great people.' No one from Southwark there. 'How about you?'

'Aw, you know. Still trucking. Long live rock'n'roll or what, hey?' she shouted, punching the air.

'So you got married, then?'

'Yup. Didn't last. Well, long enough for the lawyers to take him for a big fat settlement.'

'So you did OK out of it?'

'I suppose so. What was it you used to say—"No day is wasted"? Wasn't that one of your—what was it? Rules of Life? That's it.'

'Number Seven,' I said automatically.

'Whatever. So here I am, back in the tour business, single and looking to boogie!' She did a shimmy in her chair and for a lady of her size, it was an awesome sight. 'A little older, but no wiser. Hey—is that one of the Angel's Rules too?'

'No,' I smiled. But it would be.

'So what's cooking with you, my man?' she went on. 'Jesus, it's good to see a friendly face. This business has lost all its fun, you know. Do I lie—or what?'

'I know what you mean,' I said, trying to move my knees from her grip. If she squeezed any harder I just knew my eyes would start to water. 'You remember Werewolf?'

'The man with the magic fingers? Could I forget him?'

'That's the one. I hear he played guitar as well.'

She was about four seconds late picking that up, but when she did she roared with laughter.

'Better not let him hear you say that, Mr Angel!'

'Hell, he pays me to say that.'

'Killer! Don't stop. Badmouth me some more!' she hooted.

Across the bar, Rory blushed and buried himself behind his book. The barman turned his newspaper to the Situations Vacant pages.

'Well,' I started, wondering how to play this, 'Werewolf has asked me to do a favour for him. And it involves asking a favour of you.'

'You can always ask,' she said sweetly.

I had it now. Improvise. When in doubt, improvise.

'The favour is not to ask why I'm doing a favour for Werewolf.'

Her eyes lit up like Springsteen's do when he smells raw meat. 'Is it illegal?'

'Slightly.'

She squeezed my thighs harder.

'Is it dangerous?'

'Probably.'

Harder.

'Does it involve deviant sexual practices and me being forced to do unspeakable things against my will?'

Her face was a picture of innocence. Her grip was like iron.

'No, but I'll try and work those in if you want me to.'

'Right on!'

She released her grip, then slapped my legs with her hands. It was a painful but effective way of getting the circulation going again.

'But seriously, folks,' I said, wincing, 'I need help.'

'You got it, old buddy. Just name it.'

'As easy as that?' I asked suspiciously.

'Why not? Of course, we haven't negotiated a price for my favours yet!' As she said 'favours' she raised her voice and grinned around the bar. 'But like I said, before you showed up this tour was getting to be a drag. Dullsville, Arizona, man. And you know what being bored makes me, don't you?'

Yes. Dangerous.

The first thing was easy enough, the use of Lu-Lu's phone in Room 216 as she took a shower and changed into something less comfortable in time for the concert.

My first call was to Stuart Street and I was lucky enough to get Lisabeth. She told me there had been no messages so far and left it at that. She didn't even want to know where I was, but at least she didn't give me an earbashing about the welfare of the kittens, which Fenella would have. I told her that if Werewolf rang, or somebody called Guennoc (and I said that twice), then all she had to say was that I would be back the day after tomorrow at the latest. She muttered something about being an unpaid answering service and hung up.

Then I dug out the restaurant bill from my wallet and looked at the scribbles I'd made when I'd spotted the Mercedes in the truck park. The name of the car hire firm was Euro Limo and its sticker had said 'Chauffeur or Self-Drive Executive Cars Within Europe'. The phone number began with an 0255 code.

I checked my Seastar to find it was just after six o'clock, and decided to try anyway. From the shower, Lu-Lu was singing 'Eighteen wheels and a dozen roses' as if she was only twenty-four hours from Nashville and down to her last bottle of Thunderbird.

'Euro Limo, Harwich office, how may I help you?'

'Is that Euro Limo car hire?' I asked as if I was reading it.

'That's right, Carol speaking. What can we do for you?'

'This is the Holiday Inn, Leicester. We're trying to trace the driver of one of your cars, a Mercedes sports job, licence number G791 PNO. It's got one of your stickers in the back.'

'One moment, please.'

I could hear the sound of a keyboard being tapped as she punched in the number. I hoped she couldn't hear Lucinda, but if she did, I could always pass her off as a nearby pirate radio station.

'Hello, caller, that is one of our vehicles. What was the nature of your inquiry?'

There was a plastic folder advertising the hotel services near the phone. The first sheet in it had a colour photograph of a smiling young smoothie probably no older than his tuxedo. The legend said: *Darren Cole, Manager, Wishes You A Happy Stay.*

'My name is Cole,' I said. 'I'm the manager here and one of our guests has reported a minor collision with this car in our car park, but we don't know who the driver is. I wondered if you could help.'

'We've had no accidents reported . . .'

'Please don't get the wrong idea. The car was parked at the time and nobody was injured. Actually, the damage is really very minor but when somebody actually admits to reversing into somebody else like that, then I think we are duty bound to follow it up. Just think of the number of people who would have driven off without saying a word.'

Me for one.

'We do appreciate that, Mr Cole. Where did you say the car was found?'

'In the car park of the Holiday Inn, Leicester. The driver may be one of our guests but we have no note of that registration number.'

'Well . . . the Mercedes was booked out two days ago, for a week's hire, to a Mr Paul Gronweghe.'

'Could you spell that, please?'

She did. You pronounced it like you'd just been kicked in the nuts.

'But we have no forwarding address for him in this country.'

'Would that be Mr Gronweghe the Dutch gentleman?' I tried.

'That's right.' She sounded surprised.

'Then I'm so sorry to bother you. He's a guest in our hotel. I'll have him paged immediately.'

It didn't take a genius to put a posh car hire firm in Harwich together with the main ferry link there to the Hook of Holland.

'Is the car repairable, Mr Cole? It's the only Mercedes we have.'

'Don't worry about a thing, Carol. You'd hardly notice it had been damaged at all.'

Me and my big mouth.

Lucinda came out of the shower naked and glistening and sat at the vanity table to plug in a hairdrier.

'You can help me dress,' she said, which I thought was a novel twist. 'And tell me what you're really doing here. Just give me a minute to whoosh the old hair dry. There's booze in the fridge.'

She started up the hairdrier and I admired the view for a minute, then sprawled over the bed to reach into the small fridge, studiously ignoring the honesty sheet they give you where you are supposed to tick off the drinks you've had.

Most of the hotel's meagre offerings of miniature spirits and mixers too big for one drink but too small for two had been stuffed at the bottom. Every spare inch of space was taken with either bottles of *Rolling Rock* beer or lime-flavoured Jelloshots, sneaky little things in plastic glasses which slip down so quick you don't notice the double vodka in them. I opened two beers and put one on the vanity table in front of her, though she didn't see it at first as her great mane of hair was over her face.

'Spray me,' she said, holding out a can of aerosol behind her.

I swapped the beer for the can and read the label. It was an industrial-strength anti-perspirant guaranteed to glue your pores together. Say goodbye, ozone layer.

'It gets hot an' sweaty in there,' said Lu-Lu, standing up.

'In the concert?' I hissed the spray down her spine.

'In my suit,' she said as she turned around. 'Mmm-mm. That's cool.'

She faced me with one arm held out, the other putting the bottle of beer to her lips. I started to spray. It seemed to take longer this side.

'Suit?' I asked, though it didn't sound like my voice.

'In the closet. Get it for me, wouldya?'

I got up off my knees and swung open the wardrobe doors, then leapt back in alarm. There was a body hanging there, the corpse of a gigantic seal.

'What the hell is that? Batman's tuxedo?'

'Close, but no cigar,' grinned Lu-Lu. 'Designed it myself.'

Big of her to admit it, I thought.

I took it off its hanger and handed it to her. It was a one-piece suit, at first sight a wet suit like scuba divers use. On closer examination it turned out to be made of a combination of rubber, black leather and moulded PVC material including moulded shoulder pads. There were black plastic zips down the front, the sides and at the cuffs. In raised rubber letters four inches high across the back of the jacket section were the words ASTRAL REICH.

'I know, I know,' she said. 'It's kinda gross, but you gotta have a trademark in this business.'

She stepped into a pair of white underpants—American women haven't called them panties since Doris Day—and stretched the rubber suit out on the floor. Opening all the zips, she peeled it back and lay down on it, kicking her feet into the leg tubes.

'C'mon, Angel, give me a hand. It takes at least two people and thirty minutes to get into this thing.'

'What does it take to get you out of it?'

'A large Tequila.'

I had to ask.

Lu-Lu completed her ensemble with a pair of pointed ankle boots and half a gallon of hair gel to add the obligatory spiky bits to her coiffure. Then she sat at the mirror again and applied black lipstick, black eyeshadow and, with her forefinger, parallel lines of black warpaint to her cheeks, Comanche style.

While she did this, she tried to pump me.

'So, this favour you have to do for the Wolfman. It involves me—or what?'

'No,' I said carefully, topping another beer. 'You're not in it and that's good advice, too, so take it.'

'Yus, sir! Sho' thing, Big Boss! Is it somebody in the band?'

'Nope—but I'd appreciate it if you could pass the word to the crew that I'm an OK guy and may just be hanging around backstage for a day or so.'

'One of the roadies, then? You're after one of the crew?'

'Lucinda, I'm not after anybody.' I had a feeling somebody might be after me, but I didn't say it.

'So it's some*thing*, huh?'

'Don't ask. You really don't want to know.'

She completed one of her warpaint lines, deep in concentration.

'What weight, how much and where?'

'Can I claim the Fifth Amendment?' I tried.

'Nope.'

'How about any of the other Amendments?'

'Uh-huh.'

'Then I don't know.'

She paused, lipstick poised in the mirror.

'Truly, I don't know. I don't know what it is, how heavy or what the street value is. Just say I reckon it must be substantial.'

'If Werewolf's into wholesaling, he's in trouble. Is it crack?'

'I don't think so and anyway Werewolf's not doing it. He's just caught up in it. Innocent bystander. This time he's a civilian.'

She flicked out a long black rubber-clad leg.

'And this one's got bells on it.'

'Would I lie to you?' I said, doing a reasonable impersonation of Frank Zappa.

'Do I look that much like Shirley Temple? Or what?' She went back to her eyeshadow. 'If it's crack, you're on your own, cute feller. That's bad medicine and heavy duty retribution from the Straights when they came down on you.'

'You speak nothing but the truth, Weird Lady.'

And she did. The British cops and Customs personnel were on all-out crack alert and had been for months. As the American market reached saturation, the big bad, well-organized suppliers were looking to England, partly because of forthcoming open market policies across Europe, but also because of the black population which they regarded as an underdeveloped market. The agencies had had some success restricting the use of heroin, partly using the fear of Aids and its spread through the use of dirty

'works'— needles. But crack you could smoke and it had
the great advantage—to the supplier—that it was almost
instantly addictive. A customer who tries is a customer who
flies, as they said. The Americans were more worried about
it than anything since the appearance of Angel Dust in the
early 'eighties. But as far as I knew, there was little or no
amateur trade in crack and this whole set-up smacked of
amateurs on the make.

'I'm pretty sure it's not crack,' I said to her reflection,
which I found oddly comforting. People dressed like that
aren't supposed to have reflections in mirrors. Not after
dark, anyway. 'But, yeah, it's some sort of naughty substance.'

'And what's your cut?'

I was hurt.

'Getting Werewolf out of trouble, that's all. He was
carrying it but he didn't know it. He lost it, without realizing he'd lost it, but the end-users found him. Now they've
found me and they'll hold him until I find their stuff for
them.'

She swung around so she faced me and put her hands on
her knees.

'So why the band, huh? What's the connection?'

'Straight arrow?'

'If you want Little Lu-Lu to be on your side and not
against you, yeah.'

Put like that, I had no choice.

'It's nothing to do with the band. Or the crew, for all I
know. I think the gear is in the equipment you hired. It
was just luck of the draw you got it. That's why I'd like to
snoop about backstage.'

She took it calmly.

'Do you intend taking a truck apart or something?'

'No way. If the stuff's around, it must be in the lighting
trusses you bought in from Candlepower.'

'Stevie?' she breathed.

I shook my head.

'He's clean. Doesn't know a thing.' I was confident about that. After all, he'd let me roam about his truck. 'And I don't think the stuff's here.'

'The other lighting trusses are with Jerry.'

'That's what I figured.'

'You sure you're sure about this?'

'Nope, but I haven't any other ideas and I'm on a tight timetable.'

She slapped her knees.

'Hoakay, José, I'll do you a deal, for old times' sake. Most of us do the boo occasionally, just to relax, and one of the band at least is a dynamiter when he gets himself together. But the last thing we need is a big rap for heavy possession.'

I could relate to that. 'Boo' was smoking dope, which although slightly retro these days still went on, and a 'dynamiter' was someone who mixed cocaine with morphine. They didn't do it often, though.

'If I help you find the stuff, you get it out of here and be long gone before I count up to ten. Deal?'

'Deal.'

'Good. We may have to bring Stevie in on this, but he can be trusted. Are we in a cop-aware situation?'

'No. As far as I know the cops don't know a thing.'

'Then let's keep it that way.'

She held up her hands, palms towards me and I got off the bed and slapped mine on to them.

'Let's go for it.' She smiled. 'You see, you play straight with Lu-Lu and Lu-Lu'll help yer. I won't be treated like a dumb bimbo even if I look like one.' Just at the moment she looked like a Death Star stormtrooper but I let it pass. 'I have a brain, you know. Christ, I have more college degrees than you have.'

She did too. Fine Arts, Drama and Business Administration.

I offered her a hug.

'Thanks, kiddo. Hey—what do you say to someone with a degree in Fine Arts *and* a job?'

'Double cheeseburger and fries,' she said, tightening her grip.

She'd heard it before.

CHAPTER 8

There were times that evening during the concert when I found myself agreeing with Cardinal John O'Connor who preached from his New York pulpit against the evils of Heavy Metal. But where he was worried about the morals of young middle America, I just didn't think that metal as thrown—I won't say performed—by Astral Reich was very good. Sure, it was loud, but loud is a factor of age. The old buffers who write to *The Times* complaining about the noise level in discos once fought their way nearer the saxophone sections of the big bands even though *their* parents were convinced the racket would blow their eardrums.

Astral Reich had a few good lyrics and were better when they put tongue in cheek, like they did on a Black Sabbath rip-off called something like *Vamping till the Gates of Hell Open*. But basically they weren't very proficient musically. Still, the show was good—lights, sound, smoke—thanks to the overweight, bespectacled Elvis who seemed to be masterminding everything.

Lucinda had gone on stage and announced the band only an hour later than it said on the ticket. That was all she did, just yelled: 'It's Astral Reich!' Getting into the rubber suit just to do that seemed a bit OTT to me, but, hell, it was her band.

Then she and I had sat with Elvis backstage and watched him operate his master dimmer board and mini-computer which triggered the special effects.

'This is how they'd do Nuremberg if they were doing it today,' he'd enthused to me. 'Cue eagles . . . Bring up the orange swastikas . . . where's that Panzer hologram?'

I could worry about Elvis if life were longer.

The highlight of the first set came with the last number. I didn't catch the title but that didn't matter. This was the one the fans—and there were four or five hundred of them in the hall, none of them dressed for a Young Conservatives meeting—had been waiting for.

The band's two main minders, big wrestler types called Snap and Crackle by Lucinda, had been doing good business in the front rows of the thronging crowd selling raffle tickets. Now they cleared a yard of stage and began to draw numbered stubs out of an empty pint pot. The three or four lucky winners waved their tickets above the noises being made by the band and were swiftly—and in most cases quite painfully—hauled up on stage. As the band increased the beat these happy few had the pleasure of being picked up by Snap and Crackle, a wing and a leg each, and thrown out into the audience as far they could manage and gravity would allow.

As an encore, one of the band (Rory, I think) sprayed the flying bodies with beer from a can he'd shaken up as violently as possible. To add effect, he held it in his groin as he popped the stay-on environmentally-friendly tab, so it looked like he was peeing on the volunteer 'lemmings'. The crowd loved it. The lemmings themselves loved it. Thunderous applause all round, then Elvis cued in a tape of Judas Priest as some of the lights came up and the audience broke for the bar for refuelling.

The band had some sort of dressing-room off the hall and the anorexic Entertainments Officer from the Students' Union led them there. Lucinda said she'd better go and keep the troops happy and I didn't press her too closely on what she meant by that, and said I'd hang around backstage with Stevie and the crew.

Stevie showed me where they had plugged in a small fridge behind one of the blocks of amplifiers and told me to help myself to a can of lager. I did so, not to seem out of place. One of the student gophers turned up with a pair of carrier bags full of cartons of Chow Mein and a fistful of plastic forks. I helped myself even though I hadn't ordered any and began to quiz Stevie about his fellow driver Jerry.

We hadn't established much except that Jerry was an OK guy and I quit before Stevie said, 'Why do you want to know?' which is the roadie's favourite question after 'Where d'you want this?' and 'Whose round is it?' Then Stevie clutched at his belt, but it wasn't down to the Chow Mein, it was a small radio-pager bleeper which he'd heard long before I had.

'Sheeeit,' he said, switching it off. Then he looked at me. 'The truck alarm's gone off. Maybe kids pissing about, maybe another fault in the electrics. I'll have to check it out before the neighbours complain.'

'Do you want a hand?' I asked.

'Nah. Just tell Mitch where I am, will you? I'll be back before the next set.'

By the time I found Mitch to tell him, Lu-Lu had returned from the dressing-room and the crew were gearing up for the second half of the show. At this rate it wouldn't finish much before midnight.

Mitch took a small black walkie-talkie from his coat pocket.

'Did Stevie have one of these with him?' he asked me.

'Didn't see one,' I said, 'but I know where he's parked the truck if you want to send out a search party.'

'Go get him, would ya? We have to change the stage lay-out this set so Rory can do his dying swan act, and I need people who can move around in the dark without sticking their fingers up their own arses.'

'I'll go,' I said, then to Lu-Lu: 'Dying swan?'

'Rory does his own interpretation of ritual suicide while singing a real power number he wrote for the album. It's very impressive,' she said seriously. 'I'll come with you.'

We cut out through the Fire Exit and I led her round the corner and across the road to the old truck depot where Stevie's rig was parked. A pair of middle-aged men on their way home from the pub passed us on the street and stared at us open-mouthed. 'Kerrist, Batman and Robin,' one of them said quietly, but I pulled Lucinda along before she could start a fight.

As soon as we turned into the old Freightliner park, Lu-Lu broke into a run and about half a second later I saw why and followed on about two yards behind and a couple of paces slower.

Stevie was lying propped up against the offside wheel arch of the Volvo's cab. The door was open above him and in the light coming from the cab we could see the pained expression on his face and the blood seeping through the fingers of both hands clutching his right side.

'I've been stuck,' he said indignantly. 'The bastard stuck me!'

'Who did?' hissed Lu-Lu, kneeling down and gently forc-ing Stevie's hands away from the wound. I had to admire the Florence Nightingale routine. I didn't really want to get too close; not without gloves.

'The little shite I found in the cab.' Stevie winced with the effort. 'He'd already done the back and was ripping up the seats—Jesus, that smarts!'

'You'll live,' said Lu-Lu. 'It's a bad slash but it's not deep.'

I raised myself on my toes and looked into the cab. Stevie's intruder had certainly taken it out on the upholstery, probably throwing a wobbler when the alarm went off.

'What sort of alarm have you got, Stevie?' I asked as I took off my jacket and then pulled up my T-shirt.

'It cuts into the horns and trips headlights and indicators.' He tried to turn his head to see what I was looking at and the movement made him grunt.

'Keep still!' snapped Lu-Lu.

'Then why isn't it working?' I said to nobody in particular as I levered myself up into cab.

'That's what I said when I got here . . .'

'Shut up, will yer,' Lu-Lu yelled at him, then held out a hand for the T-shirt I'd pulled over my head.

I handed it down to her and shivered in the night air, then swung myself into the passenger seat of the cab.

'What did he use on you?' I asked, fingering the foot-long gashes in the upholstery of the seats. 'A Bowie knife?'

'It was a big bugger,' Stevie grunted as Lu-Lu folded up my T-shirt and pressed it against his side. 'But I think I fainted before . . .'

'Can it! Save your breath, Stevie. Angel's getting the first aid kit.'

I stopped rummaging at that, slightly hurt that she'd gone and ruined a perfectly good T-shirt before reminding me of the first aid kit clipped to the back of the cab.

I climbed down with it and gave it to Lu-Lu.

'He's going to need stitching back together,' she said.

I shrugged back into my jacket.

'Whoever it was,' I said carefully, 'knew what he was doing. He got the lock open without any hassle and then cut the wires in the door frame to disconnect the alarm straight away. He couldn't have known you had a radio-bleeper tied into the system.'

'I wish I hadn't,' he grimaced. 'I'd seen that bozo before, you know.'

'This pad won't stop the bleeding,' Lu-Lu interrupted loudly.

'Where? Where have you seen him?'

'He's gonna need hospitalization.'

'This afternoon. In the hall. Remember me telling you about the student wearing the Walkman and getting his eardrums blasted when we switched on the amps? I'm sure it was him.'

'Forget it, Stevie!' Lu-Lu shouted into his face. 'It's hospital time for you, baby.'

'The little sod could be back in the concert by now,' he grunted as we helped him up.

'I shouldn't think so,' I said. 'He'll be long gone.'

I knew he was. As soon as we'd seen Stevie lying on the ground, I'd let Lucinda get ahead of me so I could check on the Mercedes sports car rented to Mr Gronweghe. It had gone but the skid marks in his parking place were still fresh.

Lucinda stayed with Stevie while I ran to get the Cortina. I'd been volunteered to take Stevie to hospital on the basis that if Lu-Lu turned up looking like she did, they'd arrest her on the spot and by the time she'd got changed out of the armour-plated Batsuit, Stevie would have bled to death.

He might have done anyway if he'd had to rely on me finding a hospital with a Casualty Department open just by following the signs. Fortunately there were enough people, including a couple of policemen, around on the streets to stop and ask directions.

I left him in the Cortina while I ran inside, zipping up

my jacket so as to appear at least half-decent, and tackled the first nurse I found.

'I need a wheelchair,' I said with a smile.

'You look all right to me,' she said, concentrating on picking up a pile of towels from a green plastic chair.

'It's a friend of mine, out in the car. But he can't walk.'

'Go and register at Reception and your friend'll be seen to.' She had the pile of towels up to her chin.

'Well, if you say so,' I said humbly. 'But I wasn't too happy being parked in that space for all this time.'

'What space?' She couldn't resist it.

'The one that's marked "Hospital Administrator". But if you say it's OK, Nurse . . .' I made as if I was trying to look at her name badge.

'First corridor on the left,' she said quickly.

As I wheeled Stevie in to Casualty we rehearsed our story again. Stevie had parked his truck next to an iron railings fence, had slipped getting out and slashed himself. If they didn't wear that, then he was to admit that he'd been climbing over a fence to get to the house of his estranged wife and she'd hit him with a frying-pan and he'd slipped. Hospitals—and police—run a mile from getting too deep into domestic disputes.

In fact, nobody asked much. When we were eventually seen by a harassed houseman, things happened smoothly enough. I had taken Stevie's driving licence and filled in all the forms for him as he couldn't have done it without getting blood all over them, and left the Holiday Inn as our local address. They put twenty-nine stitches in his side and then found a bump on the back of his head, where he'd hit the wheelarch of the truck as he'd fainted.

That meant he stayed there overnight for X-rays, but by that time he'd struck up a relationship with a student nurse who had a brother who thought Astral Reich were the ultimate trip, though as he was only ten, he hadn't been allowed to the concert. At least that showed there was some sanity in the family.

As she wheeled Stevie away, the student nurse gave me a killer look when I asked if I could have my T-shirt back. I should have known. Nowadays anything with blood on it gets microwaved.

'Take care of the rig,' Stevie said as she wheeled him into a lift.

'Huh?'

'Lucinda said you'd drive it to the gig tomorrow.' He looked up at the nurse behind the wheelchair, then back to me just as the lift doors shut. 'I'm on sick leave as of now. And I might be gone some time.'

It was after three o'clock by the time I got back to the Holiday Inn. With nowhere else to stay it seemed the only place to go.

I had to press a bell to get the night porter to open the door. He looked me up and down through the glass before he opened it. I had my story all worked out: midnight mercy dash to the hospital, reporting back to big boss Lucinda, sorry to bother you, not my idea, so fourth, so fifth. I didn't need it.

'You'll be for Room 216, I suppose,' he said.

'Er . . . yes.'

'Come on then. Know your way?'

'Yes.'

'Thought you would. Get on with it, then.'

I was half way across the lobby when I turned back and headed him off at his desk.

'I have to ask. How come you were expecting me?'

He took a deep breath and fixed me with what I vaguely remember used to be called A Look of Disapproval.

'The American lady in 216 came to see me and offered me a very generous gratuity—I cannot deny that. She

asked if it would be possible for some of her musician
friends to invite ladies into their rooms—just for a drink
and a chat, you understand.'

'Of course.'

'Well, I'm fairly broadminded, so I said yes. Then she
said well, if that was the case, I wouldn't mind if she
ordered herself a man for later on in the night. And I
couldn't really refuse, could I? You'd better get a move on.
You're expected.'

It was just like old times. All the old feelings came back
and we worked together as a team, a well-oiled machine,
revelling in the surging power we conjured up between us.
I preened myself with the thought that I could coax even
more out of her if I wanted to.

I hadn't driven a truck this good in years.

It took me half an hour to negotiate the beast out of Leicester's traffic flow system (designed by a redundant air
traffic controller on speed), but once I'd found the M1
motorway and had convinced myself that I was heading
north, I put the hammer down as far as 70 m.p.h. and then
explored the rest of the controls.

We had been late leaving. This was due to having to tell
what had happened to Stevie about a million times, then
discovering that one of the band was missing—the drummer—and he was only found at about 11.0 a.m. in a local
launderette. Not that he had any dirty laundry, he just
found watching the machines go round sort of restful. Then
Lu-Lu decided we should all have brunch instead of lunch
later, so she re-opened her account at the Holiday Inn and
we pigged out. Then I had to stash the Cortina in the
safest-looking National Car Park we could find and then
there was a further delay while Lu-Lu rang somebody
somewhere to put me on the insurance policy for driving
the truck. Luckily, I had my Heavy Goods Vehicle licence

with me and not only was it clean, it was in my real name. That meant I had to be careful, something which seemed to reassure Lu-Lu, though I can't think why.

Stevie's truck had almost every conceivable comfort for a long-distance driver as standard. There was even provision for a small microwave oven, though they're reluctant to fit those these days as they have been found to play havoc with police radar traps. There was a fridge within one-handed reach, but it only had Pepsi in it, and the only music tapes were of a German metal band called Mass. I found myself making a mental shopping list to remedy these defects, then I reminded myself that this was a one-off trip and by tomorrow I'd be heading down the southbound lane because Werewolf was depending on me.

The thought of anyone having to depend on me was a sobering shock to the system. I concentrated on my driving and by the time I reached the Huddersfield turn-off I had the rest of the Astral Reich convoy in sight.

Since they closed down the mills and the mines and power-washed the old stone buildings, Huddersfield has become quite a clean town. You can stand in the middle of it these days and see the hills and the moors which surround it. Touring bands never used to stop there, preferring the more lucrative venues at the universities in Sheffield and Leeds before either heading on north to Newcastle, like the Reich were planning, or cutting over the Pennines and dropping down into Manchester. But in the late 'sixties, the Polytechnic had made a name for itself by putting on what were then called 'progressive' bands; the sort of band which always had a drummer who thought he was faster than Ginger Baker (actually, Buddy Rich gets my vote) and a guy who insisted he could play two saxophones at once. That sort of band disappeared in the softer 'seventies, with Heavy Metal the nearest logical relative in the fragmenting rock'n'roll market.

Our convoy took up just about every available parking

space near the Poly and a small slice of the town's inner ring road. One truck was already there and although it had no markings on it, I was convinced it would be Jerry's and with a bit of luck it would contain the extra 36-foot lighting trusses.

As I waited for the convoy to park in order so that the equipment needed first got nearest the buildings, I tried to work out some more home economics on the tour. Lu-Lu and Mitch rode in a four-wheel Mercedes jeep which Lucinda had hired as the nearest thing to her American four-wheel back home, the one she called 'the big, black, bastard blaster' when she was sober. The band and some of the roadies were packed into two Renault Espace microbuses driven by the minders Snap and Crackle. (I never did find out if there was a 'Pop'.) Elvis the electrician and his mate Willy drove the other two trucks, each with a roadie passenger. No one had asked to ride with me. I was an incomer and they didn't know me well enough yet. That was OK by me.

With all that transport and the hotel bills mounting, there was no way this tour was making money. Somebody was slush-funding it, but I couldn't think who. Maybe it was a tax fiddle, in which case I was well out of my depth. As I know absolutely nothing about paying tax, why learn how to avoid it?

Mitch began to do his traffic-controller act, waving people around the car park with his clipboard. The roadies travelling with the band dismounted and before any of the band could get out and get lost, Snap and Crackle drove off, presumably to their hotel.

Mitch eventually got around to me.

'Stick it over there next to Jerry's rig. You can manage reverse, can't you?'

'If it's in the gear-box, I'll find it,' I said cheerily, but it didn't seem to inspire much confidence in Mitch.

'Just do it, huh? Then bring me the keys. We only need a coupla mixing decks out of there.'

'What about the lighting gear?' I shouted as he walked away.

'For once Jerry got here early and the local gophers helped him set up. All the lighting trusses are up and flying already. Bloody miracle, we're actually ahead of schedule.'

Sod it. I cursed Jerry roundly as I swung the truck into place. To give him his due, Mitch looked suitably impressed as I did it in one fluid movement.

I killed the engine, grabbed my overnight bag, straightened my baseball cap and jumped down from the cab. I locked the doors and walked round the back of the truck to make sure the rear doors were locked. That's standard trucking procedure. So why were the rear doors of Jerry's truck not only not locked but not even closed properly?

'Keys.' It was Mitch, at my shoulder.

I dropped them into his hand.

'Where's Jerry?' I asked, starting towards his truck.

'Dunno. Probably on the phone to his bit of skirt or maybe in one of the local boozers.'

Oh no he wasn't.

'In a rat's ass,' shouted Lucinda. 'Jerry didn't do drugs. He did—then I'm Betty Ford! Bullsheet—or what?'

'Calm down, Lu, I said he *was* drugged,' I tried. 'Now if you'll stay cool and act rational, then I'll take my hand away.'

'That'd be a first,' said Mitch under his breath but I ignored him and relaxed my death grip on Lucinda.

'So what went down here?' she said as I let her go, raising herself to her full height and flicking my fingerprints off her leather jacket.

'Look on the floor,' I said.

'OK, Sher-fucking-lock, what am I looking for?'

'Beer cans.'

There were four silver cans of Grolsch lager on the floor of the truck just behind where we'd found Jerry slumped against a foam-cushioned amplifier. One, on its side, was empty, a second was half full and the other two were un-opened, still linked by plastic hi-cone rings.

'Was Jerry the type to pass out after one can of beer?' I asked.

Mitch snorted.

'Then I suspect someone asked him back here after he'd finished setting up, offered him a beer, popped the top and slipped in a fistful of crushed Mogadon or similar. Chew the fat for ten minutes or so and Jerry suddenly gets sleepy. Our number one fan gets a chance to search the truck in peace and Jerry gets to spend a night in hospital with a stomach pump.'

'Hospital? Shit! I knew I should have taken out medical insurance on these guys.' Lu-Lu the ever-practical.

'You'd better call for an ambulance,' I said to Mitch. 'Better still, find out what the Students' Union does in cases like this and take him yourself.'

'You're taking this a bit too cool,' said Mitch, promising to turn ugly. 'First Stevie, now Jerry, and all this since you showed up. What's going on?'

Lu-Lu came to my rescue.

'First things first, Mitch. Let's get Jerry taken care of.'

On the floor, Jerry began to snore quietly. He looked peaceful and probably healthier than he had for weeks.

'Hold it a minute.' Mitch raised a hand to her, then thought the better of it and dropped the gesture. 'Do you know who's doing this? I don't need to know why, just who. I want to tell my people to take care.'

I could relate to that, and it might work in my favour.

'He's young enough to be a student, but dresses like a yuppie and drives a white Mercedes Sports, registration number G791 PNO. It's a rental and has a sign advertising Euro Limo of Harwich in the back window. Goes around with a Walkman on and uses the name Paul Gronweghe. That's right, say it like you're in pain.'

Mitch glared at Lucinda, but said to me:

'Well, thank you for letting me know what's going on. I'll put the word out. In the meantime, you look like you've drawn the short straw on follow spot.'

'What?'

'Follow spotlight, for the gig. Jerry used to do it, or if he was too pissed, Stevie. Without them, you're elected.'

'Hey, that's a dangerous job,' started Lu-Lu. 'I don't think Angel should—'

'That's cool,' I said, 'I'll do it if somebody gives me a run through.'

'Get your cues from Elvis,' said Mitch, bending down to pick up Jerry in a fireman's lift.

I didn't mind flying Follow Spot at all. The job involved sitting up on the flying trusses above the stage, operating a hand-held spotlight to pick out individual band members on their solos. The job wasn't popular because you had to hang there without a safety harness, which meant you had to stay straight and, worst of all, you had to sit through the show.

But what better chance was I going to get of examining those 36-footer lighting trusses without being disturbed?

From where I sat, thirty feet above the tallest amp tower, you got a whole new perspective on the band. Not that the music improved. Far from it. In fact, I was wearing a head-set and microphone to keep in touch with Elvis at the main console and the earphones helped deaden the sound. No, it was the little things you noticed from up there. Like the fact that Rory was developing a promising bald patch; or that the bass player, who made a point of drinking from a full bottle of whisky on stage, was in fact having it topped up with ginger ale off stage.

The real roadies had looked at me pityingly when I'd started to climb the rope-ladder up to the flying trusses, because I'd refused to take my jacket off. I knew as well as they did how hot it got up there, but I also knew I had a small hacksaw and a roll of insulating tape in the jacket, which I didn't want them to see. I had taken them from my overnight bag, having pinched them from the tool kit Duncan had supplied for the Cortina. Like I said, Duncan's tool kits were the de luxe models.

Once in place on the first truss, I found my balance and settled down to wait for Elvis's orders. My first cue was for a green spot on Lu-Lu as she introduced the band, then kill that and shift position quick for a double red on the band as they came on stage and picked up their instruments. Then Elvis's computer took over for the first few numbers and all the lights on the trusses came into play. I was sweating within two minutes from the heat they threw out, but I had the gloves Stevie had given me and I wasn't worried about being seen. Anyone crazy enough to look directly into that wattage wouldn't see me behind the lamps.

There were four long trusses being flown; two together across the front of the stage and then one off each end going backstage, forming an 'E' with the middle missing. The rope-ladder, which I'd pulled up after me to ensure privacy, was attached to the stage left sections. As soon as the computer took over, I slipped off the headphones and put my ear to the aluminium tubes of the truss going off backstage. Below me, about seven hundred headbangers started to bang heads and the band played on.

I used the handle of the hacksaw to tap the truss. Clang, clang. Hollow. I tried the parallel tube three feet away.

Same result. The bottom tube to form the triangle, from which the lamps hung, involved hooking my legs around the truss I was sitting on and leaning forward and down to get my ear to it. Again, hollow.

I repeated the exercise on the truss I was sitting on. All three supporting tubes rang merrily as I hit them.

I switched on the radio mike and asked Elvis how long I had until I was needed.

'Number after next. Blue spot which should be marked number three, centre stage. Take it easy, they won't get there for fifteen minutes or so.'

'Roger.'

I licked my lips, stuffed the hacksaw into a safe pocket and started out crawling across the truss stretched over front stage. I didn't want to drop the hacksaw and impale one of the guitarists, but then this sort of audience would just think it was part of the act.

Half way across, I checked out the blue spotlight which was roughly where Elvis had promised. By rights, that was as far as I needed to go across the truss, but I kept crawling until I reached the end of that 36-footer. Then I lost the headphones again and did my listening for echoes routine again with just as little result, although at that point I almost slipped and made an unexpected comeback on the live music scene.

I squirmed around so that I was sitting facing backstage again and looking at the last truss. I was pouring with sweat and developing cramp in my thighs. It had to be this one. If I was lucky, it would be the top left tube rather than the right side one, which meant leaning out over nothing except air, or the bottom one, which meant more contortions and a rush of blood to the head.

I put my ear to the metal and tapped with the hacksaw.
Bingo.

CHAPTER 9

'Blue spot on Rory in fifteen seconds. Please copy if you're still awake up there.'

Shit. Just when things were getting interesting.

I crab-crawled my way back centre stage and breathed 'Gotcha' into my microphone just as the blue spot came on. Either it had been badly lined up, or I'd knocked it while crawling along the truss, or Rory was in the wrong place, because the cone of icy blue light I directed downwards missed the end of his fretless guitar by about five feet. Ever the trouper, he leapt sideways while playing and I picked him up from then on.

'Get it together up there, will yer?' boomed Elvis in my ears.

'All right, all right,' I yelled to myself above the music.

'And cut,' said Elvis, as Rory was joined by the rest of the band and the truss lights came on as programmed. The blue spot went off. 'You can go back to sleep now,' smarmed Elvis, 'but you can't come down until the end of the set. Have a nice day. Is that a ten-four, good buddy?'

'That's a Foxtrot Uncle Charlie Kate, Oscar Foxtrot Foxtrot,' I snapped.

I snaked back along the truss, the sweat pouring into my eyes. When I wiped my gloved hand across my forehead and flicked my fingers, droplets hissed and steamed as they hit the lamps.

I made it back to the junction of the trusses and sat up. Below me the band were working up to their lemming-slamming number, so the last place anyone would look would be up, even if they could see through the lights. And so, in (theoretically) full view of about seven hundred people, I began to hacksaw my way into the top left aluminium truss with a blatant disregard for the shavings of toxic metal and dust which sprinkled down on to the stage. What the hell, I figured, it was *supposed* to be Heavy Metal.

I cut away a crescent wedge shape, almost like you'd slice a melon, about four inches long and two inches wide in the middle. With the blade of the hacksaw I eased out the sliver of metal and put it carefully in my pocket with the masking tape. I intended to replace it with a criss-cross of black tape working on the theory that there were so many other dog-ends of black tape on the trusses where cables had been stuck down that no one would notice another bit about a foot in from the end.

Then I had to peel off a soaking cotton glove in order to get two fingers into the metal mouth I'd cut. I made contact with a papery substance and gently pulled.

It came out in a loop at first, then one end came free and I tugged some more and I found myself with a foot of it, then a yard and seemingly no end. It was plasticized paper in a strip about half an inch wide. Every inch was a bubble, just like the way you used to be able to buy aspirin on a strip so you could tear a couple off without making your hangover worse by trying to break-and-enter a childproof bottle.

These were tablets too, but not aspirin. These were smaller, about the size of a contraceptive pill, and they retailed at about £15 each.

Methylene dioxymethamphetamine was first developed during World War I by the Germans, and used as an appetite suppressant among their infantry when rations got scarce. If they'd used it on the enemy instead, they might have got a different result.

Better known as Ecstasy, or 'XTC', or—in some circles—'elastic knees', and I was sitting on a 36-foot-long tube stuffed with it.

Screw the *Front Populaire Breton*. If I knew human nature, somebody was planning *la grande partie de la maison acid*.

Mitch was waiting for me at the bottom of the rope-ladder. The stage and backstage were in darkness. Out front, the audience were cracking open cans of lager and lighting cigarettes and no doubt offering first aid to the lucky slammers who had been thrown off stage at the climax of the set. Elvis had plugged in a tape to the PA system to keep them happy and it was almost as loud as the band had been, so I had to lean in towards Mitch to hear what he wanted to say. Taking the headphones off also helped.

'Willy's found the car,' he shouted.

'What?'

'The Mercedes. I put the word out and when Willy skived off as usual to a local chip shop, he spotted it on the way back.'

He took my arm and led me off stage right. There was nothing affectionate or sinister about that, it was standard practice when a roadie came down from a flying truss into the blackout. The eyes take a while to adjust.

'Whereabouts?' I asked.

'In the car park of a pub called the Flying Horse, about two hundred yards down the road.' He gave me a serious look. 'You'd better take somebody with you.'

'Got anybody who knows how to crack a Mercedes?' I grinned.

'Sure. Take Crackle with you. Just the man for the job.'

And he wasn't kidding.

Crackle came with a tool bag and didn't say much. If it hadn't been for the obvious weight-training he'd done and the Motorhead T-shirt with the ripped-off sleeves, he could have been your average 24-hour-plumber out on a job.

I could see the lights of the pub from the Polytechnic car

park and we had less than half an hour before chucking-out time.

'Let's get it done before the pub throws out,' I said, leading off.

'Fine by me,' said Crackle, 'I'm not needed till the finale.'

'What does the band do for an encore?' I asked as we walked.

'They ain't got one. Every tune they know they do. If the show runs for more than an hour an' three-quarters, they're up shit creek without a paddle.'

I wondered why he'd stopped writing music reviews, but I kept it to myself.

There were only three cars in the car park of the Flying Horse and the Mercedes was parked in the farthest corner from the road. Even better, the driver's side was up against the back wall of the pub.

I did the obvious and checked the doors first. Locked, of course.

'OK, Crackle, I'll keep an eye out if you can do the driver's door. If I whistle, duck down behind the car.'

That would be a laugh. Crackle towered over the Mercedes and could probably lift it if he wanted to.

'Will it take long?'

He eyed the front of the sports car professionally.

'Naw, easy.'

I walked into the middle of the car park so I could see the road and the front door of the pub. There was a juke-box on inside belting out Country and Western, which turned out to be just as well.

I watched in horror as Crackle dropped the tool bag on the ground and took out a nine-pound masonry hammer, spat on his hands and then swung at the driver's door window. By the time I got to him, he was reaching inside to work the handle.

'Is that how you usually break into a car?' I hissed at
him.

'That's the way I've been doing it for fifteen years,'
he said, drawing himself up to his full awesome
height.

'Well . . . fine. Been successful?'

'Yes . . . and no,' he said thoughtfully. 'Yes, I got into
the cars. No, I kept getting arrested.'

I shook my head. Why me?

'Get the boot open, will you? Quietly.'

Crackle shrugged and picked up a chisel from his tool
bag. I was about to check to see if there was a release catch
in the Mercedes itself, but then I thought: Why not let
Crackle keep himself busy.

There was nothing inside the car except a road map on
the passenger seat, open at West Yorkshire. Huddersfield
was ringed in black ink and a route north had been traced
in the general direction of Newcastle. So he knew where the
band was going. Well, that wasn't difficult. Anyone could
have told him.

Then, on the back seat, underneath a light blue Pringle
sweater was a pair of headphones attached to a Walkman
set. Except it wasn't a Walkman. I'd seen commercial ver-
sions marketed as Whisperers, but this was definitely a
souped-up de luxe model. It clipped on to your belt and it
looked like a personal stereo, but it didn't play music; it
received, picking up and amplifying sound so you could
overhear conversations across the street.

I realized that it could have been me who had put him
on to Astral Reich. He'd been outside Candlepower when
I'd talked to Jev Jevons and he'd been in the concert hall
in Leicester. No wonder he'd ripped the headphones off
when the Reich started their sound check. It must have
blown his eardrums.

I wrapped the headphone wires around the Whisperer

and stuffed it into my jacket, then levered myself out of the car.

Crackle was pointing inside the boot, the boot lid hanging at an off-true angle suggesting it might never close properly again. I tried to remember what I'd said on the phone to the girl at Euro Limo about there being no damage to her one and only Mercedes.

'Cameras?' asked Crackle, thinking of loot.

I examined the only thing in the boot, a metal briefcase exactly like the ones professional photographers use. I tried to open it but it was locked.

'Allow me,' said Crackle, leaning forward with the chisel and hammer.

One blow sprung the lock and inside, sure enough, were a couple of cameras and a flash unit padded in a foam-rubber mould.

'Worth anything?' breathed Crackle suddenly deciding to be secretive.

'No, they're not,' I said, but mostly to myself.

Because they weren't. They were good, cheap, automatic cameras, sure, but not worth the expense of such a case.

'Gimme the chisel.'

I dug the chisel blade into the side of the foam rubber and worked it around the edge until the whole shell came up. Underneath it was another rubber mould with four cut-out shapes.

One was unmistakably meant to house an automatic pistol, one I guessed was for a three-inch cylindrical silencer and two rectangles for magazines. All were empty.

So the mysterious Mr Gronweghe was armed.

We already knew he was dangerous.

'So what do we do now?' asked Lucinda, taking charge of the Council of War we'd called in the back of Stevie's truck. Over in the Polytechnic the band started its second set.

'Three ways,' I said. 'Call the cops . . .'

'Get real,' said Mitch.

'Give him what he wants, then.'

'And just what the fuck exactly is it he's chasing?' Mitch challenged.

'That's not an option, Angel, is it?' Lu-Lu came to the rescue.

Mitch took it without question.

'Not really. So we're left with leading this guy away from the band so you can get on with your lives. And I guess that means I have to do the honourable thing for the Greater Good and all that other bullshit.' I tried to look modest.

'What do you need?' asked Mitch, not trying to talk me out of it.

'Transport—I have to get back to my wheels in Leicester—an empty suitcase, the use of Snap and Crackle for a few hours, some privacy, no questions and a big favour from Elvis.'

Astral Reich finished to thunderous applause at one minute after midnight. Much to the annoyance of their fans, by 12.15 they were being driven by Lucinda back to their hotel, the George, in the centre of town near the railway station.

Mitch had briefed his crew and the rip-down was half done before Lu-Lu's microbus had left the car park. Rip-downs are much faster than set-ups and this one would have been even faster if I hadn't rearranged the packing schedule.

Fans were still streaming out as I pulled Jerry's truck up to the college buildings head on. The lighting trusses were brought down, disconnected and hauled out to be shoved in first, then Elvis supervised various other bits of equipment and then I backed the truck off to a corner so that the other trucks could get in.

The lighting trusses, the first thing to go up, should have been the last thing to come out. And trucks should always reverse up to a hall. What we were doing looked highly suspicious.

At least I hoped so.

I let Crackle lock me in the back of Jerry's truck and set to work with my hacksaw on the truss I'd marked with insulating tape. It didn't take long to saw right through the tube and then I started to pull out the strips of plastic paper and the first one just kept coming and coming.

I began to feel like a bad magician trying to do the flags of all nations trick from his top pocket and when I had the first strip completely out of the tube, I did some calculations. There were roughly twelve tablets per foot and I reckoned the strip was near fifty feet long. That would give a street value of about £9,000 working on six hundred tabs per strip at £15 each.

I shoved my fingers into the tube and scrabbled out the other strips. It was difficult to be accurate and I may have counted some twice, but I made it twenty-five in all. If they were all as long as the first, that could be 15,000 tablets.

That meant I was sitting on around £225,000 worth of naughty substances. And I was gonna need a bigger suitcase.

'It's me, Angel.'

'Come on in.'

Lu-Lu climbed aboard. I had the lighting trusses strapped against the side of the truck and the suitcase hidden behind an amp at the far end of the truck.

'The guys are almost through,' said Lucinda. She was

wearing her rubber and leather Batsuit from the concert but had tied her hair back in a pony tail.

I looked at my watch: 1.40 a.m.

'Did Elvis do his stuff?' I asked.

'Yep, but he says you're crazy.'

'Wouldn't be the first time. No hassle from the college?'

'Hell, no. The duty electrician sloped off about nine o'clock, they always do. Elvis ran a cable off the main junction box. None of the students knew what he was doing. He says to tell you that he'll connect it to the circuit behind Jerry's cab, then he'll knock twice on the outside. Got that?' I nodded. 'Then about fifteen seconds later, he'll put the fuse in, so make sure this switch is off.'

She pointed to the light switch which operated the internal lights.

'He thinks you'll blow all his lamps and maybe the main fusebox too, and you'll only get one shot at it. You all done?'

'Ready as I'll ever be. Did you get those staging blocks?'

'They're outside; last thing to be loaded, then we'll make a big play of leaving for the hotel, like you said.'

'Snap and Crackle?'

'They'll be around, though you won't see 'em.'

'Any problem there?'

'Uh-uh.' She shook her head. 'I promised them a bonus, but even so, they'd have done it for Stevie. He was popular.'

Thinking of what had happened to Stevie when our friendly local psycho had a knife didn't cheer me up now I knew he had a gun as well. Lu-Lu read my face.

'You sure you're gonna go through with this?' She reached out and wiped the back of a soft leather driving glove against my cheek.

'You could talk me out of it, real easy.'

She put a black-gloved finger against my lips.

'I hope the Wolfman is worth it,' she said with a smile.

'It's close,' I said.

She pursed her lips.

'Now I know you don't mean that,' she said primly, 'but just how much shit did you find?'

'Over two hundred grand's worth,' I said, keeping my voice down.

She whistled. 'Dollars?'

'Pounds.'

'Werewolf who?' she said.

I had been sitting in the dark for nearly an hour when he came.

The first thing I heard was him trying the door handles, then there was a silence for a few seconds, then a metallic scraping, followed by a rapid high-pitched whine. Then the door clicked open. It happened very fast and, if I hadn't been on tenterhooks for the last hour, would have taken me unawares. I knew what it was even though I couldn't see it: he had a battery-powered lock gun, a handful of which were imported from the States for use by *bona fide* car dealers. (Now there's a contradiction in terms.) Such a stink had been raised about them—questions in the House and so on—that they'd been removed from sale pronto. I knew Duncan the Drunken would kill for one and I was impressed that Gronweghe had come so well equipped.

I'd had the roadies put two of the stage blocks in the truck near the doors. One was flat on the floor and the other was balanced on its end. The blocks were about five feet square and hollow, so I could, with a bit of crouching, keep inside the up-ended one, my hand on the light switch.

The theory was that when Gronweghe opened the door, he would be confronted with a seemingly solid-packed truck interior. He would then have to open the other door as well. The stage blocks were only half an inch thick or so, and could have been pushed aside if I hadn't been inside one, weighting down the edge. The theory went on that, even if he had a torch, he wouldn't have enough hands to open the door and hold a gun at the same time. Not that, in reality, he ought to need a gun to look inside a locked truck, having (I hoped) seen everyone pack up and leave.

For once, theory worked.

The stage blocks had hand-shaped holes cut in the sides for carrying them and one gave me a good spy-hole on him as he fumbled around the edge of the door for the release catch. As he worked it, he leant backwards, balancing on one foot on the edge of the trailer. I was about a foot and a half above him but only about six inches and the thickness of the staging block separated us. I imagined I could smell his breath, but perhaps it was my own sweat.

As he swung the second door outwards, he had to lean into the trailer and he put a hand around the corner of the block to steady himself. It was so close I could have bitten it.

Instead, I hit the light switch and stepped backwards.

God knows what wattage of spotlight hit him full in the face, though Elvis promised to work it out for me one day. All I know is that the six spotlights I'd left on one of the trusses, all with their coloured filters removed and all pointing at the door of the trailer, did come on on cue, which was more than they'd done during the Astral Reich concert.

And without my weight holding it down, the stage block wouldn't support Gronweghe, who had thrown up his left arm to shield his eyes, and he pitched backwards out of the trailer.

I kept my eyes screwed up and looked over the edge. He'd fallen flat on his back and cracked his head on the car park concrete. The staging block lay across him like a tombstone.

'I don't think we're needed here,' said Crackle to Snap somewhere in the shadows, and he sounded really miffed.

Thankfully, Crackle had brought a torch. I had forgotten one and it seemed to be the one piece of equipment Gronweghe wasn't carrying.

By the light of it, we removed the lock gun and a set of picks and keys from one of his pockets and then I ripped his jacket open to find the automatic, complete with silencer, which he'd stuck to the lining with Velcro strips. Neat idea.

Then we rolled him over and I bound his wrists behind his back with insulating tape while Crackle removed his belt and tied his ankles together with it. We were grateful for the torch, because, as Elvis had predicted, the lights rigged up to the interior trailer circuit didn't last long. I heard two bulbs crack and then the whole lot went out.

'Get him into Stevie's rig,' I ordered, and Snap and Crackle picked up Gronweghe as if he were shopping.

We had him on the floor of Stevie's trailer and I was about to climb in afterwards when headlights swung into the car park. It was Lucinda driving one of the Espace microbuses, with Elvis sitting up front with her.

'What the hell are you doing here?' I hissed as she climbed out.

'We're your back-up, man. We waited down the road until we saw the truck light up like a fucking mother ship coming in to land, then we came to see if you needed help.' Lu-Lu put her hands on her hips, defying me. 'And anyhow, Elvis needs to disconnect the power supply. And I wanted to see if my trucks were in one piece and—oh yeah—I was kinda worried about you.'

'Thanks, kiddo. Now give me five minutes with our friend, then we're out of here.'

*

For someone who was trussed up, outnumbered, guilty of several provable crimes and looking down the wrong end of his own gun, Gronweghe remained impressively cool.

'Is it now that we do a deal?' he asked calmly. He had hit his head badly when he'd fallen and there was blood in his blond hair about an inch above his left ear. He didn't seem to notice.

I held his gun on him and leaned back against one of the amplifiers. He was lying in the middle of the trailer and behind his head, carelessly propped up against the side, was a Steinberger fretless bass guitar. It made a surreal image.

I reached into my jacket pocket and took out a foot-long strip of the tablets I'd found.

'For these?' I dangled them in front of him. 'What have you got to offer?'

'I go away and leave you in peace. No more trouble. Give me the stuff and I'm gone.' He looked me straight in the eyes, ignoring the gun. I decided to reassert myself so I waved the gun some more.

'And how do you get it back to Holland? Stuff it in your camera case and go back on the ferry as a foot passenger?'

That didn't shake him, but he got curious.

'Maybe you're not as stupid as the others,' he said. His English was good and there was only a slight accent. 'How did you know?'

'Foot passengers are rarely searched, especially if they're not hippies returning from Katmandu and especially if they look semi-respectable with hire cars waiting for them. And anyway, ferry terminals aren't airports. They're big and chaotic and if the vibes are bad there are lots of places to drop an unidentified case and deny all knowledge of it.'

'You speak from experience?'

'Perhaps.'

His eyes narrowed. 'How much is Guennoc paying you?'

'Not enough. Who's paying you?'

That brought a faint smile and I felt I'd just lost any Brownie points for toughness I might have had.

'If you don't know, you don't need to know. Just remember, those tablets are our property and we intend to get them back now that Guennoc's deal has gone bad. We have our reputation to think of. Now why not let me go and you'll be left alone. We never wanted all this trouble and expense.'

The boy had a tongue in him, I had to give him that.

'Sorry, but the deal is that I'm the one who disappears. I'm out of here with the stuff and I'm gone. These people with the band know nothing. They didn't know the stuff was here, they don't know I've got it and they won't know where I am. Is that clear?'

'Then I was wrong,' he said quickly and angrily. 'You are just as stupid as the other amateurs. Stupid and dead. Dead meat.'

I jabbed the gun at him and for the first time he flinched.

'Smile when you say that,' I said, wondering where I'd heard it before.

'They don't know, do they?'

It was my turn to look puzzled.

'Your friends in this shit band. They don't know what you've found. What would they do if they knew, hey? Maybe we should tell them.' He drew a breath and prepared to shout. He got as far as 'You out there . . .' before I whapped him across the face with the silencer on the end of the automatic.

He cursed and spat blood from a split lip but I was already at the back of the trailer ripping open my overnight bag, kneeling down with my back to him so he couldn't see.

'Hey, you big men outside. Know what your friend here is doing? He's got enough drugs to make you all rich. No problems. One of the safest deals of the century. He's sitting on them and not telling you. He's cheating you out of your share . . .'

By then I had found what I was looking for: my bathroom washbag. I pushed the gun into the bag out of the way, then unzipped the washbag and grabbed the bar of soap I'd stolen from the Holiday Inn. It was still damp and slippy.

Gronweghe never saw it coming. I turned and jumped on him, putting my knees on his chest and pinning him down. I shoved the bar of soap into his mouth and kept my right hand clamped over it while I dug out the insulating tape from my jacket with my left hand.

He was writhing and bucking and almost purple in the face by the time I'd wound the tape round his head and mouth, but he did retain the sense to realize that if he relaxed and breathed through his nose, it wouldn't taste quite so bad.

I pushed myself away from him and stood up feeling pleased with myself. Psycho gunmen held no fears for me; well, not if they were unarmed and tied up.

He tried to kick me as I stepped over him to fetch Crackle and Snap, but his heart wasn't in it. Every time he exerted himself he'd taste soap.

Crackle opened the door for me.

'Do you think we could get our friend here back to his car without too many people seeing?'

'Sure,' said Crackle starting to drag Gronweghe by the ankles to the trailer doors. 'What was that stuff he was shouting?'

We both looked down at the Dutchman's face. White foam and bubbles were seeping through my makeshift gag of black tape.

'He was raving,' I said. 'Worst case of rabies I've seen this week.'

CHAPTER 10

'It's hammer time!'

We were bolting in the hammer lane with the big rigs, and that was a big ten-four. Well, it would have been if we'd been half way across Texas or Nevada or somewhere. As it was, we were leaving Huddersfield on the M1, doing about sixty in the fast lane to be sure, with Lucinda driving and it was already eight o'clock in the morning. And why was I still awake?

I had gone back to the hotel with Lucinda—fatal mistake. I thought I was going to collect the keys to her Mercedes four-wheel and split, but she had other ideas.

'You just park your ass neatly on that quilt,' she'd said, pushing me on to the bed, 'while I pack.'

'Pack?' I'd said, trying not to think how tired I was.

'Just the bare essentials. I'm coming with you.'

I'd tried to sit up but she'd held me down.

'But the band . . . The Festival of Metal tomorrow . . .'

'Aw, screwit,' she'd said. 'The band can look after itself. You're much more fun.'

I remember groaning to myself and then I'd flaked out. When I came to it was light and Lu-Lu was standing over me waving the keys to her Mercedes and saying, 'No Lu-Lu, no wheels.'

I don't think the George Hotel had ever been asked for coffee and bacon sandwiches to go before, but they did us proud and by the time we made the motorway I felt partly human, though I could have murdered another two sandwiches and four more hours' sleep.

Once on the motorway, and there was thankfully little traffic, Lu-Lu put the hammer down—well, that's what she called it. I kept asking when we were going to get out of third gear but having a 55 m.p.h. limit has done terrible things to the American psyche.

The Merc was one of the flash four-door 280GE series which would probably have been called something like a Panzerkampf- wagon had there been a war on. In the instruction book provided by the hire firm, I read that it had an on the road top speed of 96 m.p.h. and an off the road capability of up to 43 m.p.h.

Both facts were to be seriously questioned that morning.

'Hate to say this,' said Lucinda, 'but that guy you stitched last night.'

'Yeah?' I slurred, half asleep with my feet up on the dashboard, not really listening to the Doc Watson tape she'd insisted on playing.

'Did you remember to take his car keys off him?'

I sat up and looked in the wing mirror.

Oh shit.

And I hadn't checked him for the knife he'd used on Stevie, either. I had been so relieved to get the gun off him—the gun which was now at the bottom of the first canal we found on the road out of Huddersfield—that I never thought of checking his calves or ankles, which is where he'd probably had it strapped. And he'd got to it in time and cut himself free and all he'd had to do was cruise up and down the motorway as I'd more or less told him I was cutting out and heading south, back to London.

And here he was right behind us in a Mercedes sports with the driver's window busted to hell and a boot lid which flapped in the wind. And I had a sneaking feeling he was very, very annoyed.

'We could have stopped and shot the bastard,' said Lu-Lu, helpful as ever, 'if you hadn't ditched the gun.'

'That's right,' I said, 'blame me.'

'So who else should I blame?'

I made a big show of looking round the rest of the jeep.

'OK, you've got a point. A stupid one, but a point. Now are you gonna drive us out of this—or do you want a man to take over?'

She gave me a killer look, dropped a gear and put the pedal to the metal.

'Hang on to your girdle, big boy,' she said, her eyes like slits.

It never fails.

I don't know what it says in the manuals but when two Mercedes fight it out on a deserted stretch of motorway somewhere north of Sheffield, there are probably rules laid down somewhere about who does what to whom.

Lucinda hadn't read them either.

All in all, she probably adopted the right tactics. I mean, the guy was past arguing with rationally, for Christ's sake. Otherwise he wouldn't have been going so fast when Lu-Lu hit the brakes, and his nearside front lights wouldn't have got smashed the way they did. And no sane person would have leant out of a non-existent window and hurled abuse at us like he did. And, quite honestly, it was just stupid of him to try and follow us when Lu-Lu switched to four-wheel drive and took off straight up the embankment of the motorway at an angle of at least ten degrees steeper than it recommends in the textbooks.

Gronweghe's sports car, with its low axle, didn't have a chance. Even with our engine screaming, I heard him scrunch to a halt.

At the top of the embankment, Lu-Lu braked and let out a long, low breath.

'Didn't think we'd make that for a minute, there,' she smiled. Then she looked around. There were fields every-

where. In the distance we could see a line of electricity
pylons. Apart from that, nothing.

I checked the wing mirror. Fifty or sixty yards down the
embankment Gronweghe's sports car had sat down and
died, its suspension shot to pieces. It looked like it was
ready to turn on its roof and kick its wheels in the air. He
wasn't going anywhere in that any more.

'Where now?' asked Lu-Lu enthusiastically.

'Fuck knows,' I said, prising my hands free from where
they'd been gripping my seat-belt. I tried to remember if I
had a cigarette hidden somewhere in one of my pockets.
'You're driving.'

We collected the Cortina—still in one piece—from the car
park where I'd left it in Leicester and headed back in convoy to London. Lu-Lu insisted on cutting me up every five
miles or so but when we hit the outskirts of the Smoke, she
fell in behind me and I showed her the back roads across
north London to Hackney.

I made one stop, at one of the few authentic fish and chip
shops left in London and bought double portions for each
of us. By the time we reached Stuart Street they were cold,
but a couple of minutes in the microwave on death-ray
maximum would do wonders for them. The cold cans of
Carling Dry beer—the only thing I had in my fridge not
growing penicillin—did wonders for us.

'So what do we do now?' asked Lu-Lu, still scouting
around with her eyes to try and see where I'd stashed the
suitcase stuffed with naughties.

'We eat, drink, and wait,' I said. 'For a phone call from
France.'

'And then?'

'And then we do a deal. They bring us Werewolf, they
get the stuff.'

'Just like that?'

I leaned back in my one good armchair and popped another beer.

'Yeah, just like that.'

With a full stomach and a few beers, I was anybody's. It was all over bar the shouting. I'd done it. I'd rescued Werewolf. I could afford to close my eyes.

'Hey, Angel.'

'Mmmm?'

'These little cats—kittens—'

'Yeah?'

'Who taught them to open the microwave oven door?'

Guennoc rang that night. I knew he'd be earlier than he'd said he would. People in his position could never wait.

We were entertaining Fenella and Lisabeth to mugs of tea and chocolate biscuits when the phone rang. Fenella was quite happy to sit listening adoringly to the stories Lu-Lu told of her life out there in the real world of rock and roll. Lisabeth was there to keep an eye on Fenella. None of them noticed when I jumped up at the sound of the phone and hurtled to the door.

My footsteps on the stairs told the mysterious Mr Goodson from the ground floor flat that someone was expecting a call. He'd had his door half open but had gone back in before I caught sight of him. He was a man who believed in keeping himself to himself. Perhaps there were things I could learn from him.

I got the communal wall phone on the fifth ring after taking the last five stairs in one.

'Yeah?' I breathed heavily.

'Oh hello, Frank. Is Angel in?' It was Werewolf, who wouldn't have any trouble identifying my heavy breathing and who knew full well that Frank and Salome had moved out of the upstairs flat last year.

'Er . . . I'll see,' I said, trying to give him the time he was attempting to buy.

'I think he might have been away for a few days,' Werewolf said quickly. 'So he might not be back.'

'That's cool,' I said. 'Mission accomplished.'

'Well, that's the good news,' he said and then there was a grunt down the line and a different voice came on.

'This is Guennoc.'

'Hi there. How's the *Front Populaire de l'Acide?*'

Silence.

'So you have recovered our property?'

'Yes, but not without trouble—and expenses.' It was worth a shot.

'What trouble?' he snapped, not too keen to negotiate.

'From the opposition. A very professional firm in Holland.'

'Then we must hurry things along. You have established that your friend is in good health.'

'Not to my satisfaction.' Never give anything away too easily. 'I want to talk to him again.'

'That is not possible.'

'Make it possible. Where are you phoning from?'

'None of your business.'

I didn't think he'd let on, but I asked to hassle him. The call had come straight in, which doesn't mean a lot these days. You can dial a London number direct from a French call-box out in the sticks now, just by remembering to drop the '0' from the 071 or 081, not that the French telephone companies tell you that.

'We need to exchange goods,' he said.

'When do you want to come here?'

'Ah but no, you have misunderstood.' I felt my stomach do a back flip. 'You bring our property here, to France.'

'What? Are you out of your fucking mind?'

'I don't think so. You have already proved yourself very

resourceful. You will bring the goods to St Malo. Do you know where I mean?'

'Never heard of it,' I said, playing dumb. 'Saint what?'

'St Malo. You take the ferry from Portsmouth overnight.' He pronounced it 'Port's Mouth', otherwise his voice showed hardly a trace element of accent.

'I can't just get . . .'

'The ferry from Portsmouth, Tuesday night sailing and no tricks. You will be watched. Brittany Ferries. The sailing is nine o'clock in the evening.'

'Now wait a minute . . .'

But he didn't.

'When you land in St Malo, drive out of the ferry terminal and stop in the first car park you see, on your left, by the harbour. There is a gate into the old town there and the signposts say Inter-Muros. Go inside the city walls and immediately you will see a café called *Le Biniou. Le Biniou*, have you understood that?'

'Yes, but if you think . . .'

'Wait there until you are contacted. That is all. Do this or you will never see your friend again.'

'I want to talk to him now!' I shouted down the phone. 'Or no fucking deal, man!'

Behind me I heard Lu-Lu come out of my flat and look down from the landing. She must have thought I was trying to strangle the phone.

It seemed to work. Werewolf's voice came on again.

'He's given me thirty seconds, Angel. Are you gonna do it?'

'Do you want me to say no?'

'Can't honestly say I fancy that option, old lad.'

'Then I'll do it.'

'Be very careful, Angel.'

'I will,' I said, then quickly to get it in: 'I counted six of them in Guernsey. Any advance?'

'No, that's about right, but they're tooled up to the eye-balls, so like I said, be careful.'

Almost like an echo I heard Guennoc say 'Enough!' somewhere in the background and then the connection was cut and I was left holding a humming but very dead phone.

From the landing, Lu-Lu broke the silence by shouting: 'So? What's going down, Angel?'

I forced a smile as I replaced the phone.

'Ever been to Brittany, Lu-Lu?'

'Is that like Paris-France?'

'Not quite, but you'll love it. Promise.'

I made two more phone calls and I was concentrating so much I forgot not to log them in the communal calls book which hangs by a string from the wall and which Lisabeth checks at least twice a day when I'm in residence.

The first was to Duncan the Drunken, but because it was Friday night and he was down the pub, I got Doreen. So I left as much of a message as I thought she could cope with and said I'd be round in the morning.

The second was to the Sundial pub in Donhead St Agnes in darkest Dorset where I left a message for Werewolf's brother Gearoid. I got the barmaid I'd chatted up on my visit there and she told me that she wasn't expecting 'the big brother' that night but he never missed Saturday lunch-times and she'd see me around noon the next day.

Oh yes, and she did remember me. And my idea about cutting the Monk's Hood Mead with vodka, lime juice and tonic and turning it into a Mead Slammer hadn't caught on with the locals at all. And she thought I'd like to know.

Sometimes you just can't win.

I let Lucinda sleep in the next morning while I whipped over to Barking to see Duncan. I checked his lock-up gar-age first, to avoid running into Doreen, 'the wife', who would only have insisted on feeding me a second and possibly third breakfast.

Duncan was at work, showing his new apprentice how to ring the clock on a Renault 25 Diesel so that what had been a sales rep's 98,000-mile motorway-knackered company car became a 38,000-mile 'one careful lady owner's' runabout.

'Wotcha, Angel. You know Maxi, don't yer?' Duncan greeted me.

'Sure. Hi.'

Whatever her name was, it wasn't Maxi. Duncan had found her in a cardboard box one night in a jeweller's shop doorway in the City. He had literally fallen over her and at first thought he'd killed her, but then found she had enough industrial solvent up her sinuses to keep the fibreglass industry going for a year. He'd brought her back home and Doreen had fed her and fussed over her and she'd taken it but not responded, not even with speech. Then one day she'd followed Duncan to his garage and while he'd been stripping a set of points, she'd handed him the right gauge spanners without having to be asked. From that moment on she'd been Duncan's apprentice and he'd called her Maxi because the car he'd been working on had been an old Austin Maxi. She had never objected and though she did talk these days, it was monosyllables only and usually only when spoken to.

'It's about the Cortina, Dunc,' I started, smiling at Maxi but never really knowing what to say to that young hard face.

'There's nothing wrong with it, is there?' asked Duncan, moving to stick his head under the hood of the Renault.

'No, nice little runner, but it needs a few extras.'

'Such as?'

'A Green Card insurance certificate and a set of false plates.'

He straightened up and wiped his hands on a rag.

'Going on our holidays, are we?'

'Quick trip to France, that's all.'

'Mmm.' He pretended to consider this, then said to Maxi: 'Go put the kettle on, luv.'

She looked at him, then me, with expressionless eyes, then disappeared into the little office booth at the back of the garage.

'I can get you a Green Card, natch, but that'd be in your name and the Cortina's down to me, well, the business anyway.'

Subtle as a brick.

'How much, Dunc?'

'Two grand.'

'Two grand? Bloody hell, I'll bet the trade-in value is no more than twelve hundred. Where's your Glass' Guide?'

'Now you know better than that, young Angel. The Official Car Dealers Secrets Act forbids me showing the Guide to a civilian.'

He was right on that. The second-hand car trade's monthly guide to prices was a better-kept secret than most of MI5's.

'And I'm offering the Green Card and the plates in the deal. What name do you want on the documents?'

'Roy Maclean,' I said, trying to do some sums in my head.

'The old Southwark address is it?'

I nodded.

'Still using that?'

As long as I had a licence in that identity, I'd go on using it until someone rumbled that the house didn't exist any more.

I perched my buttocks on the boot of a Mazda in for repair and turned sideways so he couldn't see me count out two thousand pounds in twenties from the envelope Gearoid had given me.

'What about a buy-back price?'

'If it comes back in one piece, I'll give you nine hundred for it,' he grinned. 'Go on, tell me it's daylight robbery.'

'You have to ask?'

I didn't really begrudge it. Well, for a start, it wasn't my money, but more than that I knew I could trust Duncan. I also knew I could trust Duncan to insist on getting the last word.

I held out a wodge of notes.

'Eighteen hundred quid for the Cortina, the green card and the plates *and* you get the use of Armstrong for another week *plus* a Mercedes 280 four-by-four.'

'Owned?'

'On extended hire.'

'Make it nineteen hundred and you've got a deal.'

'Done,' I said, still offering the bunch of notes.

'I said nineteen.'

'There's nineteen there already. I knew you would.'

While Duncan and I did the paperwork on the Cortina, filling in the Registration Document's change-of-owner section and consigning it forever to the Driver and Vehicle Licensing Centre in Swansea, Maxi—without being asked—came up with a set of orange registration plates. Dutch, how apt. I said they'd be fine.

Then Duncan filled in a Green Card international insurance certificate in the name of Roy Maclean. He seemed to have a stock of them, preprinted with the name of an insurance company I'd never heard of in Chelmsford.

'How about valid for all EEC countries for a month?' he asked.

'Fine. What difference does it make?'

'None at all. You can't claim on this, the company went out of business six months ago.'

He smiled broadly as he handed it over, having signed

'Harry Ramsden' where it said 'Signature of Insurer'.

'Drive carefully,' he said.

Last word, as always.

Lucinda wasn't too happy at being dragged out of bed that
early—like before noon. Fenella was upset because we were
leaving again and she *still* hadn't found homes for any of
the kittens and how much longer did she have to assume
this massive responsibility?

Lisabeth was secretly pleased to see the back of Lu-Lu,
whom she considered as someone likely to lead Fenella into
bad ways. She wasn't as stupid as she looked.

I left them with instructions to act as normal if anyone
called and simply deny all knowledge of me, then I re-
packed my holdall with what few clean clothes I had left.
While Lu-Lu was taking a shower, I nipped downstairs and
out through the disused ground-floor kitchen of the house
and into the yard which our landlord laughingly calls a
patio and which nobody uses except the kittens. Well, we
do use it, to stash black dustbin bags of rubbish until the
refuse Vulture (they really are called that) truck comes
round on Tuesday mornings.

Anyone looking closely would have noticed that one of
the bags had a badly-disguised square shape to it, but
then I figured anyone willing to brave the kittens and
sort through bags of rubbish probably deserved to find
Lu-Lu's suitcase. I undid the plastic tie and ripped the
bin liner away. I had shoved another bag of kitchen
waste in there to distort the outline and that, wouldn't
you know it, had split and covered Lu-Lu's case with
coffee grounds and tea-leaves and those were only the
things I could identify. There was also a distinct whiff
of cat food in the air.

I locked the case in the back of the Cortina, having
checked for prying eyes up and down the street. All clear.

This was Hackney on a Saturday morning and people were out shopping or just still out from Friday night.

I yelled to Lu-Lu to get a move on, but while she was still in the bathroom, I took one other item from my book safe which I figured might come in useful if the worst came to the worst.

And in my experience, it usually does.

CHAPTER 11

I did try and talk Lucinda out of it at least twice and I thought that having to leave the big 4 x 4 behind might have clinched it, but no. She accepted that if we did run into Gronweghe again, he'd go ape-shit at the sight of it and, anyway, she'd never been to a monastery before.

I tried to explain that it wasn't really a monastery but a 'community' or 'retreat' and there was a difference. But she was hooked on the idea of meeting a monk who had an answering service in the local pub. That, she said, was her kinda monk.

'What about Astral Reich?' I'd tried. 'Who's going to look after the band?'

'They can look after themselves. I was getting bored with a capital B with them anyway,' she'd said dismissively.

'And the backers?' And when she'd looked puzzled I'd added: 'Whoever's bankrolling the tour.'

'Oh, I am,' she'd said, dead calm. 'It was my alimony so I think I can pick which toilet to flush it down.'

There was no arguing with logic like that, and so I'd got through to Gearoid down in Dorset and with the sound of the pub filling up for lunch-time, I'd told him that we still had trouble and that I wanted to come down and see him.

He had agreed immediately and gave me specific direc-

tions to get to the Community. Then I'd said I had a partner with me and did he have a spare cell where she could
spend the night, if that was in the rules. Otherwise, book
us in at the Sundial.

He'd laughed and said there'd be no problem accommo-
dating a young lady and just what sort of a place did I think
it was? They had guest-rooms these days, not cells.

I told him I knew that, but maybe a cell would be better.

'Some pile!' shouted Lucinda as we bounced across a
cattle-grid and into the driveway of the mansion that had
become—according to the sign—'*The Community of St Fulgentius of Ruspe: Peace in Body and Soul: Registered for VAT.*'

It was the sort of country house where there are eighteen
windows on the first floor overlooking the ha-ha, but you
just *know* there are only seventeen rooms up there. If it
didn't have a body in the library, I'd eat my baseball cap,
and if a butler had come to answer the front door, I
wouldn't have been at all surprised.

In fact two brothers—and these brothers were white—
came round the corner of the house, one of them wheeling
a barrowload of manure, even as we were reading the brass
plate on the door which said this was the home of Monk's
Hood Organic Products, Ltd.

They stopped dead in their tracks and looked at Lucinda.
I had told her to dress conservatively and, because I know
her, I had accepted that for her camouflage ski-pants, high
heel snakeskin shoes and a rust-coloured suede jacket with
fringe on the sleeves was conservative. Maybe I should
have had a word about the big red Stetson.

'Hi, you guys,' she started before I could muzzle her.
'Don't let us interrupt your daily monking. We're looking
for—'

'Angel! Good to see you,' came an Irish voice from behind us. 'I'll look after my guests, Stephen, thank you.'

Gearoid was wearing a brown habit and sandals, the thick wooden cross bouncing against his chest as when I'd first seen him a few days before.

As we shook hands, he whispered: 'I wasn't being rude to one of them,' and nodded in the direction of the two brothers with the manure. 'It's just that they're both called Stephen and they do everything together.'

I pretended to believe him and was about to introduce Lu-Lu when he said: 'And this must be Lucinda.'

'It certainly is,' she said, 'and it's a pleasure to meet blood kin of my old friend Wolfie.'

'Why, ah jes love that Southern accent,' said Gearoid in a passable imitation. 'Now y'all come in and have tea now, y'hear.'

Lu-Lu threw back her stetson and roared with laughter.

'Is this guy a character—or what?'

She linked arms with Gearoid and he made to lead us indoors.

'How did you know it was Lucinda?' I asked as we walked. 'I never said *who* I was bringing.'

He winked at me. 'Once described, never forgotten.'

He led us through an icy entrance hall complete with an impressive central staircase, and into what he said was 'the office'. It was a sort of reception room with a hot drinks machine and a non-matching collection of easy chairs. On shelves and in glass cabinets were samples of the Community's produce, ranging from honey and mead to organic vegetables to postcards of the house and amateurish booklets with titles such as *Contemplative Walks in South Dorset* and *Hampshire Church Steeples*.

'Would you have a few coins for the machine, Roy? I'd like to treat this vivacious creature to a cup of herbal tea.'

'I didn't know monks could talk like this,' Lu-Lu hissed at me in a stage whisper.

'Stick around,' I hissed back, emptying my pockets of change into Gearoid's outstretched hand.

When he'd got three plastic cups of perfectly foul tea out of the machine, Gearoid indicated the chairs to us and closed the door.

'We won't be disturbed for an hour or so—so fill me in. How's the emergency fund going? Is that why you're back?'

The amiable idiot act had disappeared.

'The fund is depleted, but that's not why I'm back. I need another sort of help,' I said, thinking I might as well get to it.

I told him most of what had happened since I'd picked up Astral Reich's trail, and the mysterious Mr Gronweghe had picked up mine.

'And what was the stash?' he asked. Monks weren't supposed to talk like that either.

'Ecstasy tablets—about 15,000 of them.'

He let out a low whistle. 'Why didn't they smuggle it as powder? Much easier and it takes effect quicker.' Another thing monks weren't supposed to know. I added it to the list.

'For a start, the stuff was never supposed to be smuggled here,' I explained. 'Whoever manufactured it has production line facilities, right down to a machine which presses the tablets and wraps them or punches them into strips like this.'

I did my conjuror's act and produced the strip of tablets I'd waved at Gronweghe.

'Hey! Party!' yelled Lu-Lu, then slapped a hand to her mouth. 'Oops! Sorry.'

I tried to ignore her.

'I reckon that this guy Guennoc in Brittany wants to set himself up as purveyor of acid house parties to the young, rich and French. There's money to be made in it. Last year they were talking of £100,000 a party going to the organizers of some of the big ones out in Essex and Kent, and that was without the XTC retailing concession.'

'I've heard there's almost zero drug scene in France,' Lu-Lu chipped in.

'Outside Paris and Marseilles, and leaving aside alcohol and *tabac noir*,' said Gearoid conversationally, 'you're right. And then it tends to be the top end of the market, either cocaine for the rich and foolish or heroin for the rapidly poor and hooked. There must be a large untapped youth market for something as cheap and cheerful as Ecstasy. Yes—' he looked thoughtful—'I can see somebody making a lot of money if they pick their spot, say just outside a town with a large university or a military base with a lot of young conscripts doing their national service. Do they still do that?'

'Dunno,' I said, 'but I agree with your scenario.'

'So it's a professional operation, then, is it?'

'No, I don't think so.' I squirmed around in my chair trying to find somewhere to put down the disgusting tea. 'Well, the manufacturing end is, sure, but Guennoc and these cowboys in Brittany, that's a joke. They've made a bulk purchase of laughing pills and the delivery's gone wrong and they're having to resort to outsiders like me. That's not a pro op.'

Gearoid saw my discomfort with the cup of tea and reached inside his robe. He produced a quarter-bottle of Irish whiskey.

'Have a top-up,' he offered and both Lu-Lu and I shot out our cups.

'Hey, you sure this is OK?' she asked. 'I mean, aren't there rules about drinking on duty and such stuff? What's the Father Abbott gonna say?'

'We don't have a Father Abbott,' Gearoid said gently. 'We have a Leader Elect and as he's up in Durham at a conference, yours truly here is the temporary acting deputy stand-in Leader Elect.'

'That means you're in charge, right?'

'Right.'

'Coolksi.' She sipped her tea with renewed relish.

'The Dutch hit man, he referred to them as amateurs too,' I continued, trying to get back to business before Lu-Lu and Gearoid hit it off too well. 'But I think I've rumbled their game plan.'

Gearoid slipped the whiskey away and gave me his undivided attention. 'Let's hear it.'

'Well, this whole *Front Populaire Breton* thing must be a con. I mean, they cannot be serious. But maybe it comes in handy to impress the locals.'

'Like the fishing-boat they had.'

'That's right. Whatever, I'm pretty sure Guennoc hasn't yet paid for his shipment, otherwise why would the Dutch end of things be so anxious to trace the goods? If they'd had their money, it was Guennoc's problem.'

'And you think,' Gearoid said between sips, 'that Guennoc is holding Francis and using you to get the drugs without having to pay for them?'

'Yes. If it doesn't work he's lost nothing, and if it does he repeats the Dutch deal and has twice as much dope for his money, or he cuts out the Dutch supplier altogether and so has nil operating costs.'

Lucinda was mouthing 'Francis?' at me, so I mouthed 'Werewolf' back and she shouted 'Oh'.

'He sounds to be a greedy young man,' said our host.

'And last night Werewolf said they were tooled up.'

'I was kinda wondering about that,' drawled Lu-Lu mischievously.

'It means well-armed,' I said out of the corner of my mouth. 'They have guns.'

'We had a gun, until you threw it away.' She could be really petulant sometimes.

'I wouldn't have liked to have to explain that to the nice Customs and Excise men on the cross-Channel ferry, no matter how sweetly you smiled at them.'

Gearoid jumped in. 'So how are you going to explain 15,000 Ecstasy tablets, Roy?'

'Hopefully I won't have to because they won't find them,' I said, with much more confidence than I felt.

'And just how do you intend smuggling them through French Customs, eh?'

He wasn't being sarcastic, he was genuinely interested.

'Yeah—how? Spill the beans Mr International Courier.' Lucinda, on the other hand, was being chopsy.

'Come on,' I said confidently, 'it's much more difficult to smuggle stuff into the UK. Going out, British Customs are only mildly interested in what you're carrying and when did you ever go through a luggage check at a port? Once there, well, hell, French Customs can't really believe that anybody would smuggle something into France that they would want and don't already have. Big trucks get turned over but cars and foot passengers very rarely. Still, we can't take that chance. Remember, you guys, Francis is the one who's in real trouble if we get caught and the stuff gets taken. Without it, we have nothing to bargain with. We don't even know where they've got him.'

'We?' asked Gearoid, narrowing his eyes.

'I was coming to that, and you, because you gave me the idea.'

'I did?'

'Sure, when you gave me that bottle of mead in the pub.'

It took a couple of seconds to sink in. Lu-Lu was glaring at each of us in turn like she was watching a tennis match that was being played to the death.

'We have to take out insurance against being stopped

and searched,' I said. 'Increase the odds in our favour of being waved through with no hassle.'

Gearoid got it.

'If you're thinking what I think you're thinking, we haven't got a prayer,' he said.

I beamed at him, showing off the teeth.

'Now that, I'm happy to say, is your department.'

'Bees?' said Lucinda too loudly. 'Bees?'

'Keep your voice down, will yer?' I hissed.

We were in the dining-room of the Sundial, eating steak and salad and drinking a cheeky Bulgarian Cabernet Sauvignon which tasted fine but you had to remember not to get any on your clothes. It was meditation night back at the community, so we'd left Gearoid to it after he'd shown us to the guest-rooms and given us a set of keys to the main door so we could get in late without disturbing anyone. The odds on that happening, with Lu-Lu in tow, were remote.

'Will he agree to it?' Lucinda asked between forkfuls.

'I hope so,' I said, 'I haven't any other bright ideas.'

'So what do you know about bees?'

'Nothing, except that if I was a Customs Officer, a hive of bees is the last thing I'm going to stick my hand in to see if there are any naughty substances.'

'Will it work?'

'I dunno. Gearoid is thinking it over and he'll show us the bees tomorrow. We get a guided tour of the apiary at ten o'clock, after Sunday service or whatever they call it.'

'We?'

'I thought it best if you were fully briefed too. After all, you'll be riding shotgun on them.'

'Now don't flap about, and try not to sweat. They like sweat.'

The three of us looked like extras from a training film at

a nuclear power plant, the sort of film they don't show in the Visitor Centre. We all wore white boiler suits zipped up tight—Lucinda and I checking the zips about a dozen times—and tucked into white rubber boots, and long white gauntlets stained and stiff with honey residue. Gearoid had a state-of-the-art suit with a rounded helmet rather like a fencing mask which just clipped shut. Lu-Lu and I had to struggle into the older type mesh box-masks which balanced over a topee-style hard hat and tied under the armpits. Gearoid showed us how to snap on rubber bands over the gauntlets at the wrist and put extra rubber bands around our boots to stop the bees getting up the trouser legs. Lu-Lu thought this was hysterical.

She and I moved like robots from a 1950s sci-fi movie. Gearoid hopped around us making sure there were no gaps or vents in our suits. On his modern one-piece, there was a star printed over his left breast and the legend SHERIFF BEEKEEPER. I didn't care if the bees shot him, just as long as they didn't sting the deputies too.

We pulled on the gear over our clothes in a converted stable at the back of the main house. The workbenches down either wall were littered with bits of wood, odd-looking tools and empty glass jars. In one corner was an electric honey extractor plugged into a socket in the wall.

'The place is a bit of a mess,' said Gearoid, reading my thoughts, 'but it's out of season for the bees. Well, actually their season's started but the honey flow won't begin for a while. Now, follow me and we'll go and see my little beauties. And remember what I said.'

'Don't flap,' said Lucinda, her voice muffled by her helmet.

'No sweat,' I added, through the veil over my throat.

We trooped after him in single file, across a courtyard and then through the community's vegetable garden and through a small orchard of apple and pear trees. Towards the end of the orchard the grass and nettles had been left at waist height to protect the apiary, or maybe hide it from nervous fruit-pickers.

The first sign of life I saw was a bee doing a Von Richthofen roll over Lucinda's helmet. Then I became conscious of the odd buzzing as solitary scout bees began to divebomb me.

'We'll have a look inside the first one,' said Gearoid quietly and I had to strain to hear him through the hat and the veil and the wire-meshing box around my face. 'Stand there.'

I took up position next to Lucinda and made a conscious effort to slow my breathing. No one was going to accuse me of picking a fight with *apis mellifera*.

'Most of them should be out by this time,' Gearoid was saying, 'so I'm not bothering to puff them with smoke. This lot are fairly docile anyway. A good queen, that's the secret. She keeps them under control.'

'Right on, sister,' said Lucinda, but there was a nervous note in her voice.

Gearoid eased off the flat top of the first hive. I counted at least twenty more stretching off into the long grass.

'Er . . . just how many hives do you run here?' I asked shakily.

'Thirty-two,' said Gearoid, easing the roof of the hive to the ground. 'And the answer to your next question is that there could be up to 60,000 bees in each hive, or colony. But that's in the summer. Now . . . oh, I'd reckon about 35,000.'

'Multiplied by thirty-two . . .' I said quietly.

'Over a million,' hissed Lu-Lu. 'We're in the middle of over a million bees, fer Christ's sake.'

'Relax,' said Gearoid, smiling through his fencer's mask. 'And look in here.'

Without its lid we could see into the hive and the bees

were beginning to appear, both flying in front of our faces and emerging from the hive itself, crawling across the top of wooden frames which seemed to have been slotted in there like old-fashioned fuses in a fuse-box. I decided to pretend there was a sheet of glass between me and Gearoid and I kept stock still, my eyes riveted on his hands as he levered up one of the frames with an oddly shaped metal tool.

'OK, quick lecture. Downstairs we have the brood chamber where the queen is, along with the drones. They're the ones who do nothing except mate with the queen and about ten per cent of the colony are drones. The valuable ones are these little darlings, the workers—named by Trotsky in 1921.'

Lu-Lu and I stared transfixed at the frame he held. The honeycomb pattern seemed somehow less reassuring with its thick coating of crawling, wriggling, brown bees.

'That was a joke,' said Gearoid.

'So we can laugh but we can't sweat, eh?' I whispered.

Gearoid grunted and went on: 'This is the upstairs of the hive and these frames are called Hoffman self-spacers when you buy them. Once they're in place, we call them "supers" and it's where you persuade the—Ow!' He let go of the frame with his left hand and shook it. '—Little buggers to leave their honey for you to steal.'

'Did you get stung?' asked Lucinda, leaning forward to get a better view.

I noticed a cluster of bees had landed on her shoulder and I moved to brush them off. I raised my arm slowly, remembering the 'no flapping' instruction, but half way there I froze. From the fingertips of the heavy plastic gloves to up beyond the elbow was just solid bees. I lowered the arm slowly, working on the sound principle that if I couldn't see them, they weren't there.

'No more than ten times a day,' Gearoid was saying, 'but

you get immune. As long as you're not one of the two per cent of the population who are allergic.'

'What happens then?' asked Lucinda, blissfully unaware that both her shoulders were covered now.

'I think you die,' said Gearoid.

'Didn't you ever see the movie *The Swarm?*' I added helpfully.

Gearoid picked out another frame, seemingly with even more bees clinging to it.

'Listen up, you two, they're beginning to get fractious. This is what's called a National Hive. It's your basic, popular design, but the principle's the same whether it's a home for bees or if you're transporting them. You use these Hoffman frames with a sheet of wax stretched across them and the bees make themselves at home and pull the wax out into the honeycomb shape. You with me?'

Lucinda nodded and dislodged half a squadron of bees into the air around her head. I just said 'Yes' quietly because I was busy going cross-eyed as one of the bee proletariat trundled across the wire-meshing in front of my nose.

'This National has eleven frames—"supers" if you like—which slot in to the main framework of the box. Supposing we leave some full of bees at each end, say, four at this end and three at that. The four in the middle can be dummy ones . . .'

I was ahead of him.

'Can the bees get through if you put something else in?'

'They can go under and over and round the side. Anyone taking the top off would see just bees unless they tried to remove a frame or two from the middle.'

'And how much space would that give us, roughly?'

'Oh—' Gearoid replaced the frame but the bees in the air all around us seemed to get even more narked at that— 'Roughly, a box shape fourteen inches wide by eight-and-a-half inches deep and five-and-a-quarter inches long.'

'You've measured it,' I said, sensing him grinning behind his mask.

'I've built one for you,' he said smugly. 'Some of us are up at dawn around here.'

'And you think it would work?'

'I'm not proposing we take a hive, though you could. I'm going to suggest a nucleus box—that's how you transport bees. We'll make it nine frames instead of the eleven here. One with a queen, one brood frame with pollen already on and three with honey as food for the journey, though they'd probably survive six weeks on the contents of their stomachs. The other four frames are for you. And maybe we'll take three boxes, two real and one the ringer.'

'How many bees?' Lu-Lu asked hoarsely. She had looked down and seen that too many bees to count were using her bosom as a flight deck.

'About eight to ten thousand per box.' Gearoid had closed the lid of the hive and was brushing bees off his arms with a bunch of goose feathers tied together with string. 'I've got the boxes back in the stables, come and see what you think.'

A good twenty yards away, back in the long grass, I reached out and touched Gearoid on the arm.

'If we're going to use these Nuclear Boxes—'

'Nucleus.'

'Whatever. And they're back in the stables, why did we have to come out here to the hives?'

'I just wanted to put the fear of God into you,' he said cheerfully. 'Or, I suppose, the fear of one of God's creatures. It's good for the soul and I think everyone should have something good for the soul on Sundays.'

'And what's good for yours on Sunday?' I asked, knowing I'd regret it.

'The six pints of Guinness you're going to buy me at lunch-time,' he said.

Back in the stables, we disrobed carefully—well, Lu-Lu and I did, each convinced that a mini-swarm of bees had got in somewhere and were just waiting for us to drop our guard. There was not one to be seen, but we imagined at least a hundred.

Gearoid cleared some junk off one of the workbenches and from underneath produced a box made of plywood and held together with small nails. He rummaged in a large cardboard box and produced four wooden frames, the top bar wider than the bottom so it could rest on the sides of the 'super' box which fitted on the hive.

'This goes in these,' he said, sliding the open wooden box like a drawer into four of the Hoffman frames. 'From the top, you just see the four top bars of the frames. They had sheets of wax in, but I cut them out earlier. Now over here, we have a nucleus box. I've only one but I can get another two tomorrow.'

He carried the contraption to the other bench and removed a sack from a large wooden box like a conjuror.

'This is a nucleus. OK, so it's a box with a lid which screws on, but note the ventilation holes.'

We looked suitably impressed at the panels in the top and low in the sides which were covered in a fine metallic mesh.

'Now, remember what you saw out at the hive. When I slot these frames in the middle—' he rested them in the box and then reached for more frames with wax sheets in '—and then these at each end, and remember, these will be crawling with bees, and then put the lid on—' he snapped the lid in place—'what do you see?'

Lu-Lu and I bent down and peered in through the ventilator slits.

'Nothing,' said Lu-Lu, 'except ten thousand frigging bees.'

'And I'll use old Hoffmans with honey on for the fake frames, just in case anyone takes the lid off. I doubt if they will, and not unless it's somebody who knows what they're doing, but just in case. Now your problem is, how much stuff can we get in this box?'

He opened the nucleus and took out the fake frames and slid out the box.

'That's the optimum size, I reckon. You can't go deeper than eight-and-a-half inches or wider than fourteen, as those are your two-dimensional measurements on the frame. Four frames gives you a thickness of just over five inches. So—' he pretended to do some quick maths in his head—'you have a cubic capacity of, say, about 600 cubic inches. If pushed, of course, we could make it two ringers and one real nucleus or even risk all three.'

I turned the box over in my hands.

'If we took all the tablets out of their plastic seals, they might fit and we could wad them in to stop them rattling.'

'Who's gonna hear them once they hear the bumbly bees?' Lu-Lu pointed out. 'But that's a faggin' awful job, unwrapping the tabs, I mean.'

Gearoid and I looked at her innocently.

'Did you have any plans for the next two days?' I asked.

By early evening, Lucinda had broken three nails, blunted a pair of scissors, made the two monks called Stephen run for cover into the vegetable patch (after hearing her cursing through an open window), and was into her second bottle of mead.

I decided it was a good time to make myself scarce and I joined Gearoid, still red-faced and smiling from his lunch-time trip to the Sundial at my expense, on his daily stroll around the grounds of the St Fulgentius estate.

'What about transport?' I broached.

'We'll use the community's Transit van. It's got our name down the side and they've seen it before on the ferries.'

'So you've exported to France before?'

'Yes, I thought you must have known. It's dead easy to export bees, though not so easy to import them. There's a disease, a parasite, called Varroasis which has spread across Europe a bit like rabies. Britain—and Ireland—and Norway and Sweden are the only places which are free of it. The French got it back in 1982 and we've supplied queens and small colonies to our opposite numbers ever since. We have a Health Certificate under the Bee Diseases Control Act—no, don't laugh, we have. And if you're exporting to just one end destination in France, you don't need a licence or a Transit Certificate.'

'And we have an end destination?'

'Oh yeah, didn't I mention it? I have a customer for us, well, for the bees that is, just as long as he doesn't have to pay for them. He's a monk, a real one, called Frostin and he has an apiary just outside St Lo in Normandy. I called him last night. The story, should we decide to accept this mission, is that Frostin's monastery is looking for some new varroasis-free colonies to help pollinate their cider apple trees. It could be true. Farmers round here have noticed their bean crops increasing 70% in yield thanks to my bees. It's also about the right time of year. He'll take them off our hands, but you'll get the bill.'

'How much?'

'Oh, I haven't worked it out yet, but you'd be talking around £200 for the bees, another £150 for the nucleus boxes, frames, carpentry, consultancy fees, petrol, call it £500. It'll go to a good cause.'

I gave him my straight-arrow look.
'You're beginning to enjoy this, aren't you?'
He frowned.
'Yes. I'm afraid I am.'

CHAPTER 12

Gearoid kept the Transit right behind me all the way
through Salisbury and down the A36 until we hit the
motorway which would swing us around Southampton
and into Portsmouth. There wasn't much traffic that late
in the afternoon and we'd set off far too early. I put that
down to nerves, mostly on my part. So instead of turning
off the M27 for the Ferry Terminal, I wound the window
down and stuck my arm out, making glass-tipping motions.
Gearoid flashed his lights to say he understood and put on
a spurt to overtake me.

I followed him north, out of Portsmouth on the old London road until he indicated he was turning off at a junction
marked Chalton. A few minutes later, bang on six o'clock
opening time, we pulled into the car park of the Red Lion,
a thatched pub opposite a church which wouldn't have
looked out of place on a box of chocolates.

'Oldest pub in Hampshire,' said Gearoid over a pint of
Gale's ale.

'I suppose your research into Hampshire church steeples
led you here,' I said, nodding towards the church across
the minute village green.

'Absolutely.'

'How's the cargo?'

'Bearing up. Lucinda's convinced they're sneaking into
the cab to get at her.'

'A honey for the honey bees,' I said.

Just then there came a thump from the other bar where Lu-Lu was being shown around by the landlord, followed by a muffled 'Shit!'

Lucinda appeared through a doorway to the left of the bar, rubbing her forehead.

'The people who built this place were midgets—or what?'

'By your standards, Stretch, they still are. Sit down and try the beer.'

She did, and liked it. I was beginning to think you could take her anywhere, twice—the second time to apologize.

'So, why're we here?' she asked. 'Not that I'm complaining. Nice pub.'

'Killing time, really,' I started. 'I don't fancy sitting in the queue for the boat for three hours.' Not without a cigarette, anyway.

'And it gives us an opportunity to take a final stock check of our situation.'

'That sounds to me to be a pompous way of saying do we want to chicken out,' said Gearoid icily.

'It could be me saying I feel guilty about getting you two involved,' I said quickly, then buried my face in my beer.

Lucinda looked at each of us and then downed the rest of her pint in one.

'I only get nervous if I have to do something I don't wanna do,' she said slowly. 'And I think I wanna do this— my choice. So let's get it done.'

Gearoid and I smiled at each other. Lu-Lu stood up from the table we'd been conspiring around.

'And I ain't driving, so more beer, landlord!'

Waiting in line to board the ferry turned out to be less hassle than I had expected, though we were well in advance of the tourist season and the traffic was light. In fact, mostly trucks, with relatively few private cars.

The Cortina was directed into the passenger car lane and Gearoid's van shunted off to my left somewhere among the other vans, the odd caravan towed by a car and the lighter trucks. Beyond them were the big articulated container lorries, the refrigerated trucks and the livestock trucks. French farmers were always rioting about imports of British lamb, but exports of veal calves seemed to be booming. During the holiday period, the port authorities always kept the live veal cargoes to the far side of the dock so as not to upset the kids. They also loaded them last so their plaintive mooing noises didn't echo through the car decks until everybody was topside, either trying to find the bar or fighting over the sleeper seats.

A young French crewman armed with a clipboard and wearing a Brittany Ferries tie walked down the line of cars checking tickets and giving out Boarding Passes. He stuck an orange square on the windscreen saying ST MALO. I was tempted to ask why, as far as I knew, the boat didn't make request stops en route. But I thought the better of drawing attention to myself. Then he said 'Mr Maclean' and I did a bit of a double take before agreeing with him.

He made a note of it on his clipboard. I should have remembered to warn Gearoid that they do that these days. It's nothing official really, it's just that since the Zeebrugge ferry disaster the boat companies think it might be an idea to know—roughly—who was supposed to be on board when it sinks.

There had been no trouble at Passport Control, not that there should have been. It was a genuine passport after all, just not in my name, and anyway, they never care if you're leaving a country. Why should they? You're about to become someone else's problem.

I had acquired my second passport a couple of years ago. There had been a big strike in the Civil Service which had centred on the handful of Passport Offices and had resulted in delays of six to nine months processing passport applications. To prevent would-be holidaymakers rioting and storming the striking Passport Offices, the Post Office had done a big push on the one-year Visitors' Passports (the type popular with football hooligans) for which you needed only basic ID. I had taken my Driver's Licence—well, my spare one—and got a temporary Visitor's Passport on the spot in the name of Roy Maclean. As soon as the strike was over, I sent in the one-year passport along with the right money, asking for it to be upgraded. They could, and probably should, have asked to see a Birth Certificate or proof of citizenship, but they didn't, what with the backlog they must have had. Just in case, I'd used my old address in Southwark, where mail was collected by the people next door to the space in the street where my house used to stand before it accidentally blew up.

My spare Driving Licence was also genuine, but they're easy to get. All you do is keep taking driving tests in different areas under slightly different names and different addresses. Of course, it's a bit of a blow to the old ego if you fail, but you don't have to tell anyone that.

The line I was in started moving after only ten minutes. I eased the Cortina up the ramp to where the docking bridge led into the ship, its bow doors gaping in a pretty good imitation of the shark in *Jaws I, II* and *III*. (Not *Jaws IV*. I know no one who sat all through that.)

Someone stuck out a hand for my Boarding Pass and then I was waved on board by one of the blue-overalled crewmen, and I rolled the car down and into the bowels of the ship.

I grabbed my holdall and locked the Cortina, remembering to remember which Deck I was parked on, then headed up top as quickly as I could.

The upper decks were lit up like a Christmas tree and I found an exit to the top deck after about six flights of stairs and worked my way round to the bows, if that's what they call the sharp bit at the front. From there I could look down on to the dock and after ten minutes or so I saw the St Fulgentius Transit rattle down into the decks below.

I breathed a loud sigh of relief. So loud that two really quite pretty French backpackers glared at me and moved away round the corner of the deck. I had been so anxious about Gearoid and Lu-Lu I hadn't even noticed them or their skin-tight, figure-hugging Levis.

I must be slipping.

The Brittany Ferries lady dishing out cabins for the night never even looked up. I just showed her my ticket and she went down her list until she found 'Maclean', then she ticked off the name and said, 'One, two, one' in a French accent so it came out as 'Huan, tew, huan'.

I followed a ship's plan down one deck and along a corridor until I found Cabin 121, a four-berther at the end. The door was open, as the cleaners had just left and the four keys to the door hung on a rack by the light switch. I slung my holdall on to the nearest top bunk, took three of the keys and locked the door before going up a deck to find the bar.

The boat left on schedule and by the time it had passed Hayling Island I was on my second Känterbrau beer and had broken all my good resolve and invested in a packet of Gitanes Mild and a disposable *briquet*.

The first rush of nicotine made me lightheaded and glad that I was sitting down. The weather forecast was for a relatively calm crossing for the time of year, which had calmed me if not the English Channel. I never claimed to be a good sailor and usually wouldn't set foot on board a boat unless it was big enough to have a bar on. This one had two, so why worry?

I reviewed the last two days, which had gone by quickly

in a flurry of activity yet less frenetic than you might have thought. Maybe the Community of St Fulgentius of Ruspe had a calming effect on things.

Lucinda had persevered and popped out almost all the Ecstasy tablets from their paper packaging by herself. I'd helped for a few hours but then I'd made some crack about how I hoped *she* was keeping count and she'd thrown one of her cowboy boots at me.

Gearoid knocked up two open boxes out of plywood to the dimensions which would fit under four frames in a Nucleus box and threw us a fast ball by asking if we had taken account of the weight. We hadn't, natch.

He had a point. A clever Customs man wouldn't try to dismantle a Nucleus Box or a hive, but bees are transported regularly and so they would know roughly what weight a Nucleus Box was supposed to be—no more than twenty pounds. So we had to judge everything to the weight of tablets being no more than the weight of four full frames of wax, honey and bees. Gearoid estimated that we could get away with a theoretical three pounds of honey per frame, so we had twelve pounds to play with. In the end we had a box full of tablets weighing in at just under ten pounds, with about two handfuls of tabs left over. Gearoid taped a perspex lid on the box after cutting it to size. It was so full it did not even rattle. Then, much to Lu-Lu's dismay, he took the spare tabs and ceremonially flushed them down the toilet, after inviting us both to watch him do it.

Goodness knows what the other brothers thought when they saw us all entering the hallway toilet, but no one said anything. I had a shrewd idea what Lu-Lu was thinking— and a religious retreat wasn't the place for it—and I had to admit that as I was bankrolling this shindig, all I could think of was that something like two grands' worth of street value was disappearing round St Fulgentius's U-bend.

'We should all feel better for that,' Gearoid had said as

the sound of flushing water disappeared. Probably he did.

On the Monday I had driven off to Portsmouth and booked our ferry tickets, paying cash. Then I'd found a bookshop which sold Michelin maps of France and bought two copies of No. 59, covering the Côtes du Nord and the northern half of Ille-et-Vilaine as far over as Mont St Michel in Normandy.

Then I hit a couple of banks and changed £500 into francs in each of them, trying to keep a mental running total on how the war chest was going. Down was how it was going. Even with the stash of Werewolf's, which Gearoid had handed over, funds were not plentiful. After paying Duncan for the Cortina, the Community for the bees and Gearoid's carpentry, the ferry tickets, all the gas, food and booze used up so far, I was well into my personal savings. Still, if you've got it, spend it.

For the sake of something to do, I gave the St Fulgentius Transit van a once-over. I'm no mechanic when put up against the likes of Duncan the Drunken, but Fords have the easiest engines when it comes to accessibility and even I can perform a rudimentary tune-up.

On the Tuesday morning, Gearoid had put the box of pills into its frames and then into a nucleus box. Lu-Lu and I stayed well back while he slotted in five genuine frames from one of the hives and then screwed on the lid. The hive bees, who had been slugged with a cloud of smoke from a puffer gun Gearoid called his 'Vesuvius', stayed remarkably docile. Whether this was because of the smoke (Gearoid said the smell of smoke triggered ancient instincts about forest fires so the bees immediately begin to gorge themselves to store food) or because the queen had gone, I didn't know. Personally, I've found removing the woman from the situation usually works.

Gearoid then transferred real frames to two more nucleus boxes from other hives and so we ended up with three queens and about 28,000 bees in three undistinguished and indistinguishable boxes in the back of the van.

Despite Gearoid's assurance that the bees couldn't get out, Lu-Lu and I hung back and took his word for it that if you looked in the ventilation slits, all you could see were bees.

Once I'd told Lucinda that she would ride up front with Gearoid, she'd borrowed the Cortina and driven to the village shops to buy a can of insect spray. At least she had the sense to keep it out of sight of Gearoid.

The plan was for me to travel alone just in case Guennoc did have somebody planted on board the ferry. Also, I had no problem getting on the ferry. My passport was genuine and the ticket honestly paid for. (Also, my passport said I was a Civil Servant, which usually goes down well with Immigration. Never, never put 'Student' on one, not even if you are one. And if anyone asks what sort of Civil Servant, say 'outdoor clerical' and claim you work for the Forestry Commission or the Highlands and Islands Development Board, or, at a pinch, the Ministry of Agriculture. You won't get any more questions.)

Lucinda was to pose as an American journalist with some suitably 'green' magazine (if asked—Americans don't have to put their occupations on passports) doing a story on natural foods such as honey. She'd asked if honey was 'organic' and Gearoid had said yes, every bee he kept promised only to visit plants which hadn't been sprayed with anything.

Gearoid, of course, would go as a monk, though he'd refused to put on his full habit until he was in the queue for the ferry.

This meant he raised one or two eyebrows, even from the most hardened *routier*, as he entered the ship's bar with Lu-Lu on his arm. But let's face it, even dressed conservatively in jeans and a dark blue fisherman's smock, Lu-Lu could turn heads, so maybe it was her they were clocking.

The bar wasn't crowded, but I waited until Gearoid had ordered drinks before I stood up and carried my beer outside to stand on deck and watch the last lights of England disappear. I checked through one of the bar windows that Lu-Lu and Gearoid had taken the table I had been at. They had, without trouble, so they would have found the two spare keys to Cabin 121 I'd left on the seat.

I wandered around the deck until I was chilled to the bone. If Guennoc had put someone on board to watch me, I never saw him. But then, why should he worry about where I was on the boat? I wasn't planning on getting off.

I decided there was nothing to be gained from trying to spot a tail if there was one, so I hit the Duty Free shop for a carton of cigarettes and a bottle of twelve-year-old Macallan. Might as well be happy and poor.

Then I treated myself to a chicken salad in the boat's restaurant, on the assumption that if you are going to be seasick, it is better to have something to be sick on, before working my way down the stairs to the cabin deck.

Gearoid was lying on a bottom bunk, reading a paperback edition of Simon Schama's history of the French revolution, *Citizens*. Lucinda was in the adjoining bathroom, the sound of her singing 'We are Sailing' drowning out the noise of the shower.

'Bees settled down for the night?' I asked, sitting on the lower bunk opposite him and unpacking the Scotch from the Duty Free bag.

'No problem. It's cold down in the car deck and that'll slow 'em down. They'll be in an evil mood tomorrow when they start to come round, though,' he said without looking up from his book.

'That might be useful,' I said, getting the top off the Macallan.

Gearoid's right hand came up from behind the book. He

held one of the tooth glasses the boat provided. He'd left it to me to provide the filling.

'Any problems at all?' I asked as I poured.

'None. Sailed through. The only time I was worried was as we were waiting to drive on board and Lucinda noticed an American destroyer docked across the harbour.' He put a leather bookmark decorated with a Celtic cross into the paperback to mark his page.

'What? Did she think she knew someone on it?'

'Not yet.' He sipped whisky. 'So what's the plan tomorrow morning?'

'We get off the boat in one piece. I never asked, how good's your French?'

'Better than Francis's and I can also get by in Breton.'

'Can Werew . . . Francis understand Breton?'

'Ah, sure.'

'That might be a help, too.' I took a drink straight from the bottle. 'The plan is simple: do what they've said so far. That is, I said I would go straight from the boat to this café—*Le Biniou*.'

'The bagpipes.'

'What?'

'*Biniou* are Breton bagpipes.'

'Oh, thanks for that. Now I can sleep easy. Anyways, I show up there as planned. You take the van on and pull in to the first car park you find. I think there's one near the old gates, where the tourist coaches stop. Stay there until I come.'

'And what will you be telling them?'

'We have the dope but they don't get it until we see that Werewolf is alive and kicking.'

Thinking about Werewolf's wheelchair-bound condition, I suppose I could have chosen my words better.

'That's it, is it?' he said from behind his book again.

'That's what?'

'The plan. Is that it?'

''Fraid so.'

'Then we'd better start praying on overtime.'

The howling from the bathroom stopped and Lucinda came into the cabin wearing one towel around her head and another around her breasts which would have been re-spectable for someone under five foot six, but was touch and go for someone six foot four.

'Hiya, guys. Ready to hit the beach at dawn? Last one out of the landing-craft gets to play in the minefield.'

She flounced by me, pausing to pat my cheek, then she climbed the small ladder up to the top bunk above Gearoid, heedless of the view she was presenting him with. I'll swear his hands shook.

Lu-Lu turned around, sitting on the bunk, her long legs dangling over and began to towel her hair.

'Wassamatter with you guys?' she asked.

'We were talking about the power of prayer,' said Gearoid hoarsely, burying his nose in his book.

Through the open jaws of the ferry I could see France, or rather ten feet of slimy harbour wall, a couple of Porta-kabins and a line of articulated trailers missing their truck units.

I had been to France many times, working the same roadie route around the provincial universities which Werewolf had been doing when he came a cropper, and I had also done a spell as a bus driver and courier when times had been hard, making up the running commentary as I went along. You'd be amazed at how many different places Joan of Arc got barbecued.

A few years back I had spent a week or so in Brittany on a scouting mission for a South London garage. The pro-prietor had this idea, which I went along with, that the old style Citroën 2CV van could be turned into a cult vehicle among students and suchlike. The French post office, the PTT, had thousands of them, which periodically they dumped at depots along the northern coast. Apart from being left-hand drive, bright yellow, and having about 200,000 kilometres on their clocks, they were perfect. They were certainly cheap. I found at least three PTT officials who would have been delighted to get rid of them as they had no second-hand value in France. The deal fell through, though, due more to the pending imprisonment of the South London car dealer than anything else. Since then, of course, Citroën have stopped making the 2CV saloon—the one invented by combining a lawn-mower engine with two dustbins—and, natch, they have become cult cars and the deal would have been worth it to corner the market in spare parts alone. Still, no use crying over spilt Citroëns; file it as How To Become A Millionaire, plan 467, and put it down to experience.

The car at the front of my queue started its engine and I closed the Cortina's window and air vents before I did the same, not wanting to passive smoke the others' exhausts. In the tourist season, this was where you sat for about an hour while all around you kids started crying, engines stalled and marriages disintegrated, but nobody was prepared to do anything other than a Le Mans start to get off the boat.

With very few vehicles, or at least very few passenger cars, it all went much quicker and within five minutes a guy in Brittany Ferries overalls was waving us off. The Cortina bounced once on the iron ramp with a disconcerting metallic clunk and then I was on the concrete dock, following the brake lights of the car in front.

There were few people about at that time in the morning and no one giving instructions. I followed the guy in front, who followed the white arrows on the road. There was one sign saying DOUANE and pointing off to the right, but it seemed to be *Fermé*, with no lights on and no one hanging about to force the issue. Then there was the obligatory sign reminding English people to drive on the right. I suspect the French would like to forget that one if they thought they could get away with it.

Then there were two French policemen hunched in their capes in the lee of a truck, sheltering from the cold morning breeze. Both had lit cigarettes cupped in a hand behind their backs. With their free hands they simply waved all the cars through and suddenly I was at a roundabout and the city walls of St Malo were in front of me.

I cut up a PTT van of all things—a canary-yellow Renault 4, I noted—swerving around the roundabout and then turning right into the car park which ran in front of the west wall of the town, alongside the east dock of the harbour. I had a choice of spaces, so I parked as close to the harbour edge as was legal and killed the engine.

I didn't risk getting out of the car yet. There were still too few people about for my liking. Where were the nosey, interfering, busybody general public when you needed them?

From the glove compartment I took out a pair of small but deceptively powerful Zeiss opera glasses which I had acquired from a sad old man who hadn't used them for birdwatching in the conventional sense. I focused in on the ferry at anchor across the harbour. Big trucks were still emerging from its bowels but there was no sign of a white Transit with *Community of St Fulgentius of Ruspe* stencilled down its side.

I scanned the dock until I saw it, well clear of Customs posts and the dock itself, on the road and following the signs towards *Centre Ville* until I could see it no longer because of the city walls. To have got so far so quick must have meant a clear run off the boat, like mine, with no stops or checks at all. It was disgraceful, really. We could have had anything in the back of that van. If I had been a French taxpayer, I would have complained.

Maybe we didn't need the bees after all.

I treated myself to a celebratory cigarette but threw it away once I had convinced myself that my hands weren't shaking any more. Then I hauled my overnight bag over from the back seat and rummaged around in the waterproof wash-bag until I found the thing I'd brought from Hackney in case things went from shitty to worse.

I was quite pleased with the way I had stuck the label of a well-known brand of breath freshener over the small aerosol tube. But this wouldn't do your halitosis much good. It was a handbag-size cannister of mace for personal rape-attack protection, which I had taken from a nutter of an animal rights campaigner just before she'd done the business on a burly policeman. I had confiscated it for her own good and somehow forgotten to return it. I gave it a shake and popped it into my jacket pocket, keeping my hand in there and having a quick practice to make sure I could flip the top off without trouble.

Then I dug into the washbag again and took out the three disposable Bic razors. I had absconded from the Community for an hour after we had flushed the excess Ecstasy tabs down the toilet and made busy with a tube of superglue. The handles of the razors are hollow and I dropped twenty or so tabs into each and then sealed the ends, rather like a bee seals a honeycomb with wax, with a blob of clear glue. They were not heavy enough to arouse suspicion and unless you actually peered down the handle, you wouldn't see anything amiss.

Checking to see there were no early-morning, sniffer-dog-walking citizens about, I cracked the razors open and tipped the tabs out on to a Michelin map opened across my knee. Then I took a small bottle of (genuine) seasickness pills from my bag and emptied them into the ashtray, counting the XTC back into the bottle. Fifty-seven in all, at street value £15 a hit.

So maybe I hadn't been totally honest with Gearoid. Life's like that.

I shovelled the broken razors back into my bag, zipped it and flung it back on the back seat. Then I adjusted my Angels baseball cap in the mirror and climbed out of the car. I looked every which way as I locked the Cortina but there was nobody suspicious around except me.

The archway through the city walls, just wide enough for one small truck, was across the car park about fifty yards away. An ice-cream truck too big to enter had parked outside and a white-coated driver was ferrying cold, steaming boxes on a porter's trolley. He paused to light a cigarette and muttered '*Bonjour*' to me.

I nodded at him and flicked a mental switch and said good morning back, and motioned to the steam coming off the ice-cream cartons, adding the equivalent of 'nice cool job you've got there' in French.

He told me to tell him something he didn't know, and grinned.

So far, the natives seemed friendly.

Couldn't last.

CHAPTER 13

As Guennoc had said, I couldn't miss *Le Biniou* once I had walked through the archway into the city.

It was one of the few remaining cafés just inside the walls which had not been touristified and still catered for the locals. You could tell that just by looking at it from across the cobbled street. For a start, it was open so early—and not even the *boulangerie* up the road was open, which for France meant *early*. And it did not advertise pizzas or Marlboro cigarettes, which were rapidly replacing Pernod and Gauloises as the in things to put in your mouth in France.

I sauntered by the entrance and took a good look through the steamed-up glass in the door. Formica-topped tables, yellow Ricard ashtrays, a coffee machine which looked like part of the set of James Whale's *Frankenstein*, and two guys in work clothes propping up the bar holding small balloons of cognac to go with their coffee or hot chocolate. A little piece of the old France we all knew and loved, maybe. A hotbed of Breton nationalism? I doubted it.

There was little point in me wandering the streets. Nothing was open yet and I would only be drawing attention to myself. I walked back to the café door and got there just as the two cognac-drinkers came out. Neither so much as gave me a glance.

Inside, a middle-aged madame who must have got up at 4.0 a.m. to apply her make-up, served me with *café-au-lait* and croissant, and I could tell from the sound it made hitting the plate that it was yesterday's bread. I picked a table near the door and a seat backed up to the wall before I started to dunk it in the coffee to soften it.

I was just about in a position to suck it to death when they arrived.

Guennoc came in first and stood in front of me. The Cowboy stood in the middle of the empty bar and scanned it, trying to look tough, like he'd seen in the movies. When the proprietress appeared from the kitchen, Cowboy asked for two *petits cafés* in a thick Breton accent and she busied herself at the coffee machine.

With his back to her so she couldn't see, Guennoc unzipped his brown leather blouson and showed me the gun tucked into the waistband of his trousers. Then he un-

wrapped a long black wool scarf from around his neck, took
the gun out and laid it on the table opposite me. Before he
covered it casually with the scarf and sat down, I identified
it as a Walther P38 automatic.

No big deal. I'd seen plenty of war films and anyway it
was so sparkly clean you could read 'P38' stamped into the
frame of the thing.

'Your boat docked early,' he said smoothly.

I said nothing, just stared him down.

'Do you have my merchandise?'

Cowboy took two small cups of coffee from the madame
so she wouldn't have to come to the table and brought them
over. He unbuttoned his raincoat and it sagged with the
weight of a gun in each pocket. As he sat down his coat
made a clanging noise against the legs of the tubular steel
chairs. Guennoc frowned at him. Then turned back to me.

'You have not answered my question.'

I reached into my jacket pocket and slid the bottle of
seasick pills across the table to him.

'Your merchandise is in France,' I said, cool as I could.
'That's just a sample. Want to drop a couple to see if it's
kosher?'

He unscrewed the lid and poured a couple of tablets into
the palm of his hand. He examined them, showed them to
Cowboy and even sniffed them in an attempt to look as if
he knew what he was doing. I realized that I could have
probably passed him junior aspirin or white M & Ms and
he wouldn't have known the difference.

'My merchandise was—' for a moment he struggled to
find the word in English—'packaged. Wrapped.'

'We had to unwrap it for ease of transportation,' I said,
instantly regretting the 'we' but he was too keyed up to
notice.

'Where is it?' he hissed.

'Where's my friend?' I countered.

He narrowed his eyes.

'You know we have your friend.' The reasonable approach.

'You know I have your stuff.' Time to offer him a facesaver. 'But your Dutch partners also know I've got the stuff, so I am in a weak position. It is all I have to bargain with—for my sake as well as my friend's.'

He thought about this and took a slug of his coffee, then he translated for Cowboy and most of what he said was accurate, though I tried not to let on I could follow.

'Where is your car?' he came back.

'Not far,' I said, reaching into my pocket again for the keys.

I flipped them into the ashtray between us. I was bluffing in that if they didn't know what I was driving, then it might give me an edge, but it was worth playing it out. They wouldn't find what they wanted.

'Go help yourself,' I offered, 'you won't find anything.'

For a moment I thought he was going to pick them up. Instead, he drummed his fingers on the tabletop next to the gun covered with his scarf.

'Were you followed?' he asked, which wasn't what I was expecting at all.

'I thought you said you had a man on the boat,' I countered.

This was crazy, we were just trying to out-tough each other. Still, boys will be boys.

'That was to keep you alert,' he said with a half smile, and then I understood the question.

'Oh, you mean by our Dutch friends? I don't know, but nothing would surprise me. Young Mr Gronweghe seems very good at what he does—and he certainly doesn't have a high opinion of you.'

That hit home.

'Just what was the deal originally?'

'That is none of your business.' Tough talk again, but real sweat on his forehead and desperate not to let Cowboy see it. 'Your problem is keeping your friend alive.'

'Did you say you'd buy the stuff and then spend the money on something else?' Last chance; he couldn't be pushed much further.

In fact, he showed remarkable restraint. I could see him make up his mind on something, the give-away being the momentary flicker of his eyes. Suddenly he wouldn't meet my stare.

'Do you have a map?'

'I can get one,' I said, giving him nothing.

'Drive west, into Côtes d'Armor. After Ploubalay, take the coast road to Matignon, the D786. Understand?'

I nodded. Even if I had had a pen and paper I wouldn't have written it down, I was so cool.

'Stay on that road until you go through the village of Port à la Duc across the sea-wall. There is a café on your right and a sign saying that it sells mussels and ... huîtres ...'

'Oysters,' I offered, too quickly.

'And by that café is a small road running alongside the bay. Drive exactly two kilometres down that road and stop. Be there at exactly eleven o'clock.'

'And you'll have my friend Francis there, ready to exchange?'

'Yes,' he said not looking at me. 'Of course.'

We were going to need the bees after all.

I let them get well clear of the *Biniou* before I paid the madame behind the bar and left her to the other early-morning customers.

Instead of going back to the Cortina, I cut through the town and dog-legged a couple of times just in case they were tailing me. I couldn't spot anyone and I thought it unlikely. They'd be heading out to where they'd invited me to come and be ambushed.

I found a set of steps leading up to the ramparts and walked around the town on top of the wall, enjoying the view across the harbour, especially the elegant sight of the Jersey hydrofoil taking off with its first load of commuters. Now that was a class way to go to work, if you had to work, that is.

Above the main gateway I scanned the car park below me until I spotted the St Fulgentius Transit. Lucinda was leaning against the passenger door, smoking nervously and trying to look inconspicuous. Dressed in a sack and in another country, she might have had a chance.

Then I spotted Gearoid walking towards her, doing what a few million other Frenchmen were doing, whether dressed as monks or not. He had a long stick loaf under his arm and a newspaper. The loaf had a jagged white edge where he had already nibbled off one of the crusty ends. I have a theory that only about one per cent of French bread ever gets home intact.

I strained my eyesight and cursed that I'd left my binoculars in the Cortina, but I couldn't spot any suspicious characters around the car park. Apart from those two.

Gearoid snapped off a piece of bread for me as I approached.

Lucinda put her hands on her hips and said: 'Well? Did it go down—or what?'

'I should've known,' I said, spraying her with breadcrumbs, then reaching out automatically to brush them off her sweater. 'They want a meet out in the country at eleven this morning. We exchange there. The stuff for Werewolf.'

Gearoid tucked into another chunk of bread.

'And you believe them?'

I gave him the old up-from-under look.

'Sure, and when we've done the business I'll let him sell
me a second-hand car.'

Gearoid grinned. Lu-Lu looked like she was going to ask
why I needed another second-hand car.

'First, we need some better maps.'

'Where are we going?'

'Out to a place called Port-à-la-Duc.'

'I know it,' said Gearoid, 'it's on the way to Cap Fréhel
and Fort de la Latte. That's where they filmed *The Vikings*,
you know.'

'You mean *The Long Ships*,' said Lu-Lu. 'With Richard
Widmark.'

'No,' said Gearoid sternly. '*The Vikings*.'

'Anyway,' I tried, 'once we have a big-scale—'

'Was that the one with Kirk Douglas and Tony Curtis?'

'—map, we can—'

'That's the one. Curtis loses a hand and Kirk gets his eye
scratched out by an eagle—'

'—suss out the lie of the land because I think they must
be holding Werewolf close—'

'And they have to storm the castle in the last reel.'

'That's it. The Vikings run up and throw their axes at
the gate . . . Where are you going, Angel?'

'To get something for my headache.'

I found a Maison de la Presse just putting its lights on and
I persuaded a grumpy old-timer to find me two copies of
the *Série Bleue* map for the area in question. It turned out
to be No. 1015 Sud, covering the coast from St Cast over
to Pleneuf and some of the Côtes d'Armar's leading holiday
resorts. The *Série Bleue* maps are much bigger scale than
Michelin, a sort of less cluttered Ordnance Survey map,
and I found Port à la Duc immediately.

I reckoned it could take an hour to find the right spot, so
we had little time to plan anything elaborate. The track

Guennoc had said led up the side of the bay, the huge, tidal
mud Baie de la Fresnaye, was marked and appeared to me
to be just about the only road in France without a single
sign of human habitation. Not a good omen.

But then again, if there were no people about, it would
give the bees more room for manœuvre.

I walked through the town again, the shops opening by
now, the cobbled streets filled with kids and old women all
carrying bread. The *Biniou* was doing good business and
none of the customers looked like they were plotting to
secede from France.

I picked up the Cortina and drove around the walls until
I rendezvoused with the Transit. I gave Lu-Lu one of the
Série Bleue maps to study while Gearoid drove. I told him
to follow me out to the Matignon road.

'We go over the river Rance on the big tidal barrage.'

'I know. It's a generating station.'

'That's it. Once over there, I'm going to pull over and
we switch cars. You remembered to bring the bee suits?'

'Just two,' said Gearoid, tugging at his beard.

'That's all we'll need,' I said.

'Good. You'll be keeping her out of it, then?'

'Hell no. She's the cavalry—if we need rescuing, that is.'

'Then God help us,' he said, shaking his head. Then: 'I
know, I know, that's my department. Don't worry, I've put
in a word.'

After Ploubalay on the D786, I turned left on to a very
minor road signed to a hamlet called St Galléry and pulled
off into the edge of a small wood.

Gearoid parked the Transit up behind me and retrieved
the beekeeper suits from the back. Lu-Lu stayed away from
the rear end of the van and came to watch me changing the
number plates on the Cortina for the orange ones I'd
bought from Duncan the Drunken.

'OK, Chief, so what *is* the plan? The Holy Man back there tends to get kinda evasive when I ask him.'

'That's because I don't believe in briefing my shock troops until the last minute,' I grunted, dropping a screw from the number plate into the mud.

'Shock troops?'

Too right. She scared hell out of me.

'You, dear Lu-Lu, are the cavalry. You wait in reserve where we'll show you. Then you give us until, say, ten past eleven and then you come down the track after us. Go exactly—'

Dammit, Guennoc had said two kilometres and the Cortina's milometer worked in miles and anyway, Americans didn't have a clue about kilometres.

'—one and one-tenth miles and then stop. If you can see us by then, you've come too far. I can't help any more, I don't know the layout. Just get as close as you can without making too much noise. If we give a blast on the horn or you hear shooting, come in fast and I mean Hammer Time.'

'OK, boss, gotcha, but like I said, we should never have ditched that gun.'

I gave her the shrugged shoulders routine and walked round the front of the Cortina to do the other plate.

'Are those things gonna protect me?' she said sarcastically.

'They might. They're Dutch and the last thing our friend Guennoc wants to see is his Dutch friend Gronweghe. Think about it, it might work.'

She put her hands on her hips.

'Angel, if I thought you'd planned that, I'd take my hat off to you. How did you know to get Dutch plates?'

I didn't like to say they were the only spare ones Duncan had in stock.

'Foresight, intelligence, tactical—'

'Dumb fucking luck, you mean,' she snapped.

'Well, you know what my Rule of Life Number One is.'

'Always get somebody else to do your dirty driving for you?'

'Close enough.'

We found Port à la Duc without hitch, me driving the Transit with Gearoid up front and both of us in beekeeping suits except for the helmets, Lu-Lu following in the Cortina. I had told her that they drove on the right in France and she'd said fine and that in the first town we came to she'd stop and ask a woman just to be sure.

We convoyed across the long, low bridge which crosses the River Frémur as it trickles into the tidal mudflat of the bay, and the first thing to greet us on the west side was a sign offering shellfish for sale. There was a café, not yet open, surprisingly, a car park and an unmade road leading off down the line of the bay.

I signalled and pulled over to the right into the car park and Lu-Lu brought the Cortina alongside. She killed the engine and got out and came over to my window.

'Don't get out, you guys,' she said, indicating our white bee suits. 'They'll think I've brought the Ku Klux Klan with me.'

'You know what to do?' I asked, more in hope than anything.

'Yeah, yeah, stay out of the way unless you *men* get into trouble and then come like a bat out of hell. I sure wish I had my four-by-four here—and a gun.'

'Don't tell me,' said Gearoid, asking for trouble, 'I bet you can ride better, drive faster and shoot more sharper than any man.'

'You're damn right,' she said seriously, 'just as long as I remember to put my contact lenses in.'

'Enough, enough. Let's save it for the bad guys,' I said. I had to say something, I was between them.

'That's neat,' said Lu-Lu. 'Who said that? Burt Lancaster in—?'

'No,' Gearoid chipped in, 'it was—'

'It was me; just now. I felt my lips move. Now listen, there are some binoculars in my hold-all in the back of the Cortina, you might need them.'

'I might need that gun you threw away.'

'Shut up about the gun, will you? We have enough armament right here.'

'Oh yeah, where?'

I jerked a gloved thumb backwards towards the rear of the van.

'Any trouble and we'll sting them to death.'

'Have you told the bees that?'

'No.' I jerked my thumb at Gearoid. 'He has.'

'I have not,' he said, like Oliver Hardy would say it.

'Shit. Then we're in trouble.'

Lucinda threw back her head and laughed, then leaned forward and kissed me on the cheek.

'Go get 'em, kid,' she said loudly. Too loudly, even for her.

It was good to know someone else was as scared as I was.

As we bounced down the track—me trying to keep an eye on the milometer to work out two kilometres—Gearoid said, one hand on the dashboard:

'Now she's out of the way, what is the plan?'

'I thought we'd open all the nucleus boxes, stir up the bees a bit and tell Guennoc to help himself.'

'You like to keep it simple, don't you?' It wasn't really a question.

'We negotiate. We demand to see Werewolf.

'You're sure they won't bring him?'

'Positive.'

'And you're sure this'll work?'

'I never said that,' I admitted. 'Oh yeah—and I have a technical beekeeping question.'

'What's that?'

'What do you do in one of these suits if your bladder suddenly throws a wobbler?'

'Tie a knot in it.'

I took my eyes off the track just long enough to give him the killer look.

'You can be a real comfort some times.'

As near as I could guess to two kilometres down the track, we stopped. There was nothing ahead of us except more track going up a slight incline. To our left, grass, heather and scrub. To our right, about ten feet of the same and then a drop down into the bay. The tide was still in, but on the turn. I knew that when it went out on this coast it was like somebody pulling a plug and all you were left with was the rancid stink of sea mud. In an hour or less we'd probably see white-shirted waiters from the local restaurants wading out there to hack the lunch menu off the rocks.

Gearoid helped me into my beekeeper's hat and veil and then snapped on his own space-age version. I was sweating already inside the suit and gloves, thick with old honey stains, were stiff and clumsy. I felt as if I were an old-fashioned deep-sea diver, pre-Cousteau, trapped in a rubber suit and walking against the pressure of water. Then I thought again about the clubs and private establishments where people paid good money to get dressed up like this, and contented myself with the thought that there's always someone weirder and sicker than you are.

I let Gearoid open the back of the van and only stood back a couple of yards as he lifted two of the nucleus boxes out and on to the ground, then pulled the third one near to the lip of the van. He fumbled around in the back of the Transit until he found a screwdriver and began, clumsily, to unscrew the lids, although he made no move to take them off. That didn't matter. I could hear bees and feel them in the air even though there weren't any.

'You take the top off that one while I do this, OK?' said Gearoid, though I had to strain to catch the words through my headgear.

'Which one's got the stuff in?' I seemed to shout.

'Mine. Don't worry. If they want a closer look, they'll be welcome.'

There was a hard Irish lilt to his voice. The sort of accent you get on warning messages.

'What if nothing happens?'

'Kick the box over, but don't tell anyone I told you that. And we've got company.'

It might have been his suit and the flash spaceman's helmet which let him hear them first, or just the fact that he was more used to wearing the stuff than I was, but he was right.

They came both ways. A Renault 4 down the track the way we'd come from Port à la Duc, and an old Peugeot station wagon from the track up ahead. Both pulled up about twenty feet from us within seconds of each other. I was impressed.

'It's showtime,' I said to Gearoid, and I think he grunted something, but I couldn't be sure.

Through my netted visor and the curtain of sweat I was producing (with no way to wipe it off), I saw the doors of the Peugeot open first. It was getting more dreamlike every minute.

Guennoc got out first, from the driving seat. He had a gun, a pistol, already out. Then from the back seat two even younger hoods trying to look cool in leather jackets and Levis and scarves, just like Guennoc, clambered out. And they had pistols too. Walther P38s, just like the one Guennoc had flashed in *Le Biniou*, and they were holding them in a double-handed grip like they'd seen on *Cagney and Lacey*.

I took it all in my stride. Three guns pointing at me and none of them seemed real. Correction, five. The Renault's doors opened and Cowboy climbed out of the driver's seat, with the big one I'd christened Sumo squeezing out of the passenger door. They had Walthers. They pointed them at me as well.

'Change of plan,' hissed Gearoid. 'Tell them we're from the power station down the road and there's been a radiation leak.'

'Think that'll scare them more?' I hissed back.

'More than *what*? I don't notice them running for cover.'

'Then we'd better do something about that.'

We; meaning me.

'Where is our friend Francis?' I shouted.

Guennoc took a step nearer and waved his gun casually.

'What do you think you are doing?'

I had to give it to him, it was a good question.

'Waiting for you to produce our friend.'

'What about my merchandise?'

He had to keep coming forward. He couldn't know what we were up to and he couldn't bring himself to ask what we were doing in the Ku Klux Klan outfits. Not with his troops there, looking for a lead. And then I recognized the two with him in the Peugeot; I had last seen them on the deck of the fishing-boat in the harbour in Guernsey. So these were the troops which were going to liberate Brittany.

'Your shit is here, man, right under my feet.' I put a boot on the box nearest to me. 'Where's Francis?'

'He will be released as soon as I have my property.'

Guennoc was getting louder too. Nervous. That was a good sign, or at least I told myself it was.

'No deal. We talking to him or else.'

'Or else what?'

He was waving his gun now, and Cowboy and Sumo were getting closer too, though it was difficult to judge distances with the hat and veil on.

Even my Wellington boot seemed a long way down, but it wasn't that, it was the thought of what was under it, in the box.

'Or else you get it yourself!' I yelled.

'Do it,' Gearoid said and flung off the lid of the box he was hovering over.

I fumbled mine and took an involuntary step backwards.

Nothing much happened, and suddenly Guennoc and one of the fishing-boat kids and Sumo all seemed to be very close, crowding me. I lashed out and gave the box a hefty kick; well, hefty enough to hurt my toes through the rubber boot.

The box didn't go over, it just rocked, but a squadron of bees took off like hunter-killer helicopters: straight up, in formation, and the air was filled with a buzz which scared me and I was expecting it.

Gearoid went one better and picked out one of the frames and smacked it against the rim of the box. A couple of thousand bees, probably not good tourists to begin with, got really pissed off about that.

The air was thick with them and as they looped-the-loop in front of my visor, I saw one of the fishing-boat kids drop his pistol and clutch at his neck. Then Sumo screamed, had his gun up in front of his face, flapping at them with it. The bees were not impressed.

Guennoc reacted faster, doing an immediate runner for the Peugeot, slamming the door and winding the windows up. The two from the boat just ran up the track, and Sumo did the same in the opposite direction. I couldn't make out where Cowboy was, but maybe he wasn't as stupid as he looked and had locked himself in the Renault.

'Keep still,' Gearoid was shouting at me. 'Don't flap. Just walk through them. They'll go back to the queens. Just walk slow.'

I followed him like an automaton. The back of his suit, around the neck and down one arm, was covered in bees. I could feel them, or thought I could feel them, bopping against my arms and neck as well.

Gearoid walked over to the Peugeot and gently tapped a gloved finger on the window. Guennoc was inside, frantically brushing imaginary bees off his leather blouson. When he reacted to the tap on the window, he scrabbled frantically for the door lock until it clicked down, then he tried the ignition.

I stood in front of the car and held my arms out. There were bees all over them, but they were beginning to drop off and zip back to the nucleus boxes. I must still have been a pretty impressive sight.

'We just want our friend,' I shouted, though he almost certainly couldn't hear me. His face was white and his expression rigid.

Gearoid tapped on the window again and then shouted in French: 'Back off fifty metres and then we can talk.'

Guennoc nodded gratefully and started the car.

CHAPTER 14

He did what we told him. He had to. He'd been thrown badly by the bees and had lost all the advantages his henchmen and their guns had given him. He needed a way out.

'Just back up and wait. We'll get rid of the bees,' Gearoid shouted slowly at him, still in French.

Guennoc nodded and put the Peugeot into reverse. Behind me, I heard the Renault start up and I turned my head slowly, still seeing bees whip across the face veil. Sumo, the fat one, was clambering into the back seat. Cowboy was driving and looking up the incline towards us. Guennoc flashed the lights of the Peugeot and Cowboy answered back with his full beams, then began to reverse and turn around to go back towards Port à la Duc. I hoped Lu-Lu had the sense to get out of sight.

Gearoid made soothing waving motions towards Guennoc, miming him to stay put after he had pulled back twenty yards, then he headed back to the Transit and fumbled for several minutes until he had his Vesuvius smoke gun lit. I stayed back, not wanting to front the bees in case they remembered who kicked them. They seemed to have forgiven me in that they continued to drop from my suit and hat and hover back to the nucleus boxes. Gearoid encouraged them by puffing smoke over me and then getting me to do the same for him.

'They'll find their own way home,' he said, helping me take off the hat and veil when we were sure we were clear. 'Let's go talk to The Man. Hold it!'

He shot out a gloved hand and caught a bee in midflight, one that had clung to the shoulder of my suit and had decided on a kamikaze attack on my cheek. Gearoid's forefinger and thumb squashed an inch or so from my eyes.

'Jesus!' I breathed. 'Are there any more?'

'Don't think so, but let's walk.'

'You keep your helmet on, OK? Guennoc hasn't seen you yet.'

'Fair enough.'

It was a relief to be able to move my head and see the world not through a fine mesh grille. I walked quickly towards the Peugeot, trying not to show the paranoia I felt about the bees I just knew were still on my back. I could smell myself, and it was not pleasant, a mixture of smoke, sweat and stale, sickly honey.

The two younger hoods from the fishing-boat were beyond the Peugeot up the track, sheepishly making their way
back. One of them was clutching both hands to his chest,
the other had one hand up to his neck and was scuffing the
scrub and grass to the side of the track looking for something. I guessed he had dropped his gun as he did his runner. Amateurs. Still, Guennoc seemed to have enough
pistols; he must be buying them wholesale.

He still had his and he lowered the car window and
pointed it at us. His eyes flipped around the inside of the
car, though, still convinced the bees had got in there with
him.

'Stay there!' he yelled. 'I should kill you for that.'

'And who'll get your stuff for you?' I countered. 'My
comrade can remove the bees and have your merchandise
back here in twenty-four hours.' I heard Gearoid snort
at 'Comrade'. 'But we have to see our friend Francis
first.'

He made up his mind quickly.

'Just you,' he said, pointing the gun at me. 'And we go
now. You—' the gun at Gearoid now—'stay here. Hervé!'

One of the fishing-boat crew, the one who had lost his
gun, came closer and Guennoc switched to rapid Breton. I
picked up the gist of it in that he was telling them to stay
put and make sure Gearoid didn't follow us. Then he
looked back at me.

'Get in. You go back to the van and stay there. My men
will be watching.'

'Good luck,' said Gearoid to me. 'Say hello to Francis for
me.'

Guennoc made me kneel down on the floor in front of the
passenger seat and put my arms around it, then he used
brown plastic tape to tie my gloved hands together. With
my face squashed into the back of the seat, I couldn't see

much anyway but just to make sure, Guennoc put another strip of tape across my eyes.

Happy enough that I couldn't cause him trouble while he drove, he called to Hervé again and gave him his gun, telling him, in no uncertain terms, not to lose that one. Then he slammed the passenger door shut and I yelped as it trapped my left arm against the back of the seat, but Guennoc didn't seem to care.

The car turned through one hundred and eighty degrees and bounced off up the track. I had tried to sneak a glance at my Seastar just before Guennoc slapped the tape over my eyes, but with my beekeeper gloves on and my hands round the other side of the seat, it was impossible. So instead I counted in my head and got as far as five hundred and something before the car bounced heavier than usual and then the ride became smoother and we swung to the right. Guennoc changed up the gears and accelerated and in no more than another three or four minutes I felt him brake and then heard the plink plink of his indicator going. We turned right again, my weight falling on my trapped and rapidly cramping left arm, then we hit what could only have been cobbled stones and the car squeaked to a stop.

'Stay where you are,' Guennoc ordered, and I heard him get out.

I tried to move about to uncramp my knees, but Guennoc wasn't gone long. He opened my door and then the back door and I felt him grab my bound wrists and jerk them up over the top of the seat. I yelped again and sat back on my heels, the Peugeot dashboard crunching into my back. I howled again as he ripped the tape from my eyes.

'Get out.'

He had another gun, a Walther same as the others. He must be getting a good discount rate. He waved it in my face again.

'That's getting very boring,' I said. 'If you were going to use it you would have done so by now.'

'Shut up. Over there.'

He waved the gun some more. We were in a farmyard except it was no longer a farm. The farmhouse and the out-buildings had been subdivided and tarted up and turned into a small complex of six or seven *gîtes*, the small, basic cottages which the French use as holiday homes during the good summer weather and the British hire out the rest of the year. But as we were still well short of the tourist season, the place was deserted except for me and Guennoc.

Then I saw the old man standing in the doorway of one of the converted stables. Guennoc shouted at him in French and I pretended not to understand.

'Change of plan, Monsieur Cadic. Your sons will be back soon. First, we have to show this one the mad Irishman.'

M. Cadic grunted something and jerked a thumb into the interior of the *gîte*. Guennoc prodded me in the back with the pistol and I started walking, looking round me as furtively as I could.

Between two of the *gîtes*, I could see the water of the bay stretching out to the sea. And that reminded me of where I'd seen the old man before, on board the *Cendrillon*. That made six of them altogether, as Werewolf had tried to indicate to me.

The old fisherman shrugged himself deeper into his dark blue, dirty oiled pullover and avoided my gaze as I drew level and he moved aside to let me into the *gîte*.

I felt Guennoc's gun in my back again and then I stepped over the threshold and into the gloomy interior. The door slammed behind me and I heard the lock turn.

'You took your time, you old bastard.'

'Hiya, Werewolf, got anything to drink?'

'There's sweet cider, dry cider or Calvados. If it can be made from apples, they drink it round here. Don't seem to have heard of wine.'

My eyes accustomed themselves to the low level of light allowed in by the shutters on the windows. The downstairs of the *gîte* was one big stone-floored room with a long wooden table, a sofa and a couple of benches.

Werewolf propelled the wheelchair, his plastered leg out in front of him, and did a handbrake turn at the kitchen end of the *gîte*. There was a fairly modern kitchen unit built into the wall there, with cupboards, a hob and a small fridge. Someone had spent some money on the place recently.

Grabbing a bottle from the cupboard and two glasses, Werewolf zipped back to the big rectangular table.

'You're getting pretty stylish on those wheels,' I said as he poured.

'Needs must, my son, needs must. Want me to undo your hands? They've removed all the knives from the kitchen but I could maybe spoon you free.'

'They'd notice,' I said, 'better not.' In fact, my wrists being bound together like that actually helped conceal the fact that my hands were shaking.

I took a slug of the fiery apple brandy and nearly gagged. 'What's with the spacesuit?' Werewolf asked.

'It's a long story.' From outside I heard the distinctive sound of a Renault coming into the courtyard. That would be Cowboy and the fat one, Sumo, returning. 'And we won't have long, so you talk. You must have heard something.'

'We're somewhere on the Côtes d'Armor, I'd say the eastern side of the Fréhel peninsula. They have a boat, a fishing-boat, which can dock at high tide in a little cove of rocks about half a mile down the cliffs. There's a path leads right up to the back of these *gîtes* and it's the limit of the tide. At very low tides they can't even get that close. It's owned by the old guy—'

'I've met his two sons,' I interrupted.

'They're his grandsons actually, but he calls them his sons, Hervé and Loic. There are two other hoods, the ones you met in Guernsey. I've not seen anyone else.'

'Do they know you can understand them?'

'No. They slip into Breton if they think it's important but I soon picked up one thing: the old man, Cadic, and the two lads from the fishing-boat, they don't know what's going down. Guennoc keeps them in the dark. They think Guennoc is selling the guns for cash, they don't know about the naughty substances. I doubt if the old man would approve . . .'

'Guns? What guns?'

'The guns they're trying to sell to somebody called The Dutchman, except they're not selling them, they're trading them for—for whatever you found.'

'Ecstasy tabs.'

'How many?'

'Fifteen thousand.'

'Jesus! How did you . . . ? That suit . . . that smell. Bees. You smuggled them in a beehive?' He reached for the Calvados bottle again, shaking his head. 'I wish I'd thought of that. Where . . . ?'

'From Brother Gearoid.'

'Oh. Is he here?'

'He's on the team,' I said, worrying now because there wasn't time to worry. 'So's Lucinda Luger, but don't ask why. Just go back to the guns. What guns?'

'Don't get hysterical. For a bunch of morons with so much hardware, they haven't actually shot anybody yet. As far as I can put it together, Guennoc's family owned this place and he inherited it and used the family cash to turn it into holiday homes. I think Cowboy and the fat yob—'

I smiled, noting that Werewolf had adopted the same nick-name for the thin one with the flashy boots—'are some sort of local builders. Anyway, they were working here on the conversion last summer and they turned up a false floor in one of the barns, a sort of cellar where there shouldn't have been one. Guess what? They found cases of pistols, Wal-thers, left behind by the Nazis in 1944, all wrapped up carefully and packed in grease. Perfect working order. A couple of cases of ammunition too, but some of that is a bit dodgy. I overheard the Cowboy complaining about misfires when he'd been doing some target practice out on the cliffs.'

I was impressed with how much Werewolf had gleaned without either losing his temper and arguing with them or getting drunk and letting it slip that he understood. I was also impressed that he knew the French for 'misfire' but I always think about totally irrelevant things when I'm scared.

'So our friend Yannick sees a chance to make more dosh than the holiday homes business by pushing guns. Then he thinks of even more easy money by swapping the guns for drugs. You can buy a gun easy enough in France, but the druggy market could be fashionable and ripe for expansion. At the moment, it's a supplier's market.'

From outside I heard footsteps on the cobbles.

'I'm out of here in one minute,' I said quickly, 'so listen. I don't know what's going to happen. We're trying to deal but I don't trust Guennoc as far as I can throw him. But one way or another, we should get you out tomorrow. Twenty-four hours, tops. Be ready to move.'

Werewolf reached out, leaning forward in the wheelchair and grasping my taped wrists in his hands.

'Watch yourself, good buddy,' he hissed, 'and keep an eye on Gearoid. Don't let him do anything stupid, will yer?

You've got to make allowances for him. Remember, he's the black sheep of the family.'

Christ, what a family.

Guennoc stood in the doorway with a roll of brown insulating tape. Cowboy stood to his right with two pistols levelled at hip height. I stepped forward and stood in front of him.

'I'm satisfied,' I said formally. 'Can I suggest we repeat the exchange at the same place, same time, tomorrow?'

'Very well,' said Guennoc, tearing off a strip of tape.

'And just to make sure . . .'

'Shut your mouth,' he said, slapping the tape over my eyes.

My ribs suffered as Cowboy prodded me across the courtyard with the muzzles of both guns. They helped me into the back seat of the Peugeot this time, making me lie across the seat with one of Cowboy's guns pressed into my temple. I hoped he had the safety-catch on—or at least had chosen some duff ammunition—as the car bounced off the road and on to the track.

When it stopped, I was hauled unceremoniously from the rear and dropped on the ground. I felt another gun muzzle at my temple and though I knew it was only Guennoc trying to re-establish his authority in front of his gang, the disorientation of being dumped on the ground and being bound and blind finally did the trick and I lost control of my bladder.

'Tomorrow, here, same time. And no tricks this time. Do you understand?'

'Yes, yes,' I said quickly. Then the pressure of the gun was gone and there was a chatter of Breton which I didn't catch and then the car doors slammed and the Peugeot's engine started up. I could smell petrol fumes and exhaust smoke and heard the distinctive pitch change as Guennoc went from reverse into first gear and turned around.

I hooked my thumbs under the tape over my eyes and ripped it off. Gearoid was running up the track towards me, still in the beesuit and helmet.

'Are you OK, Roy?' he shouted.

I raised my taped arms and made to stand up.

'Apart from a loss of circulation and a rather embarrassing mess in your suit, just dandy. Francis is fine, too. We've got to talk, though, I've a lot to tell you. Where's Lu-Lu?'

'No sign of her,' he said as he unwound the tape from my arms, clumsily because of the gauntlets he was wearing.

'Shit. Finding her is priority number one. Then we have to plan a pre-emptive strike. These guys may be amateurs but they won't fall for a stunt like this twice.'

'Where are they holding him? It can't be far, you weren't gone that long.'

'You're right. We may have to cruise the area but if I see the place I'll spot it. We need the car, though. If they see the van again, they'll do a runner.'

'And Francis can't run, you say?'

'That's one of our problems.'

'Oh, just the one, eh? What's the other?'

'Working out how to tell Lu-Lu she was right all along. We should have brought a gun with us.'

Gearoid made me put the hat and veil on again as we neared the St Fulgentius van. He estimated that eighty per cent of the bees we had shaken out had found their way back into the nucleus boxes. There were still enough to unnerve me just floating about in the air.

'We can't wait, so this lot will have to claim French citizenship,' said Gearoid, screwing the lids back on the boxes. 'But keep the suit on until we're clear of the area. I'll drive.'

About a kilometre away he stopped and we got out and helped each other out of the suits. My shoes and holdall were in the Cortina with Lu-Lu, so I had to pull the Wel-

lington boots on again and try not to think of the damp
patch at my crutch.

As we approached the car park near the café at Port à la
Duc, I counted four cars, but not the Cortina. All were
locals, with the 22 Côtes d'Armor registration number.

Gearoid read my mind.

'It's lunch-time.'

He was right, it was only just on noon. We had been in
France for less than seven hours but it felt like a week.

'Which way?' he asked as we approached the road.

'How do I know where the crazy bitch took off to? She's
probably looking for a bar that sells Budweiser. No, wait,
I take it all back.'

As I spoke the Cortina screamed into the car park,
Lucinda doing her best to negotiate a left-hand turn from
the right side of the road in a right-hand drive car. She
parked next to us, jumped out and came running to my
door, her hair flying and her face flushed.

'Cavalry scout corporal Luger reporting, sah!' She
flapped a salute, then she pounded a riff on the door panel
of the van with the palms of her hands.

She backed off as I climbed out.

'Where the hell have you been?'

'Following you, boss, or rather following the fat guy who
got stung to hell—I would pay to see that again—and his
polecat friend. I saw them come in this way, so I figured
they'd leave this way. I got the car—and boy, is that a
piece of shit for wheels, or what?—as close as I could, but
off the track, behind a big rock, and did the rest on foot.
When I saw you kick the bees loose, I hightailed it back,
thinking they'd be outa there double quick. Sure enough,
boss, they were doing hammer time as they went by and
didn't even notice little ole me following them.'

'You found the *gîte*?'

'The what?' she beamed.

'The farm place . . . the house with the cottages . . .'

'You mean the place where they bundled you back into the car and they all waved guns about?'

'Yes!'

'No idea where that is, boss,' she said deadpan. Then she let herself grin. 'But I could find it with my eyes closed.'

'She's a diamond, Roy, a true diamond,' said Gearoid, giving her a bear hug.

'Control yourself,' I snapped. 'You're supposed to be a holy man.'

Gearoid stepped back.

'Which reminds me,' he said. 'Frostin.'

'Frosting?' asked Lu-Lu, slipping her arm round him.

'The real holy man, the one who'll take the bees off us. I must give him a ring.'

'Does that bar have a phone?' Lu-Lu nodded towards the roadside café.

'Probably,' said Gearoid. 'And I am hungry enough to find out.'

'OK,' I said, trying to restore some order, 'as the rest of France closes up for two hours at lunch-time, we'll refuel here and discuss our next move.'

'I could eat a horse,' said Lu-Lu.

'I'll check the menu,' said Gearoid.

As it turned out, I did the ordering while Gearoid talked one of the waiters into letting him use the house phone in the kitchen. I asked for *soupe des poissons, crêpes aux œufs et au jambon* and a bottle of *cidre bouché* to cover all of us. Lucinda asked why we were drinking apple juice, though she changed her mind after trying the cider. I remembered that for Americans you have to specify *alcoholic* cider just like they sometimes specify *hot* tea.

'Frostin will meet us in St Malo this afternoon,' Gearoid reported back, diving a hand into the basket of bread chunks on the table.

'We'll find somewhere to unload the cargo and he'll take the bees off our hands. He's offered us board and lodgings if we want them, at his monastery near St Lo. We could catch a ferry back from Cherbourg or Caen that way.'

'That's good thinking,' I admitted. 'They might be watching the St Malo terminal if we manage to stitch them up. But not tonight. For tonight we need something closer. There's a place back there on the coast called St Cast. Tourist town. Bound to have hotel rooms out of season.'

A young waiter brought us our soup, nervously conscious of Lu-Lu's fixed gaze on the rear of his tight black trousers. She said nothing, just sighed. Then we showed her how to coat the thin slices of bread with garlic paste and sprinkle them with the grated cheese before floating them on the fish soup.

' 's good,' she slurped. 'What's this about stitching them up?'

'I thought we might pay the Breton Liberation Front, or whatever the hell they like to call themselves, a visit in advance of the meet we set for tomorrow.'

'Unarmed?' she said, too loud. 'Are you thinking straight? Are you thinking at all?'

Gearoid patted her hand and stole the last of the grated cheese from in front of her.

'I had a word with Frostin for you.'

'Now look, I appreciate you putting me in your prayers, which is not something I say to just any man, but—'

'There is no problem buying a handgun in France, but you can only use one inside your house to protect your property,' said Gearoid quietly. 'However, anyone can walk in off the street and buy a shotgun over the counter. To use it, you need a hunting permit and they are like gold dust, but to actually buy a twelve-bore, no documentation needed at all. And Frostin knows a good gunshop in St Malo.'

'I'm not sure that's a good idea,' I said weakly, but I meant it.

'Got any better ones?' asked Lu-Lu drily.

'No.'

And I meant that too.

Over the rest of lunch I told them what Werewolf had told me and after the part about the guns, and their silence, I began to think that we would need a shotgun each. And grenades. And maybe air support.

I made Gearoid take the van and head off to St Malo. We had left it in full view of the road for too long already. Reluctantly he agreed and said that Frostin had arranged to meet him in *Le Biniou* at 4.0 p.m. I wanted to do a recce of the *gîte* and surrounding area while it was still fresh in Lu-Lu's mind. By the next day she could easily have forgotten which country we were in. The risk of Gearoid deciding to do something on the spur of the moment that close to Werewolf was too great.

I made Lucinda plot the route on the *Série Bleue* map as I drove. Beyond Port à la Duc, in a village called St Aide, we took a right on to a minor road heading north-east up the peninsula, parallel to the coast track we had been on that morning. After about five kilometres she said slow down because it was somewhere here, and then yelled 'Right!' in my ear and I turned on to a smaller road not even worthy of a signpost. Lu-Lu told me to pull over into a small copse of trees and despite the groans of the Cortina's suspension, I made sure it was well out of sight.

She handed me the binoculars she'd taken from my bag and said: 'The farm place is across the road, about fifty yards away, set back down a drive but you can see right down into it from the edge of the trees.'

I followed her through the trees until we could see but stay in cover. Through the glasses, I could see the *gîte* where Werewolf was being held. One of the others, a larger one and probably the old farmhouse, had smoke coming from the chimney. All the others looked deserted. Beyond the *gîtes* was the cliff edge and then the bay and the sea.

'I want to get closer, down to the cliff edge.' I pointed to the left of the farm. 'All the windows of the *gîtes* look into the courtyard. Keep low until we get across the road and into that field. If anyone spots us, turn back and run for the car.'

Lucinda wrinkled her nose.

'Is this fun—or what?'

I just shook my head and sprinted to catch her up.

The old farm had a six-foot high wall around the front of it, forming, with the buildings, a neat square and ensuring privacy from all except the seagulls. The wall had been restored when the *gîte* conversion had been done, but there was no gate any more. In the courtyard, the Peugeot was parked next to the little Renault. The gang were at home, hopefully not interested in some unscheduled target practice.

Once we had dashed across the road, I was sure we were out of sight of anyone in there unless they had been standing in the gateway. We climbed over a strand of rusty barbed wire and made our way down the side of the field which ran down to the cliffs. After another strand of wire, the field turned into heather and open rock. The topsoil was probably about an inch deep where there was some.

I made Lu-Lu get down with me and crawl through the last few yards of heather to the cliff edge. The wind off the sea whipped her long hair across my face as we peered over. The drop was about ten feet on to a shelf of rock which sloped down to our left.

Using the glasses, I could pick out what was obviously an old thoroughfare. There were even old, crude steps chiselled out of the rock in places. Way down to our left, where the bottom of the cliff curved out into a small spit, was a square of flat rock and to it was tied the *Cendrillon* fishing-boat.

The boat bobbed around on the emerald water in what was probably the only accessible anchorage on this stretch of cliff. I could see the old man, Cadic, on board, moving lobster-pots around the deck, then one of his grandsons appeared from the wheelhouse and I could make out that he had some kind of bright yellow poultice on his hands. From the mast flew the black-and-white flag of Brittany, a mono-chrome Stars and Stripes except the Stars were the Breton *ermine* symbol.

'This path leads up to the farm?' hissed Lucinda.

'I reckon so,' I said. 'I wonder if they sleep on board?'

'Why?'

'It would cut down the odds at breakfast-time.'

CHAPTER 15

I put my foot down, anxious to get some distance between us and them as I was convinced we had pushed our luck enough. We made good time and I detoured up the coast to St Cast-le-Guildo to find a hotel. I explained to Lucinda that we should go for the biggest one we could find as big hotels ask fewer questions than small ones and, if things went to the plan which I was beginning to form, we would want a place where we could leave at dawn without causing a stir.

St Cast, out of season, looked like a ghost town, with sand blown off the beach drifting down the main streets instead of tumbleweed. On the cliffs above the town were the usual collection of Gothic houses which dominate all the resorts on the Côtes d'Armor—or the Côtes du Nord as they used to call it, looking like a line of Bates motels. The hotels down near the beach, though, were square, modern and functional; the one we chose still had building work going on as another extension was added. The tourist trade seemed to be booming.

I left Lu-Lu in the car and tackled the Reception at the *Hôtel Anne de Bretagne*. A bored teenage girl said there would be no problem booking two rooms for the night and didn't bat an eyelid when I offered to pay in advance. She did go on the defensive when I said we would want to leave by 7.0 a.m. and told me in no uncertain terms that the restaurant opened at 8.0 a.m. and not a second before. I said that would be OK and filled out a registration form in the name 'Mr and Mrs Maclean' and one for 'The Rev. Dromey' but the girl didn't even look at them, just folded them inside the visitors' book.

Lucinda slumped down in her seat and slept most of the rest of the way back to St Malo, waking only as we approached the city walls.

'Hey, sorry about that, Angel,' she said, rubbing her eyes. 'I guess I'm just not a morning person.'

'You did OK.'

I spotted the St Fulgentius Transit in the car park where we had met that morning, but there was no sign of Gearoid. I parked as far away from the van as I could and led Lu-Lu by the hand through the old town.

We walked by *Le Biniou* arm-in-arm, my head on her shoulder, so I could sneak a look through the windows. There was one customer, a broad, thick-set, middle-aged man with a red face, wearing an off-white monk's habit. There couldn't be two.

'*Père* Frostin?' I introduced us, once inside.

'You must be the Angel I have heard about,' he said in English.

'And this is the outstanding Lucy—is that correct?'

'It'll do,' grinned Lucinda. 'Are all you monks so charm-
ing? And do I call you "Father"?'

'Was your mother in Cherbourg in nineteen-sixty?'
Frostin asked, deadpan.

'No,' said Lu-Lu, not getting it.

'Then Frostin will do. Gearoid has been here and
says he has to go shopping and he will need some
money.'

I was impressed at the way he pronounced 'Garrodth'
correctly and I was taken by the twinkle in his eye when he
added:

'I think it best if I do not ask what he is buying.'

'I think that's wise,' I agreed. 'Can I get you anything?'

Frostin asked for a glass of tea and I seconded that.
Lu-Lu wanted a Coca-Cola, just about the most expensive
drink in a French café. I hoped Gearoid wasn't running up
a large bill.

The woman who had opened the café that morning was
still on duty and served our drinks, her make-up recently
renovated, probably in Frostin's honour. She rattled something off in a thick Breton accent which I didn't have a
chance of following, and Frostin replied, then questioned
her, and the exchange ended in shrugs of shoulders and
pursed lips on both of them.

Lucinda made a face at me and I made an 'I dunno' face
in return.

'I understand you have problems with some young
anarchists,' said Frostin when the café lady had returned
to the kitchen.

'Hardly anarchists,' I said. 'These people seem to be
dedicated capitalists to me. They go under the name of
Front Populaire Breton.'

'Stupid,' Frostin snorted. 'They do not exist.'

'I suspect they're rather new at the liberation game.'

'Students. Idiots.'

'But dangerous.'

'They have no popular support,' Frostin persisted. 'Not here, never. Perhaps in Finistère or Morbihan.'

'What you guys talking about?' asked Lucinda, reaching into my pockets for a cigarette.

'Brittany is made up of four provinces,' I explained, looking at Frostin for confirmation. 'Ille-et-Vilaine, where we are now, and Côtes d'Armor where we were this morning, are the more cosmopolitan areas, although that would probably be taken as an insult. The two Atlantic provinces, Finistère and Morbihan, are redneck country. That's where the Breton nationalists traditionally operate.'

'You are absolutely right,' said Frostin. 'The nationalists who suggest breaking away from France are completely mad and they have never been popular on this coast.'

'But, with respect, Frostin, things are changing. This morning we have seen a lot of new building and almost all holiday homes.'

'We did?' muttered Lu-Lu.

'And near St Cast, I spotted new building plots and all the planning applications posted on the road are in the names of English people.'

'You are very observant,' said Frostin as if he wanted to add 'for an Englishman'. 'You feel that these holiday homes will become a cause for the nationalists?'

'It's happened elsewhere. Firebombing second homes is a recognized tactic.'

'Not in France.' Frostin shook his head. 'If that was the case, the Dordogne would be an inferno.'

He had a point. The rarest flora and fauna in the Dordogne these days were the French.

'No, these people who call themselves the *Front Populaire* are not true Breton nationalists. They are young and foolish. The cause of Brittany is not a fashionable one, not a young man's cause.'

'How did you know they were young men?' I asked quickly.

Frostin smiled faintly.

'It is, of course, none of my business, but the good lady who runs this café was telling me that the other foreigners were also hoping to meet some young Bretons here today.'

'Other foreigners?'

'She described a handsome young man who looked like a film star and said they had heard that *Le Biniou* was a place where Bretons met and drank. They were not English, they were German perhaps?'

'Not German,' I said thoughtfully. 'Dutch.'

Lucinda and I exchanged glances.

'Maybe we can visit with Frostin,' she said to change the subject. 'See how our friends the bees like their new home.'

'It would be a pleasure,' beamed the monk. 'I believe we have you to thank for such a generous gift of new colonies.'

'Oh, think nothing of it. We are staying nearby tonight, but perhaps tomorrow . . .'

I didn't say that perhaps tomorrow we might be in need of sanctuary as that was the moment Gearoid returned.

'Ah, good, you've got to know my old and distinguished comrade-in-bees Father Frostin. I hope they're not leading you into temptation.' Then he grabbed at my arm. 'And I'm sure Lucinda will keep you amused while I have a quick word outside with young Roy here.'

I felt myself being lifted out of my seat and I smiled weakly as Frostin waved us away and turned to Lucinda to say: 'And what could you possibly know of temptation, my dear?'

I would have been interested in hearing the answer to that myself. Instead, Gearoid bundled me out on to the street.

'Give me four thousand francs,' he hissed.

'What for?'

'I've found a gunshop and we can get a pump-action twelve-gauge and some shells. It was like Frostin said on the phone, no questions, no papers.'

I counted out a wedge of notes, leaving a thin and flimsy pile in my wallet.

'It could come in handy if we have to knock over a bank to buy breakfast tomorrow,' I said, but he ignored me.

'Now give me the keys to the Cortina.' I handed them over as well. 'I'll get the gun and stash it in the car. Keep Frostin talking for half an hour before making your way back to the van. Where is the car, by the way?'

'Same car park. What are we going to do with the bees?'

'I thought we'd let Frostin take the van,' he said, stuffing the money into the back pocket of his jeans. He had changed out of his monk's habit when we'd put on the bee suits. Pity. If he'd worn it this afternoon, he would probably have got a discount in the gunsmith's.

'I stopped on the way here and took the pills out of the nucleus box. They're under the driver's seat in a plastic bag. Don't open the back of the van as there are bound to be bees floating about. They weren't too keen to go back in the box.'

'Temperamental little buggers, aren't they?'

'Right, see you back at the car in thirty minutes. Oh, and stop off somewhere and buy a couple of candles.'

'Candles.'

'Yeah, candles.'

'What for?'

'Don't ask.'

I mentioned the candles to Frostin as we strolled back through the town; he acknowledging the greetings of the good and faithful, me trying to look round corners before we got there.

The candles were no problem. We paused outside the

main church and he asked me for some money. Why should he be different? I made the mistake of letting him too near my wallet and he removed a fifty-franc note with surgical precision. He disappeared inside the church and emerged a minute later with two long, thin offertory candles which I stuffed inside my jacket when Lucinda whispered loudly: 'Well, I ain't carryin' them in public.'

Gearoid was waiting for us at the Cortina, sitting in it, keeping low. I knew something was wrong straight off.

'I think it's a good idea if Frostin takes the van,' he said in a tone which defied anyone to argue with him. Then he said, in French: 'The bees are docile, but cold. They should settle tomorrow.'

Frostin thanked him and asked if he would see us tomorrow and Gearoid said yes, or we'd ring the monastery near St Lo, but he wasn't to worry if he didn't hear from us. The Community back in England knew where the bees were heading so they could arrange for the return of the van. He didn't say *if the worst came to the worst*. Not in words, anyway, and it was obvious that Frostin had cottoned on to the fact that he didn't want Lucinda to understand too much.

Frostin shook hands with Gearoid and wished him luck, then embraced him. Then he turned to Lu-Lu and began to say how he hoped she would visit St Lo, so forth, so fifth. In my opinion, Lu-Lu would descend on St Lo like the 82nd Airborne came down a bit further north on D-Day.

Gearoid flicked his head and I moved a yard away from them. A wise move anyway, as Lu-Lu was determined to give Frostin the full hug treatment.

'About five minutes ago,' Gearoid said under his breath, 'a flash Renault—a big turbo job, smoked windows—cruises by. Window goes down and someone takes a very close look at the Transit and makes a note of the number.'

'Cops? Customs? It couldn't be Guennoc, he's familiar with it,' I said, not convincing myself.

'The Renault had Dutch plates and it didn't give me and this wreck a second glance, but it checked out all Brit registrations.'

He looked at me like he was expecting a masterful decision.

'Let's fuck offski,' I tried.

'I agree. Sound move.'

Lu-Lu had just about released Frostin, his face redder than ever but his eyes twinkling like landing lights.

'Mister Angel,' he said and we embraced, and he whispered into my ear: 'Do not let any harm come to her.'

I didn't think it was a good time to tell him she was there to cover my backside.

He didn't hold the embrace for very long and I couldn't blame him. I was badly in need of a shower.

'Your hat,' he said, 'is a baseball hat, right?'

'Yep, the California Angels,' I said proudly.

'It's good to have angels on your side.'

I hoped Werewolf felt the same way tomorrow.

It was dark by the time we got to the hotel in St Cast. Gearoid was sulking because I made him put on his habit, complete with the six-inch wooden cross hanging round his neck, on the basis that the hotel would ask even fewer questions if we checked in with a man of God in tow. Lucinda was sulking because I wouldn't let her find a place to practise with the shotgun. I finally won the argument by telling her that shooting someone's sheep in the dark was still a hanging offence in Brittany.

One of the reasons I had picked the hotel was that it had a small off-street parking space where the Cortina couldn't be seen from the road. We parked and checked in, each of us carrying a holdall. Gearoid left the shotgun in the back

of the Cortina, still wrapped in corrugated brown paper—
ironically, the stuff that beekeepers like to burn when
'smoking' bees—and covered with his duffel coat. I took
charge of the bag in which he had stashed the box of
Ecstasy tablets and I just walked in with it like it was
duty-free cigarettes or something.

The receptionist didn't look as if she remembered me, or
cared, but she accepted that we had rooms booked and paid
for and, yes, weren't we the people leaving early? And did
we want to eat in the restaurant because reservations were
necessary.

I said we would—and no, Lucinda, we were *not* going
out on the town because I didn't think there was much of
a town to go out on. But I suspected that the reservation
was just to ensure that the chef didn't go home early.

In our room, I tossed Lucinda for first use of the shower
and won. As I closed the bathroom door I heard her crashing about trying to find a phone to call Room Service. Fat
chance, I thought, but when I emerged wrapped in a towel,
she was sitting cross-legged in the middle of the floor, a tray
at her side with a well-damaged bottle of Muscadet and
two clean glasses.

Gearoid sat cross-legged opposite her and was burning
one of the candles I had contributed to the Catholic church
for.

At first I thought I was witnessing some strange druggy
ceremony, then I saw the ten 12-gauge shotgun cartridges
lined up on the floor in front of him. He had a penknife as
well and had prised open the triangular ends of each shell
so that they looked like sinister orange flowers. Carefully
he dripped molten wax into each shell and when he was
satisfied there was enough in each, he blew out the candle
and very gently pushed the ends back in with the point of
his knife.

I hadn't said a word up to now. Lucinda said nothing

but poured me a glass of wine. I knelt down to join the huddle and took a sip.

'When the wax hardens,' said Gearoid quietly, still concentrating on his work, 'you have in effect converted a birdshot cartridge into a solid shell. All the little pellets of birdshot and the wadding become one big mother of a bullet. Up to thirty yards or so, these babies will go through trees.'

'How come,' said Lucinda softly, after a silence, 'you know stuff like this?'

Gearoid paused before looking at her.

'Don't you think I wish I didn't?'

I was right about the hotel restaurant. We were the only customers, which suited me fine as we could discuss our plan, such as it was, for the morning.

When the waiter—another surly teenager anxious to get home before 9.0 p.m.—brought us coffee and Armagnacs, it was clear he was going to leave us alone. I poured out a thin stream of salt on to the paper tablecloth until I had an almost complete square.

'Look, the farm buildings which are now *gîtes* are walled in except for this one gateway. There isn't an actual gate, so if we can sneak up on them and park here—' I jabbed a finger at my salt model—'then the Cortina's the cork in the bottle. They can't get out. If we can do it early enough and quietly enough, we can get Werewolf out before they know we're there. He's in a *gîte* here.'

I stabbed again and wrecked my salt square.

'But the point is he's here, actually near the gateway. Guennoc and his two hoods must be in the main house, the old farmhouse, the farthest away from the gate.'

'And the other three?' Trust Gearoid.

'They sleep on the boat.'

'You sure of that?' Trust Lucinda.

'No, but it's a fair bet and early tomorrow morning there'll be a tide in the bay so the boat will be afloat.'

'Don't get yer,' said Lu-Lu firmly.

'There's no point in staying on board a boat that's stranded on a rock at low tide, is there? So the odds are they stay on board when it's afloat.' That sounded quite convincing, I thought.

Lucinda shrugged as if she was willing to concede that one.

'That means three-on-three,' said Gearoid, damn him.

'Then we take one each and jump them—if we have to. And, Lu-Lu, I don't want this to be the OK Corral. OK?'

'Hey, does that rhyme—or what?' she grinned.

'I'm serious. I want you to use that cannon Gearoid bought to knock out their cars, not their brains. Got it?'

'If you say so, boss. But if the going gets tough, this lady gets tough.' She jerked both her thumbs into her chest. Her chest won. 'Which one do I take?'

I looked blankly at her.

'If there are three of them and three of us, which one do I get if it comes to a firefight?'

'I'll take the fat one,' said Gearoid. 'He looks like a good Catholic boy, the sort wouldn't hurt a man of God.'

'Then I'll take the smart-ass with the gun, the head honcho. Guennoc. I presume I'm in charge of the artillery?' Lu-Lu flicked her head at us both.

'Don't look at me,' said Gearoid, burying his nose in a glass.

'You can shoot better, drive faster—' I started.

'OK, so I'm elected. You get the skinny one in Cowboy boots.'

The one with a black belt in karate knowing my luck.

'So we disable the opposition, grab Werewolf and then what?'

She was ahead of me. I could never take this much gung-ho while sober.

'Then we hightail it across country to Frostin's monastery in St Lo,' I said, hoping they wouldn't realize I was making this up as I went along. 'And if we intend to catch them snug in their little duvets, then we kick out of here at six, agreed?'

They nodded.

'So let's pay the bill and hit the sack. Today's been a long day. Tomorrow could be longer.'

Lucinda put her right elbow on the table and opened the palm of her hand.

'Then let's do it, guys. Let's go get Werewolf.'

Gearoid and I gave her five. Then she screwed up her forehead.

'Hey, that's a line from a movie, isn't it? No, the line is something like "Let's go get *Angel*," that's it. Now what the friggin' hell was the movie?'

It was *The Wild Bunch*, but I didn't tell her.

I knew how that film ended.

Rule of Life No.71: When sleeping in a strange bed, always wake up first.

Actually, Gearoid made it first, as he'd said he would. I could hear him clumping about in the next room. He'd also used up all the credit in his monk's habit to squeeze out of the hotel an alarm clock for Lu-Lu and me. I woke two minutes before it was due to explode and stuffed it under the covers next to her head. Boy, was she a grouch in the mornings.

To be fair, Gearoid had exercised more of his Irish charm (and my wallet) to get somebody from the kitchen to prepare us four huge sandwiches of soft cheese in foot-long loaves of only slightly stale bread, to take with us. The thought of breakfast got Lucinda moving and she didn't say

that she could kill for a cup of coffee more than thirty times
before we hit the road.

It was still dark when I found a garage opening up about
ten kilometres outside St Cast. The other two hadn't said
much, just piled into the Cortina, Lu-Lu stretching across
the back seat using a holdall as a pillow, Gearoid hunched
in his duffel coat, hood up, against the chill morning.

I filled up the Cortina with BP Supergreen, working on
the basis that we might not be able to stop and refuel later
and after a bout of haggling, I paid over twenty pounds for
the garage attendant's Thermos flask of sweet, black coffee,
just to keep the troops happy. I hoped that Frostin's monastery took credit cards because I was down to loose change
by now.

The coffee did the trick, along with the chocolate bars I
had pilfered while the young lad at the garage had been
getting his Thermos for me.

We shared it in the two cups made from the outer and
inner lids of the flask after pulling off the road a couple of
kilometres from the garage. Dawn was struggling in and
not putting up much of a fight, but Lu-Lu came awake with
the coffee as if she'd taken a jolt of electricity straight from
the mains.

'I wanna try the gun out,' she said.

Before I could say anything, Gearoid put a hand on my
knee and squeezed.

'OK, it's quiet enough.'

Quiet enough? We hadn't seen a car all morning and
there wasn't a house in sight.

Gearoid opened the boot of the Cortina and began to
unwrap the gun. Lucinda opened her door in the back so
the interior light came on and she began to rummage
through her shoulder-bag, her hair falling down loosely and
hiding what she was doing.

I turned in my seat, nursing the last of the coffee and

tried to see what she was doing. When I did, my stomach churned. She looked up and read my face.

'So I need contact lenses,' she snarled. 'Gonna make something of it—or what?'

The noise Lu-Lu made cranking a shell into the chamber of the shotgun scared me. When she fired at a tree-stump about thirty feet away, I actually did jump backwards.

The three of us walked over to the tree and I flicked on the rubber-encased torch I'd taken from Duncan's ace tool kit. There was a hole four inches in diameter right through the tree. So it hadn't been a very thick tree, but it was big enough.

'Those shells of yours are mean suckers,' said Lucinda quietly.

As we walked back to the Cortina, Lu-Lu emptying and reloading the shotgun to get the feel of it, me dropping behind to talk softly to Gearoid, I saw he was biting his lower lip, his short beard curling up as he did.

'Second thoughts?' I asked.

He shrugged.

'Just thinking about something Frostin said.'

'Worried about the gun?' I remembered that Gearoid had dragged me out of *Le Biniou* rather than talk about buying the shotgun in front of Frostin.

'Partly. I had to make him a sort of promise—without telling him too much.'

'What sort of promise?' My stomach was throwing a wobbler again.

'In essence . . . well, basically, whatever happens we don't let them get the drugs.' He wasn't looking at me and that was a bad sign too.

I thought up some counter-arguments: these weren't exactly hard drugs, it was his brother after all, we could always call the cops and grass on them.

'We'll work something out,' was what I said. It didn't put a spring in his step.

'Frostin also said he would pray for us.'

'Don't worry. They won't lay a finger on us,' I said cockily.

'He wasn't talking about our bodies,' said Gearoid seriously.

We went through Port à la Duc and followed the route Lucinda had shown me, heading up towards Point de la Latte, running parallel to the line of the bay.

When I estimated we were within three kilometres of the *gîte* complex, I stopped the car on the main street of a small village and pulled out the *Série Bleue* map.

'We're here,' I pointed, 'and I estimate that the farmhouse place is here.'

I made them both look at the map and say they understood. I wasn't going to say 'in case anything happens to me' but they knew what I was getting at.

'Whatever happens, I'll keave the keys in the ignition, OK?'

They both said OK and I was about to give them my 'over the top' speech when Gearoid breathed: 'Would you fucking credit it?'

Not more than twenty feet in front of us the door of the local *boulangerie* had opened and a young man with four long French loaves under his arm had emerged and was mounting a small 250 cc Peugeot motorcycle, one of the putt-putt types which infest the roads of France, ridden by schoolkids, pensioners and nuns in equal proportions.

This young man never even glanced at us, just climbed on, fired up and pulled away. Didn't even look over his shoulder. A careless driver just asking for an accident.

He didn't see us, but Gearoid and I saw him clearly.

And his flashy cowboy boots.

I clicked in my safety-belt and Gearoid did the same, deliberately catching my eye.

'One down, two to go,' I said, starting the engine.

CHAPTER 16

I stayed about half a kilometre behind the Cowboy, which meant keeping the speed down to about 30 k.p.h. until we had cleared the village and the road ahead showed no sign of habitation. The only other vehicle we saw was an ancient Citroën van coming towards us. Once he was lost in my mirror, I put my foot down.

As we came up behind the motorcycle, I wound down my door window. Above the rush of incoming air I said:

'And now to demonstrate one of the advantages of having a right-hand drive car in a country where they drive on the right.'

I drew out and level with the Cowboy and for the first time he looked at the Cortina on his left, and then straight at me. Just as his jaw dropped open in recognition, I took my right hand off the wheel, reached out of the window and pushed him hard on the shoulder.

The force of my shove and a natural reaction to lean away from the Cortina, which never actually touched him, meant the little Peugeot curved gracefully away on to the grass verge. It bounced twice, then the front wheel disappeared into a ditch and suddenly he was doing a wheelie the wrong way up. It didn't last long as the bike decided to stay in the ditch. Cowboy, however, chose to travel on, horizontally, but only for as long as gravity let him.

'Way to go!' yelled Lucinda from the back seat, almost deafening me.

I stopped the Cortina and we all got out, Lu-Lu bringing

the shotgun with her. As we approached the inert figure lying face down, she worked the slide. There was no response from Cowboy.

'I thought the *justaposée à pompe* was worth the extra cash,' Gearoid said dreamily.

'What?' I said, my mouth suddenly dry.

'The gunsmith tried to sell me a *super posée*, an over-and-under, but I paid the extra for the pump-action. It has a much more intimidating sound, don't you think?'

I stared at him bemused. I couldn't afford to have him crack up on me now. Then I twigged. He couldn't—just as I couldn't—bring himself to ask if the Cowboy was dead.

'He's still breathing,' said Lu-Lu; good old Lu-Lu, the only one of us willing to get close enough to see. 'Want me to blow him away?'

'No!' Gearoid and I shouted together.

'Only kidding, boss,' she grinned, and then leaned over and pulled up Cowboy's jacket to reveal a Walther P38 pistil stuffed down the back of the waistband of his jeans. She pulled it out and offered it to me.

'I've done my bit,' I said.

She held the gun out to Gearoid, who shook his head. She shrugged and pushed it down the front of her jeans.

'Do we just leave him here?' she asked.

'Why not?' I said. 'The bike's not going anywhere again.'

That was certainly true. The front wheel was totally buckled and it would have taken a circus clown to ride it in a straight line. Gearoid and I tipped it over so that it fell into the ditch and could not be seen from the road. I checked, and Cowboy's prone figure couldn't be seen either.

'Let's saddle up, we'll be there in five minutes.'

I shivered inside my bomber jacket and it wasn't just the chill morning breeze coming off the sea.

Lucinda strode out back to the car, the shotgun across

her shoulders, her arms draped over barrel and stock almost as if crucified to it. I let her get a few yards in front, then I dug in my pocket and took out the metallic aerosol canister and offered it to Gearoid.

'Prefer this?'

'What is it?'

'Mace. Anti-rape protection.'

'It could come in handy.'

Back at the Cortina, I rearranged things as we had agreed, dropping the back seat down so that Lucinda could lie in the rear full length among our bags, including the carrier bag with the tablet box in, and be covered by the white bed sheet I had appropriated from the hotel in St Cast. Yet another reason we wouldn't be invited back.

By the time she was comfortable and securely wedged in, it was almost impossible to tell there was a Lucinda in there, just an anonymous mass of luggage and stuff under a sheet.

'OK, team?'

'Yo, baby! Let's rock'n'roll.'

I swapped another glance with Gearoid.

'Got any tape?' he asked, which threw me for a moment. 'Sticking tape.'

'Yeah, somewhere.'

I opened Duncan's tool box and handed him a small roll of black insulating tape. He bit off a strip about six inches long and handed back the roll. Then he opened his duffel coat and flipped out the big wooden crucifix he wore.

'Hold that,' he said, offering me the end of it stretched out on the leather thong round his neck.

I held it as he taped the gas canister of mace to the back of the wooden upright, then he took the top off the aerosol and put it in his pocket.

'What a world,' he said, shaking his head.

*

One last check through the binoculars. The farmhouse/*gîte* complex deserted. No sign of life, the Peugeot and Renault cars parked in the middle of the square formed by the cottages and the wall. The gateway without a gate wide open.

'They'll be in the big house dead opposite the gateway,' I told Gearoid. 'Werewolf—sorry, Francis—is in the second one on the right. It'll be locked and I would think Guennoc keeps the key.'

'Turn the engine off and coast down,' he said.

'Good idea,' I said, wishing I'd thought of it.

After another ten seconds, he said:

'Well do it, then.'

So I did.

The Cortina coasted into the courtyard and we had just enough momentum to carry us beyond the parked Peugeot and then I swung the wheel over to the left and we came to rest about ten feet from the door of the farmhouse, facing away from it.

Gearoid was already out. He had opened the passenger door as we had slid down the hill and held it until we had almost stopped rolling. I hit the handbrake and fumbled for my door handle.

By the time I had got round to the boot of the Cortina, he was at the door of the farmhouse, pressed into the wall and holding the crucifix out in front of him like a demented vampire-hunter from a very B picture. Still, in his brown habit and that pose, he was good enough to impress an atheist.

I clicked the catch on the boot of the Cortina and began to raise the door, but before it was half way up, the farmhouse door opened and out stepped the fat one, Sumo, blinking in disbelief at what he saw.

What he didn't see was Gearoid, who reached out and

grabbed a fistful of the fisherman's smock Sumo was wearing and pulled.

Sumo staggered two steps out of the doorway with a loud grunt, trying to set his feet firmly to get balance. Once he did, nothing short of an earthquake would shift him.

Gearoid screamed at him—something in French I couldn't catch—then thrust the crucifix close to his face. Sumo gave up any thought of anything else then. All he was concerned about was the feeling that his eyes were being poked out by blowtorches from the back, as the mace hit him. He put his hands to his eyes and bellowed like a buck deer looking for a little something for the weekend. Then he staggered forwards, crashing into Gearoid, the two of them going over in a tangle of legs, monk's habit and body fat.

The boot of the Cortina was up and I was reaching for the sheet, doing it all half-turned to the farmhouse to watch Gearoid. Out of the corner of my eye I saw Guennoc inside the house, leaning over a table and picking something up and coming for the door, one hand over the other, working the action of a pistol.

I had the sheet off and I dragged it after me as I twisted round and down to get behind the Cortina and under cover. As Guennoc made the door he froze, trying to take in Sumo and Gearoid writhing on the cobblestones, but mainly looking into the rear of the Cortina and hearing Lucinda work that very loud slide on the pump gun. He lowered his right hand and the pistol fell back into the house. He stayed frozen, his arms out from his sides.

I stood up and looked into the Cortina myself.

Lucinda was lying on her back, her shoulders and neck propped up by our holdalls, her legs open wide and her knees up. The shotgun pointing out and up, lay across her stomach, the barrel seemingly growing from her thighs.

'Impressive, isn't it?' I said cheerily.

*

Lucinda eased her way out of the Cortina without taking the shotgun off Guennoc. It was an impressive display of her buttock muscles.

'Over there,' she waved the gun. 'Sit down. Hands on head. Translate it, Roy.'

'I understand,' said Guennoc, and he did as he was told. No threats, no 'You'll never get away with this,' no visible anger. Trying so hard to stay cool, but most of it was probably shock. It had all gone very wrong for him.

Gearoid had disentangled himself from Sumo and was dragging him, Sumo on his knees still, over to where Guennoc had sat, cross-legged, on the cobbles. He still had his hands over his eyes and was whimpering.

'Which one did you say Francis was in?' he gasped, breathless.

Then a full bottle of something, probably cider (he wouldn't waste Calvados) came through the window of the *gîte* to our right and smashed as it hit the ground.

'That one,' I said.

'Yeee-hah!' came the accompanying yell. 'It's the cavalry!'

'Sounds like it,' said Lucinda. 'But let's get these guys out of the way first.'

'Good thinking, Batgirl,' I chirped, suddenly on top of the world. Guennoc and Sumo didn't look to have much fight left in them to me.

'Keys,' I said to Guennoc, and he reached into a shirt pocket and produced a bunch of three which he handed up to me without looking at me. 'Pick up the other gun,' I told Gearoid and then I jogged across the courtyard and did a quick scan of the three *gîtes* there.

The end one nearest the gateway had been made out of some outbuilding and looked solid enough. The second key I tried opened the door. This *gîte* had yet to be furnished, its interior totally bare, not even a kitchen unit yet, just a cold flagstone floor. There were two windows with shutters but no back door. Perfect.

'In here,' I shouted, and Lucinda prodded Guennoc upright with the shotgun.

Gearoid helped Sumo up by the collar. He had picked up Guennoc's pistol but was holding it like it would bite him. They marched over and I stood aside to usher Guennoc into the *gîte*. Still he wouldn't look at me. Sumo wasn't looking at anyone. He was crying now, which was probably the best thing he could do. Staggering into the door frame didn't improve his spirits any, though.

I pulled the door shut and locked it, testing the handle. Then we looked at each other.

'We've done it,' I said.

'Or what!' Lucinda yelled, then swung on her hip and brought the shotgun up to her shoulder.

She fired three times in rapid succession, aiming at the wheels of the Peugeot and the Renault, and then at the rear window of the Peugeot. The noise was stunning, the effect amazing.

'Jeeesus!' she said, lowering the gun.

I blinked and snorted to clear my sinuses of cordite and then I saw what she meant. Where Gearoid's patented modified cartridges had hit, they had left buckled metal, shredded rubber and no glass at all in the rear window.

'Was that absolutely necessary?' asked Gearoid, who hadn't seemed too worried by the shooting.

Lucinda seemed to think about this.

'Yes,' she said, jaw set.

'At least they can't follow us now,' I offered.

'What the fuck's going on out there?' came an angry cry.

We all sprinted across the yard and I fumbled the keys out again, getting it right on the last one.

Werewolf was backed up against the side wall in his

wheelchair, the wall which stayed in shadow when the door opened. He had a full bottle of cider by the neck in his right hand, ready to throw, and three more lined up on the floor at his side. His broken leg, the plaster dirty and scratched, stuck out in front of him ridiculously.

He lowered the bottle, offering it.

'Well, hello Lucinda, nice of you to drop in. Fancy a quick one?'

'Love one,' said Lu-Lu tossing her hair back. 'But with your leg in that position it could be hazardous. How about a drink instead?'

'I take it they know each other,' Gearoid said drily.

'You guessed.'

'You did what?' shouted Werewolf, his hand shaking as he offered the bottle around.

'We locked them up across the yard,' I said. 'Don't bother to say thanks for rescuing you or anything.'

'Which one?'

'What?'

'Which *gîte*? Show me.'

He wheeled himself to the door.

'Have you ever seen such an ungrateful little shite?' said Gearoid in a most unChristian way.

I got behind the wheelchair and pushed him out of the door. 'That one, across there, if you must know'.

'Holy shit! Get the gun. Get them out of there. You dumb fuckers, you've—'

He was flapping his arms so much I thought he would jump out of the chair. But then suddenly I wasn't aware of anything except the sound of tinkling glass.

I stared in horror as the windows of the *gîte* near the gate were smashed outwards. Then there was the flash and the sound of a shot and a bullet whanged off the stone wall about two feet to my left.

I dragged back Werewolf's wheelchair, spinning it round into the room again. I heard Gearoid say 'Hell's teeth' as more shots rang out and one of the windows of our *gîte* smashed. Then Lu-Lu had the shotgun up again and let fly once before slamming the door shut. The noise of the shotgun was truly deafening inside the cottage.

Gearoid and I pulled the wheelchair behind a solid piece of wall and crouched down below window level. Two more shots came and more glass popped out, but at least we had the internal wooden shutters closed, which gave us a bit more protection.

I hoped.

'You utter airhead,' snapped Werewolf. 'You locked them up in the old barn. They've got enough guns and ammo under the floor in there to start a small war!'

I didn't think saying 'Sorry' was a good idea, not then. So I saved that for later and kept quiet.

'Then let's give 'em a small war,' said Lu-Lu excitedly, ramming more shells into the breech of the shotgun, looking exactly like she knew what she was doing.

'Can we do a deal for the stuff?' said Gearoid, ducking as a bullet thwacked against the wooden shutter above his head.

I knew how much that cost him.

'Well, Mastermind?' Werewolf accused me.

'I have another idea,' I said. 'Let's run away.'

'Hold this. Don't drop it,' I said, giving Werewolf my Angels baseball hat.

'You sure about this?' he asked, stuffing the cap inside his shirt.

'No,' I said honestly. 'But if Lu-Lu can keep their heads down for a few seconds, I should be able to get behind their cars. They won't be able to see me then and I can get to the Cortina and bring it to the front door.'

'They'll see you then sure enough,' said Gearoid.

He offered me Guennoc's pistol which he had been holding all the time without making any attempt to use it.

I shook my head. Werewolf took it instead and began to
examine it. 'Where's the safety?'

'Come here,' said Lu-Lu, putting the shotgun on the
table and showing Werewolf how to use the Walther.
'Don't use it until I run out of shells. I'm better than you
are.'

'How do you know?' snarled Werewolf.

'Trust her, brother dear,' said Gearoid, patting his plaster cast.

Lu-Lu checked the other pistol she'd taken from Cowboy
and pushed it down the front of her jeans again.

'OK, this is how we play it,' she said, taking command
much to my relief. 'Wolfman, you stay where you are and
get ready to open the shutter things if it looks like I need
back-up. Remember to aim low. Big Brother G, you get the
door. When I say "Go" you rip it open. I'll take out their
windows which oughta keep their heads down. Angel, you
come through my legs and keep low. I've got five shots,
remember. By the time you hear number five you should
be behind that station wagon.' She meant Guennoc's Peugeot, the one that she'd recently improved the air-
conditioning on by blowing out the rear window. 'Don't
stop to chew the fat with anyone.'

'There must be another way,' said someone and I realized it was me. 'That's what you're all supposed to say to
talk me out of it.'

They stayed silent.

'Thanks a bunch.'

Gearoid edged his way to the door handle, then looked
at Lucinda. She nodded once and cranked the pump-action
again. I crouched down on the floor behind her, taking a
last look at her tightly-jeaned buttocks.

Ah well, if you had to go . . .

'Go!'

The door was ripped open and Lu-Lu stepped forward and braced her legs apart. As she let fly with the first shot, I was brushing her inner thighs, crawling furiously, my hands scraping the cobblestones, then my knees.

Boom—boom. That made three.

No answering shots, that was good, I remember thinking. Then I was on my feet somehow and stumbling, crouching and gasping but above all *running*.

Boom. Four. Boom. Made it.

I collapsed behind the Peugeot. The damage Lu-Lu had done earlier to the nearside wheel meant the car had lurched over and there were shards of glass everywhere, but I didn't mind. I could have hugged it.

There were more shots, this time from Guennoc's side, one of them sparking as it ricocheted off the cobbles. They weren't aiming at me, though, so Lu-Lu really had kept their heads down.

I risked a look and could see why. The two windows of their *gîte*, shutters, frames and all, had disappeared leaving two square holes. There was also a hole in the door. If they weren't scared in there, they should have been.

From the *gîte* where they'd held Werewolf, I saw the nose of a pistol come through the hole in the window where Werewolf had thrown the bottle. Two snap shots and then it withdrew.

I looked around me, suddenly frightened. What if *their* cavalry suddenly arrived in the form of old M. Cadic and his fishing grandsons? There was no sign of them down the path to the cliffs, which I could see from where I crouched. Maybe down at sea level they couldn't hear World War III up here.

Don't worry about it; get crawling.

I snaked my way round the rear of the Cortina, keeping

an eye on Guennoc's *gîte* from underneath the car. I reached up and opened the driver's door and climbed in, keeping my head down.

There was another exchange of shots and I risked a peek. It was more than a little farcical, almost like an old cartoon of a Western where the gunslingers shoot at each other from saloons directly across the street.

I made myself as low as I could in the driver's seat, tilted the mirror down so I could see behind me, licked my lips and started the engine, dropping reverse gear and letting off the handbrake.

I fired up the engine, that was Lu-Lu's signal, and let out the clutch. The Cortina roared back, almost into Guennoc's farmhouse. I jammed on the brake and crashed first gear, bucking forward and yanking the wheel over to miss the Peugeot. I had to look over the wheel now to see where I was going.

Lucinda had the door open and had stepped out into the yard, one of the pistols in a two-fisted grip in front of her. She fired once, swung the gun and then again, spacing her shots one per window. I hit the brake as I reached her and she went down on one knee, using the engine of the Cortina as cover, resting the gun on the engine.

'Move it!' she screamed.

Gearoid appeared in my mirror, yanking open the boot. I put the gearstick in neutral and leaned over to open the passenger door. There were more shots and a bullet banged into the driver's side—my side—of the Cortina somewhere.

I crawled over the passenger seat to get out to help Gearoid. He was back in the *gîte*, hauling Werewolf out of his chair and into a fireman's lift across his shoulder. Werewolf's plastered leg swung wildly and I heard him scream: 'Be gentle with me, you clumsy bugger!'

Lucinda loosed off two more shots as I made the *gîte*. At least the Cortina was between us and the opposing camp now but I didn't want them to disable it as Lu-Lu had done their wheels.

'Can you manage?' I gasped.

'He's my brother,' said Gearoid, 'and he sure is fuckin' heavy.'

'In that case, women and comedians first,' I said, turning back to dive outside again.

As I climbed into the passenger seat again I yelled, 'Get ready,' to Lu-Lu.

'Go, go, go,' she said, not taking her eyes off her targets.

Gearoid appeared in the door, Werewolf's backside next to his head. I was back in the driver's seat and I still hadn't been shot. I couldn't believe it. Then I couldn't believe much at all any more.

Over the engine, with Lu-Lu's arms stretched out holding her pistol, I looked out of the open gateway and up the track to the road.

At the top of the track there was a flash new Renault with smoked windows parked so that it blocked the whole road. Half way down the track was the Cowboy, staggering forward, clutching his ribs. Behind him were four men in overcoats, one of them a stylish Drizabone raincoat with matching Australian stockman's hat. A good four hundred quid's worth of keeping the rain out. And it wasn't even raining.

They all carried short stubby things which I didn't like the look of, and the one in the Drizabone was almost certainly Gronweghe.

'Back inside! Get back inside!'

'What the shit . . . !'

'Run!'

Gearoid had been about to upend Werewolf into the rear of the Cortina. He staggered, corrected his balance and turned back to the doorway. Lucinda gave me her killer look and only moved when I gunned the engine.

As soon as her arms were off the bonnet I pushed in first gear and careered forward. I hadn't time to see if they had made it. A bullet went through the windscreen, but it didn't star as they do in the movies, and then I was almost at the gateway.

I swung down hard right and rammed the Cortina into the far gatepost, the rear end swinging round to clip the other post and smashing off the open rear door as it did so. Then I was out of my door and running across the court-yard.

I heard a different kind of shooting—a light, rapid, sub-machine-gun—and then a series of twangs as bullets hit the car, then I was diving through the open door and rolling over on the stone floor and Lu-Lu was slamming the door shut.

'What the fuck's up?' Werewolf shouted at me. He looked ridiculous, sitting on the edge of the table where Gearoid had dumped him, holding his leg out with both hands.

'You've blocked us in!' shouted Lu-Lu from the window.

'And written off the car!' Gearoid chipped in.

'Relax, will yer? Everything's under control.' I stood up, panting. 'How many of those cannon shells have you got left?'

I picked up the shotgun and handed it to Lucinda.

'Two.'

'Good. Open the door and lie down. I want you to hit something.' I joined her by the window and pointed to the Cortina wedged between the gateposts as if someone had dropped it from a helicopter.

'See there? Just behind the rear wheel, low down. Hit that, it's the gas tank.'

'Then what?'

'Then we run like stink the other way.'

'What other way?' griped Werewolf in frustration. 'The

other way is blue, wet and called the English Channel.'

'Exactly. And we know where there's a boat, don't we?' I patted Lu-Lu's arm.

'Sho' thing, boss, I like the style.'

'Then let's do it quick because our Dutch friend Gronweghe is coming down the hill fast and he's brought some muscle with him. And I think this lot know what they're doing.'

I grabbed the door and pulled. Lucinda dived down, crawled forward on her elbows further out than I thought safe, then put the shotgun to her shoulder.

I looked at the opposing *gîte*. There was no sign of life. Then an upstairs window shattered and I could see Guennoc clearly, pistols in both hands, but not pointing at us. From up there he could see what was coming down the track as well. He began firing over the Cortina, probably grateful to me for putting it there. Then his fire was returned and he ducked back as bullets sprayed the wall around the window.

Lucinda fired and the Cortina moved as the slug hit but that was all. She worked the pump-action.

'Last one,' she said and pulled the trigger. Again the car jerked and went on buckling as one of the latecomers at the gunfighters' ball began to spray it with rapid fire from outside.

'Nothin'', said Lu-Lu.

'I can see petrol coming out,' said Gearoid from the other window.

'Give me the handgun,' ordered Lu-Lu, and I grabbed it from the table for her.

She held it out at arm's length and turned it on its side before firing. I don't know whether she hit the cobbles or what, but it did the trick. The petrol leaking from the ruptured tank caught fire and I saw the flames run in several directions under the car. Then the tank went up with a whoomf noise and clouds of thick black smoke began to billow out. Just what we needed.

'OK, team, let's go. Down the side of the farmhouse; the track leads right down the cliffs.'

Gearoid turned and bent his knees so that Werewolf could mount him piggy-back.

'This had better be good, Angel,' he said as he linked his arms round Gearoid's neck.

Lucinda was on her feet outside.

'Come on, I'll give us cover,' she coughed as the smoke swirled. We couldn't even see Guennoc's *gîte* through it.

She fired a shot in the general direction.

'Christ knows where that went in all this pollution,' she moaned.

'Don't worry,' I said, grabbing her arm and pulling, 'it's unleaded.'

CHAPTER 17

'My bag was in that goddamned car!' she bitched as we ran.

'So was mine.'

'But my passport . . . everything.'

I hadn't thought to tell her to keep things like passports about her person. I had just assumed she did so, like I did.

'Christ, I've just torched all the XTC tabs, haven't I?'

'Frostin will be proud of you,' I wheezed as we ran towards the cliff path. But from the look on her face as she glanced back over her shoulder, I reckoned she would exchange a blessing for a fire-extinguisher given the choice.

We caught up with Gearoid as he staggered, bow-legged under Werewolf's weight, just as the path dropped down below the top of the cliff. The wind whipped in on us and

the emerald green water looked rough and a long way
down.

Lucinda clicked the magazine out of the Walther she
held and counted out three bullets, then she slotted them
back in the magazine and stuffed that in her jacket pocket
and threw the gun over the cliff edge. Then she reached
behind her and pulled the second Walther from her jeans
and worked the slide mechanism.

'I'll stay here and give cover.'

'No way,' said Werewolf.

'You—' I said, pointing at him—'don't have a vote.
Wait until we get to the turn in the path down there and
then come on.'

'Yo.'

I helped peel Werewolf from Gearoid's back and with his
arms round our shoulders and a leg each, Gearoid getting
the plaster one, we trundled down the cliff, grunting and
sweating and weaving drunkenly from side to side.

If they were still shooting up above us, we couldn't hear
a thing down here. The wind and the sea made sure of that.
By the time we made the gap in the rocks I had indicated,
we could hear only our own rasping breathing.

'Stop here,' I gasped, lowering Werewolf and then sig-
nalling to Lucinda, who set off after us like an Olympic
sprinter.

I tried to get my breath back and motioned Gearoid to
follow me around the rock. Down below us was the spit of
rock curving out to sea, providing the small natural harbour for the fishing-boat bobbing there. The steps in the
rock lay just below us, then the path was partly sheltered
from the boat by other rocks jutting seawards.

'If you get down the steps without them seeing you, you
can get to within a couple of hundred yards,' said Gearoid
between pants.

Lucinda had reached Werewolf. She had an arm round

him and was bending over to get her breath back. I waved her over and told her what Gearoid had said.

'Can you carry Wolfie?' she said to him and he nodded. 'Then let Angel and me go for the boat. They got guns?'

'I don't know,' I said truthfully. 'I'm more worried about them casting off before we get there, because then the only way left is up.'

'All hell was breaking out up there,' she grinned, 'but you can't hear a thing down here.'

'Then let's get it done,' I said. 'Wait until we're down there before you show yourself. Unless, of course, somebody comes over the hill . . .'

Gearoid just waved us away. 'We'll manage. We're an awful hard family to kill.'

'I've noticed,' I said and started down the slippery rock steps.

We made it down the stepped section of rock and then we were covered by the outcrop, although we couldn't see them either. I stumbled and fell twice and once brought down Lu-Lu by accidentally tapping her ankles. She swore at the tear in her jeans and waved two broken fingernails at me. For the first time I noticed that she was bleeding from a nasty gash on the neck. She said it had been a ricochet and not to worry and did I look any better?

I had to admit I probably didn't. The knees of my jeans were slashed in three or four places where I had crawled around the courtyard. The palms of my hands were filthy and bloody, only the dirt stopping the blood flowing. I hadn't noticed either hurting as yet, and at least the ripped jeans were still fashionable.

The path twisted through a tunnel of rock and then into the open, a sloping plate of granite down to the sea about ten feet wide and at several points the sea crashed against and over it.

Lucinda fell back against a rock and took her pistol out to flip off the safety-catch.

'It's about a two hundred yard sprint,' I said. 'Downhill all the way. Don't slip.'

I shoved my head around the rock for another look.

'The old man's on deck and there's one in the wheelhouse. The other's probably below deck. Don't let them cast off. What more can I say?'

'Nuthin'. Leave it to Lu-Lu.'

Then she was up and running with me on her heels.

We were half way there when the old man saw us. He pulled a pipe from his mouth and flung it on deck and started to shout.

For a man of his years, old Cadic came off the boat with the ease of a chimpanzee, landing two-footed on the wet rock and making straight for the mooring ropes which held the boat to two iron stanchions hammered into the cliffs twenty feet apart. He got the stern rope loose with a furious jerk and without looking to see Lucinda bearing down on him, he made for the bow rope.

I was aware that the engine of the *Cendrillon* was being fired up, but it didn't catch first time.

Then old man Cadic was at the bow rope stanchion and reaching for the knot. Forty or fifty yards still to go and the rock path slippery with seawater under our feet.

Lucinda stopped dead and spread her feet in a policeman's crouch, the Walther at arm's length, two-handed. She fired four times in rapid succession, putting two shots at Cadic's feet and two actually on to the iron stanchion he was reaching for. Old man Cadic froze and stared at us.

'Touch that rope, penis-breath, and I'll blow your fucking eyes out!' she yelled above the waves. Then, to me: 'Translate it, Roy.'

'I think he got the message,' I wheezed.

*

I asked old Cadic if they had any guns on board and he said no. He had Lu-Lu's Walther in his right ear at the time, so I believed him. The two grandsons stood on deck looking lost. Back up the cliff I could see Gearoid start down the steps with Werewolf piggy-backing again.

'Get on board,' I told Cadic in French. 'We will not harm you unless there is trouble.'

I made them stand near the wheelhouse and helped Lu-Lu climb aboard the boat which was swaying even more now it was secured with only one rope.

'I'm going to help the others,' I told her as she took up her pistol-range stance. Then in French I said: 'Kill them if it becomes necessary, otherwise don't harm them.'

She didn't understand a word of it, but they did.

I ran back up the path, uphill and harder now, my legs starting to tell me they were tired. My brain had news for them; it was, too.

Gearoid was speechless and very relieved to see me when I met them. Werewolf was just rigid with frustration.

'Christ, will yer put me down? Let me make it under me own steam.'

'Shut up, you tart,' I gasped, picking up a leg and an arm.

The two younger Cadics, Hervé and Loic, took our arrival with dead calm, but I think this had more to do with them being totally gobsmacked by the sight of the gun-waving, hair-flying Lucinda.

I was trying to think how to get Werewolf on board when the old man said loudly to his grandsons: 'Don't just stand around, help the man.'

And they did, just like that. They even offered Gearoid and me a hand up over the pitching side and on to the deck.

'Thank you,' I told him. 'We have to leave here quickly.'

'I know,' he said, and nodded to a point over my shoulder.

I turned and looked up. At the very top of the cliff were two figures waving something at us. I saw a flash of fire but heard no sound and we were too far away for the bullets to come anywhere near. Still, no time to hang about.

'We have to leave very quickly,' I revised. 'Will you start the engines? We do not want to hurt your family and we do not wish to steal your boat. Merely borrow it.'

Cadic looked me in the eye and then looked down at Werewolf. Then he looked at Gearoid in his monk's habit and shabby duffel coat. But most of all, he looked at Lucinda.

'American?' he asked, and I said yes.

'Okay.'

He barked orders in Breton and Hervé and Loic jumped into action, one disappearing down into the engine-room, the other to the wheelhouse. The *Cendrillon*'s engines coughed again and then roared, smoke belching from the exhaust pipe running up the side of the wheelhouse.

Old Cadic jumped over the side again and loosened the mooring rope, scrambling back on board before it had cleared the stanchion. He hauled the rope in and waved instructions to the grandson at the wheel and the boat inched backwards until it had cleared the spit of rock. The swell was more vicious here now that the sea proper could get at us.

I held on to the guard rail and tried mentally to glue my feet to the deck. I am not a good sailor.

Gearoid walked by me as if he was in church and touched old Cadic on the shoulder.

He spoke in Breton, but I got the gist. He asked him why he had suddenly helped us and Cadic simply said 'Americans'. Then he said something else and all I caught were the words 'liberation' and a date, the year 1944.

'He's paying off a debt,' Gearoid said softly to me.

I looked over at Lucinda, still holding the gun on any Cadic she could see.

'Tell her it's because he's scared of her,' I said.

The *Cendrillon* turned into the waves and began to pull away from the rocks. For a moment I thought I saw figures running down the pathway but perhaps I was wrong. No one shot at us any more. Apart from the increasing swell of the boat, life was looking up.

Cadic headed the boat out to sea and we saw Port de la Latte disappear on our left.

'Where we heading?' Werewolf asked.

'I don't know,' I said. 'Let's pool our resources. Money?'

'None,' they all said together.

'And no passport,' added Lu-Lu.

'Same here,' said the Dromey brothers together. They were beginning to work like a double act and that scared me. I kept quiet about my passport in my inside pocket.

'But we have these,' said Gearoid, his eyes twinkling as he produced a bottle of Calvados from each of his duffel coat pockets. 'I liberated them.'

'Well, we could drop round into St Malo, but with no dosh, no transport and no passports, it could be tricky,' I started, but they weren't listening.

Gearoid got the top off a bottle and casually tossed it over the side. He offered Lu-Lu first swig.

'Firewater—or what!' she yelped.

'Monsieur Cadic,' Werewolf shouted. 'Would you join us in a small drink?'

The old man shambled over and peered at the bottle. 'Ah, Calvados,' was all he said, then he took a hit. His expression said 'not bad,' then he made waiting motions and said he would be back in an instant.

He disappeared below deck and emerged a minute later— Lu-Lu keeping the Walther handy just in case—

with a pair of clear glass bottles containing an amber liquid.

'Try this,' he said, offering it first to Lucinda.

She took a swig and screwed up her face, then, suddenly, her expression relaxed.

'Kinda sweet, but *very* interesting.' She handed the bottle to Gearoid, who raised it to Cadic and then took a drink.

'It's mead!' he said joyously. Then, to Cadic in Breton, something about bees, and when Cadic nodded he said: 'We are going to get on famously,' and put his arm round him.

After a few more rounds of drinks, with Lu-Lu even taking a bottle to young Loic in the wheelhouse and staying there quite a while as he practised his English, Cadic asked us where we wanted to go.

I held his shoulder, more to steady myself than anything else, and pointed to the near horizon where the early morning Sealink ferry was chugging in what I hoped was the right direction.

'Follow that,' I said.

It was hard to believe that it was still not 8.0 a.m. when the *Cendrillon* left Brittany, so much had happened. It was over thirteen hours later before we chugged into sight of the lights of the English coast, having avoided larger ships, drunk everything on board (which was not inconsiderable) and eaten the Cadics out of boat and home. And I had only been sick twice.

The old man produced a chart, a very old chart, of the English coast and told us we were approaching Portland Bill.

'Who's he?' asked Lu-Lu drunkenly.

'It's a place, dipstick, near Weymouth on the Dorset coast.'

'Can we get ashore without going into a harbour with

Customs?' Gearoid asked, trying to pull the chart under the wheelhouse light.

Lucinda fell against young Loic and they both laughed, but Loic's laugh was the nervous one.

'I could get us to the Community somehow,' said Gearoid, 'and we could hole up there.'

'What's this place?' Werewolf jabbed a finger at the map and missed.

'Osmington, it says,' I read. 'Looks like just a landing beach for yachts and windsurfers. No harbour.'

Gearoid rattled off something at Cadic and he replied equally quick.

'The old man has a rubber raft,' he translated, 'but it only takes four so we'd have to buy it off him.'

I sighed and counted out the last of my French francs, about £150 worth.

'That's all I have,' I said, 'and about two quid in English change.'

Gearoid handed it over to the old man, who thanked him. I doubted it would buy him a new raft but the deal was the principle.

We could see the lights of Portland Bill and the promenade lights of Weymouth quite clearly as we anchored offshore.

Hervé and Loic set about inflating the raft on deck. I could make out the dark shape of the Dorset cliffs and gave thanks that the sea here was millpond calm.

Werewolf explained to Cadic about the guns and about the drugs. Cadic nodded sagely and then said that he had known all along that Guennoc was no true patriot—and by that he meant Breton—but the cause was the cause, if we knew what he meant.

Gearoid and Werewolf said they did.

We shook hands all round and Lucinda kissed them all, the old man getting one smack on the mouth. He grumped and spluttered and wiped his mouth with his sleeve, and he loved it.

The Cadic lads helped lower Werewolf into the raft and then took a long time lowering Lu-Lu down. Then they handed down two paddles and we made a complete mess of it by going round in a circle before striking for the shore.

'What did you do with the gun?' I asked Lucinda.

'Oh, I threw that overboard hours ago,' she said casually.

'Good. Have you still got my hat?' I nudged Werewolf.

'What? Oh yeah, here.'

He pulled out my crumpled Angels hat from his shirt and I jammed it on my head.

'I think it important to be properly dressed now we're back in England,' I said.

We got Werewolf ashore first on to the pebble beach that acted as a landing hard at Osmington and then Gearoid opened the air valve on the raft and we pushed it back into the water.

Hanging between Gearoid's and my shoulders, Werewolf hobbled up the street into the village, Lucinda going on ahead as scout.

'There's a pub up ahead, with a restaurant,' she reported back. 'Nothing else. This village is the sticks, or what?'

We staggered into the pub, which had about ten customers and just over an hour to go before closing time. The barman looked at us with deep suspicion.

We set Werewolf down at a table laid for dinner and Gearoid whispered, 'I'll handle this.' He put up a good blag but the barman wasn't having it. He didn't care if we were underprivileged hospital inmates out for a drive to the seaside and everything had gone wrong when our minibus broke down. After all, he had a business to run, and it wasn't his normal practice to ring a monastery the other

side of the county to establish a line of credit for four din-
ners and several pints.

While this was going down, and Lu-Lu had disappeared
into the Ladies to find hot water to wash with, I sat next
to Werewolf and palmed a knife off the table.

I set to work on the peak of my Angels cap, picking open
the sewing I'd done back in Stuart Street. A rectangle of
plastic popped out into my hand. I stood up.

'American Express?'

The two brothers both called Stephen turned up in the
spare St Fulgentius Transit at about half-one in the morning. The barman was past caring by this time and even
offered us a VAT receipt for my huge Amex bill, which
included, thanks to Werewolf, a bottle of vodka for the journey home.

The Stephens drove us back across Dorset, all of us in
the back, bouncing around and singing. Lucinda kept proposing toasts to 'St Livertin', something one of the Cadic
boys had taught her on the boat. I pointed out that St
Livertin was the patron saint of headaches and she roared
with laughter and punched me on the arm. Gearoid said I
was right, so she punched him too.

It was 4.0 a.m. when we fell into various beds and it was
4.0 p.m. the next day when I surfaced after a much-needed
shower and shave with an old-fashioned cut-throat razor
someone had thoughtfully left out for me.

I followed my nose to the Community's communal
kitchen where someone was brewing coffee. After my third
cup, I spoke.

'You did ace, kid,' I told her.

'Thanks.' She was wearing a dressing-gown and thick,
towelling socks.

'So why the depression?'

'I've been on the horn to the band.'

'Bad news, huh?'

'Yeah, the worst. The sons-of-bitches just go and make themselves *the* hit act of the Festival of Metal while I'm not there, don't they? And the TV cameras turn up and catch the act, so next day they're on national radio and the day after they've signed a record deal, freezing yours truly right out of it. Do I turn my back for one second and get shafted—or what?'

'Christ, Lucinda, you're their manager. You must have it in writing.'

'You wish.'

'Then sell your story to the papers. "My Life With the Double-Crossing Superstars'—' stuff like that. Get a lawyer.'

She perked up and then levelled a finger at me.

'You're right. I'll get a lawyer. You get me a cab.'

And she was off, padding down the corridors of the Community of St Fulgentius of Ruspe singing 'Hi-Ho Silver Lining'.

We had dinner that night in Werewolf's room. Gearoid offered mead but I'd had enough of bees and I passed.

'Treasurer's report?' Werewolf asked after the meal.

'Bad,' I said. 'I've spent your dosh and even mine. I'm skint.'

'You'll be pleased to know the van's safe,' said Gearoid. 'So we don't have to fork out for that.'

'You've contacted Frostin?'

Gearoid nodded. 'Rang him this afternoon. He'll get one of his lads to drive it over. And before you ask, there's nothing clear about what happened. French radio is giving out that there was some big shoot-out up near Fréhel. Loads of bullets found but no bodies.'

'Has Frostin found a set of English number plates in the Transit?' I asked.

'Not that he's noticed,' said Gearoid wickedly.

'Good.'

'How bad is the old cash flow, Roy? Seriously.' This from Werewolf.

'Can you lend me the train fare back to London?'

'I haven't a bean, chum, not if you've used the stash I left here.' Werewolf looked genuinely concerned.

'Well then, I'll throw myself on Aunt Dorothea's mercy tomorrow. After that, it looks like I'll have to get a job for a while.'

'Shit,' breathed Werewolf. '*That* serious?'

Gearoid drove me over to Aunt Dorothea's the next morning, pulling up outside the gates of her cottage and laughing at the nameplate.

'Heaven's Gate—I like that.'

I offered him my hand.

'It's been an experience,' I said.

'Funny, that's just what I was going to say.'

I climbed down. 'See you again,' I said.

'Not if I see you first.' He grinned and drove off.

I sauntered into Aunt Dorothea's garden and then froze at the sound of a dog barking, and a barking, advancing dog.

Round the corner of the cottage came Bishop, Dorothea's ancient Labrador. He bounded up to me and rose on his hind legs to plant his front paws on my chest and lick my face.

'Hey there, down, boy! What's got into you?'

The last time I had seen him he was hiding behind the kitchen Aga.

Dorothea emerged from round the back of the cottage. She was wearing her gardening clothes and gloves and had a spade over her shoulder.

'Oh, it's you, is it, Fitzroy? Had fun, have you? Gallivant-ing off while I look after your livestock?'

'And it's nice to see you too, Aunty. Now don't tell me Springsteen has been any trouble? Has he?'

'Less charitable people than I might say so,' she said haughtily.

'What's wrong? And why is Bishop here—down, boy!—so full of beans? You haven't been giving him hormones or anything?'

'Certainly not,' she said testily. 'You'd better come and see for yourself.'

I followed her round the back of the cottage, wary of run-ning into the Akita cage now I knew it was there. The cage was still there, but I couldn't see the dogs.

'Where's the killer couple?' I asked.

Dorothea pointed into the shadows of the old woodshed which was where the animals slept.

'They haven't come out of there for four days. Their nerves have gone, shot to pieces. I'm sending them back to Japan. Bloody useless as attack dogs.'

'But why, Aunty?'

She looked at me over the top of her glasses and then just pointed a finger upwards. My eyes followed it. There, on the flat roof of the cage, his tail dangling down through the chicken wire into it, lay Springsteen, sound asleep.

I sighed.

'Sorry about this, Dotty. Is there any way I can make it up to you?'

I hadn't, after all, hit her for my train fare yet.

'Not unless you've ever considered breeding from that killer of yours. There must be money to be made from a new strain of guard cats—vicious ones, that is, like him.'

I looked down at her. She was serious.

I thought of Fenella back at Stuart Street and I just knew

she wouldn't have had the heart to get rid of Ella, Billy, Sarah and the rest of the band.

I put an arm round Dorothea's shoulder.

'Funny you should mention that, Aunty.'